MW00720091

Ketchup & Carbonara

Steven Bale

Trevor

Thank you for
all your support!

Steve

Black Rose Writing | Texas

First printing

This story is based on real events. Some names and identifying details have been changed to protect the privacy of individuals.

ISBN: 978-1-68433-686-9
PUBLISHED BY BLACK ROSE WRITING
www.blackrosewriting.com

Printed in the United States of America
Suggested Retail Price (SRP) $18.95

Ketchup & Carbonara is printed in Book Antiqua

*As a planet-friendly publisher, Black Rose Writing does its best to eliminate unnecessary waste to reduce paper usage and energy costs, while never compromising the reading experience. As a result, the final word count vs. page count may not meet common expectations.

Praise for Ketchup & Carbonara

"The text flows fast and sure and it's a real page turner. The chapters are well structured and just the right length to keep the story moving. Also, the alternating narrator structure might have been an issue and instead it works very smoothly. The two "voices" are so distinct and all the characters are well defined.

The book is also funny. It has some very nice comic moments to it. I laughed out loud more than once, and that's rare."

–Angela Montgomery PhD - Author of *The Human Constraint*

"Yours is a book about love…the writing is excellent: pacey, rich yet not contrived, chapters of the right length. The images that you create for the reader are vivid and they lend themselves to a Netflix series, way better than much of what you see these days. Actually, I believe the book has all the elements to be quickly transformed into a TV series.

Last but not least, the stance you take on love is positively (and appropriately, given this day and age) "gender neutral"; it's not "chick lit", it is not conventional, you could not say if the author is male or female, straight or gay, contemporary or different century. You raise an issue touched only marginally by the current "cougar" debate. You take it to a different level.

You may be onto something new: values based fiction. How about that!"

–Domenico Lepore PhD - Founder: Intelligent Management Systems

Acknowledgments

There are two who need the most recognition.
The first guides my heart when I have the humility to listen.
Grazie Dio.

The second stole my heart, and keeps it in the palms of her loving hands.
Grazie Simona.

Ketchup & Carbonara

Chapter 1
Rome Sweet Home

Laura

I wondered if other immigrants felt the way I did: torn between two worlds. Choosing such a life was never my first choice. I loved my country too much to ever want to leave, but as it turned out, it was the only way to get away from a past I wanted to avoid.

As I wandered off the airplane lost in thought, a young man charged past knocking me against the smooth walls of Fiumicino Airport, a not-so-subtle reminder that I was back in Rome.

"*Aaoo! Piano cretino!*" I yelled at his fleeing back. I had a short fuse on the best of days, but after thirty-five hours of traveling, airline delays and apologies, I wasn't just ready for a fight—I *wanted* a fight. There was no better way to get ready for Rome than a good old-fashioned *litigata.*

Unfortunately, the young man must have heard my eagerness to confront, because all he could say was a feeble "*Mi scusi*" as he disappeared into the crowd of people at the baggage claim area.

Too bad; I'd wanted to let off some steam. At least he didn't say "sorry" like they did in Port Angeles. Four years of polite "sorries" was enough to make me *want* the chaos of Rome again.

Nonna's voice came to mind. "*Mogli e buoi dei paesi tuoi.*"

"Stick to your own people" was the general gist of the phrase. It was a saying she often repeated when I was a little girl. I was too young to understand it at the time, but after living and dating abroad, those words seemed all too real.

After about fifteen minutes, my suitcase finally came tumbling down the carousel and in no time, I was heading for the exit. People surged around me like a broken dam of humanity. Dodging plumes of cigarette smoke, I made my way to the taxi area. It was always strange to be thrown back into the cauldron of Italian chaos as the world reeled around me.

Before I could make it ten steps, however, a strong arm ripped the suitcase from my hand.

"*Signorí*," a man said with a thick Roman accent. "This way. I have a taxi waiting."

This man was an *abusivo*, a taxi driver without a license. Men like him swarmed tourists in the hopes of getting double fare. Thankfully, my suitcase was so heavy with new clothes that the *abusivo* nearly pulled his arm out of his shoulder.

I always brought Mamma clothes from the U.S., where brand names were cheaper than in Italy. My ex-boyfriend, Luke, told me my shopping habit was going to kill him one day. Luckily for me, it nearly killed the *abusivo*.

"*No grazie!*" I commanded in an even thicker Roman accent. Right away, he knew he had chosen the wrong woman as he dropped the handle and moved onto easier prey.

Outside, I arrived at the end of the taxi lineup behind a couple that drew my attention. His clothes screamed wealth, but his taste whispered elegance. It was nice to see a well-dressed man again. She, on the other hand, exuded a style reflecting her much younger age. With a skirt that was as short as her stilettos were long, she dressed with a class quite contrary to her companion. She spoke with a "twenty-something" exuberance that would have made eyes roll. Hoping I was never that annoying at her age, I couldn't help but eavesdrop.

"I want the other bag. The one with the gold trim," she commanded to the much older man, who nodded apathetically.

"*Si, amore. Si.*"

I couldn't tell if the woman was his daughter or his lover. His left hand had a faded wedding band. She was far more beautiful than he was handsome, even if she was overly apparent.

"Are you listening to me, amore?"

"Si. Si. You want the gold trim bag."

Sensing that she had lost his interest, she reached over with a well-manicured hand, stroked the back of his neck and gave him a kiss that made *me* blush.

Definitely not his daughter.

After the kiss, Miss Shop-A-Lot continued her demands. "Then I want to go to Milan . . . soon."

The whole scene made me think of my father and all the lovers he had cheated with behind Mamma's back. They reminded me of another reason why my decision to return to Italy was so difficult: cheating.

I wished I was innocent of this affectious crime. As it turned out, my mister's name was Giancarlo and he was the biggest reason stopping me from returning to Italy. I could have easily had him wrapped around my finger, if he didn't have a ring wrapped around his. Miss Shop-a-lot glaringly reminded me of my past failure.

I wouldn't fall into that trap again, even if it was the thing to do in Italy. After the pristine purity of the Pacific Northwest, I felt I was ready to resist the charms of the Roman glitterati, including Giancarlo.

I knew he would try to get me back. Mamma had reported his phone calls at home had become a weekly expectation. Such persistence was the reason I gave into him in the first place. He had a way that made me think every idea he had was a good one, and at the same time, making me believe they were my own.

Even sleeping with him.

Being a strong woman, I couldn't understand how I had been caught with my guard down, and how he had seduced me. In the end, the only way to get over him was cold turkey. Pure denial. I had to forget my feelings otherwise they were going to eat me alive. He was married and that meant I would have always been the "other woman."

Now, after living long enough in the land of Thanksgiving, I had learned that cold turkey was best left in America. It was time to woman-up and face him again.

When he tried to seduce me, I would just ignore him. Plain and simple. It shouldn't be difficult after the conscious-clearing tranquility of Port Angeles. He wouldn't stand a chance against me now. No way. Not a shopaholic's chance in Nordstrom on Black Friday.

He wasn't *that* good-looking. I didn't need to run my fingers through his dark full hair anymore, even though it had the perfect amount of wave without being curly. Why would I? He wasn't ever going to leave his wife. I didn't want another woman's man, even though he made me feel like no man had before. He could keep his taut, tanned skin and sophisticated ruggedness to himself.

Never mind his beautiful chest that suited an off-the-rack Zegna suit perfectly. For some reason it framed his body flawlessly, accentuating his broad shoulders. They weren't too wide, like a bodybuilder's. That would have been overkill. They were just wide enough to emphasize his long straight back that lead to his narrow waist and his perfectly tight...

"*Signora*," the man behind me motioned to a taxi that had just pulled up. Shaking myself back to reality, I silently scolded myself as the driver loaded my suitcase in the boot.

Why was I still thinking of Giancarlo? I had barely been back an hour, and my past was already haunting me. Beating myself up was something I had done since I had left Italy, but before self-criticism could gain momentum, my phone rang.

"Mamy," I answered. "Yes. I'm home safe and sound. I'm on my way ho—"

Her voice shouted from the other end. Being short of hearing, she thought if she couldn't hear her voice, no one else could.

"Ma, I'll be home in forty-five minutes. I just left Fiumicino. We can talk then . . ." She wasn't listening. "Okay, Ma. Okay. I'll see you soon. I'm hanging up now. Ciao, Ma. Ciao."

As I settled in for the ride home, my thoughts wandered back to Giancarlo. I shook my head.

Oh yeah.

Returning to Italy was going to be a piece of cake. A piece of you've-still-got-a-thing-for-Giancarlo-cake.

Merda.

Chapter 2
Missing Will

Alex

Great-aunt Anne was the hussy I had never met. The story I was always told was one of a beautiful temptress whose scruples were so few that she had to steal them from men. At least, that was how Mum described her. Using these unfortunate souls to fulfill her own ends eventually lead to Anne's lonely demise and the reason I was standing in her Tuscan apartment with Mum and two undersized Carabinieri officers.

The taller one was the first to notice us. All I could see was the tip of his curved nose where the brim of his hat nearly touched.

"*Chi siete?*" he squawked. After three months of Italian tutoring with Laura, I understood what he said, but I looked over to Maria to see if she would do the talking. I would have felt more comfortable if a native Italian speaker did the conversing. I really didn't want to say anything out of place with the police.

Maria and her mother, Francesca, were Anne's friends. They were being kind enough to help us navigate the labyrinthian task of trying to find Anne's will three months after her death. She had left nothing with a lawyer, so I hoped it was somewhere in this apartment.

Maria had the same Italian warmth that Laura exuded, though I had to say, Laura was much sexier. It should have felt strange thinking about my fifteen-year-older tutor that way, but for whatever reason, it didn't. Maybe I had just grown tired of girls my own age who only really cared about how many likes their last post got.

Dates with "Instagirls" always felt like I was intruding on their social media life. They usually filled moments of silence with texting instead of talking. I guess that was why I preferred being outdoors by myself. Nature always had time for me.

"This is Anna's family. They've arrived from America," Maria replied.

"Well actually, I'm from Canada, but we live in America. My friends call me the Camerican," I said, trying to add some levity to the tangible tension in the room. Everyone looked at me blankly. Laura and I had talked about Carabinieri in one of our lessons. She had compared them to the FBI. Obviously, they shared a similar sense of humor.

"How do you spell that?" he asked seriously while raising a pen to his notepad.

I looked around for help, but Mum and Francesca were both frowning at me, and Maria was too busy snickering to explain it was my dumb attempt at humor.

At least someone got my joke.

"Relax, kid, I'm only kidding," he said dryly. "Nice to meet you, Camericano. My name is Officer Pizzi, and my partner's name is Marco. Someone has broken into Ms. Anna's home. How are you related to the deceased?"

Exhaling loudly in relief, I looked over to see that Mum was already looking around, assessing the apartment's contents. I wondered if she was as surprised as I was. Anne's apartment wasn't anything like I was expecting. I had imagined the telltale signs of a woman of leisure. Golden faucets and silk curtains. Maybe a mirror on the ceiling and dark, lurking shadows hiding all manner of untold impropriety.

Instead, we'd found sunny yellow walls, simple decorations, and modest furniture that showed a fondness for Tuscan wood. The only thing that was remotely ornate were the lavish rugs that looked more like frescoes than carpets.

"My name is Alex. I'm her great-nephew, and this is my mum. Anne's niece," I told Officer Pizzi.

The officer scribbled in his notepad. His big hat covered his face each time he looked down to take notes.

"*Avete documenti?*" he asked.

I nodded and produced my passport.

He pointed to Mum. "*E lei?*"

"*Si, certo,*" I replied. I asked Mum to pull out her passport.

"Can we get some air in here? It's so stuffy," Mum asked. Maria obliged as she opened the door leading to an outside balcony. Fresh air bellowed the lace curtains.

The officer took our passports and began jotting down our information. In the meantime, Officer Marco came over to see who we were.

"*Chi sono?*" he asked his counterpart.

"*Sono la famiglia della Signora* Watson. They are Camericani."

Office Marco shrugged as he continued his inventory of the contents of the apartment.

"Your aunt's safe is empty." His short, hairy thumb pointed in the direction of the bedroom.

"What did they take?" I asked.

"I do not know. Now that you are here, perhaps you can help us with that."

"Did you happen to find a will?" Mum asked eagerly. I translated for her before Pizzi answered.

"No. The safe is empty. There was nothing left inside. Please, have a look." Pizzi led us into a yellow sunlit room which perfumed of roses and figs.

Anne kept a tidy place. Across from her bed, a stylish painting of an enormous angel hung for all to see. It was impossible to miss as it held a sword over a writhing snake under its feet. Golden wings spread wide across a cerulean sky. "Arcangelo Michele" was engraved in the frame.

Not your everyday art.

At the end of the bedroom, a collage of frames decorated the wall. Photographic memoirs of a life past.

"Are those all pictures of Anne?" I asked.

Mum walked past the officers and examined them, her mouth pursing. "Yes. They're all Anne all right."

In each photo, she posed with a different person. Men, mostly. Trim and well dressed, her beauty was stunning. In her younger years, she had blond hair and tanned skin; I could tell even though the pictures were black and white.

I thought about Mum's description of Anne for a moment. Maybe she was right? Maybe Anne was a little loose socially? One of the pictures had been removed, exposing an empty safe. The gentleman in the picture was obviously younger, though she didn't seem to care as she stared at him admiringly.

"That's a great hiding spot," I said.

"It seems your Aunt was pretty savvy," Maria said.

"Not as savvy as she should have been. They still found the safe," Mum replied.

I looked back to the pictures of Anne, which revealed little of the woman Mum had described during our flight from Seattle. "She seems happy. She couldn't have been that bad, Mum."

Mum shook her head and said nothing. She was peering over Pizzi's shoulder into the safe, her features stern.

Looking around, I noticed that there were several other photos of the same man dotting the walls. In fact, there were more photos of him than any other man. Taking one of the pictures from the chest of drawers, it became obvious that he was important to Anne.

"Can I take this?" I asked the room. When no one answered, I shoved the small frame into my pocket. I was certain no one would miss it. And having a memento of my mysterious aunt felt justifiable.

After all, if Anne truly was a hussy, why were there so many photos of her with this man? I had a feeling there was more to my aunt than Mum had led me to believe. Looking up to Arcangelo Michele, the sun twinkled off of his eye as though he had winked, confirming my thoughts.

Who was my great-aunt Anne and where would we find her missing will?

Chapter 3
La Signora's

Laura

Italian elevators. Another good reason to stay away from Italy. If I chose not to return to my country, it would be to avoid stepping into one of these death boxes again. Why was everything in Italy designed to suffocate me? First Giancarlo. Then that smelly taxi. Now elevators! Dealing with Giancarlo was one thing, but surrendering my claustrophobia to this Mussolini relic was making me ruin my blouse with nervous sweat.

And I never sweat!

Drawing in a big breath, I pushed my fear way down to the bottom of my stomach and stepped inside, dragging my suitcase behind me. The elevator squeaked under the strain of my presence. There was barely enough room for both of us in the lift, and for a second, I felt like sending my suitcase up without me.

But because Italians liked to make everything difficult, I had to be inside the elevator to close the safety door to pick a floor, making it impossible to send it up without me inside. There was always the option of dragging my suitcase up the five flights of stairs to Mamma's floor. Mussolini had made sure the stairs in Italy were long and grandiose, like he had in all the common housing he built throughout Rome.

Not gonna happen.

The elevator groaned as I pushed the button to Mamma's floor. My heart rate jumped every bump and creak as the elevator agonizingly pulled me up.

Please don't break. God. Please don't break.

Finally, coming to a shuddering halt, I flung the door open, escaping with my life intact. Within seconds, I was standing in Mamma's apartment, asking the emptiness where she was hiding. "Mamma?"

I had forgotten how small and dark her place was. It was a far cry from our home in Eur, which had been more like a palace than a villa. Papà had taken that away from us during the divorce. Mamma's decision to leave Papà came after he had beaten me so violently one day that I had passed out. After that, her choice was one of two: live a life of wealth all the while waiting for him to kill one of us, or live a life of less - and stay alive. She ended up finding this dark hole for an apartment. The nunnery beside our building added a sense of serenity to the neighbourhood, which was probably why she chose this area.

At the time, I blamed the divorce on her. I had hated her for it, but seeing how she had survived in Rome all these years by herself had changed my thinking. Now, she was the bravest woman I had ever known, even if she drove me nuts.

Mamma came from the kitchen, her mouth twitching more than usual, a remnant of the beatings my father had given her. I could tell she was nervous, so I gave her a big hug. She seemed to get smaller and softer every trip, but it felt good to squeeze her again.

Quickly dismissing my embrace, she pushed me away, leading me to the kitchen. Physical contact wasn't her love-language, especially after the violent contact she had with Papà. Unfortunately, I loved cuddles, which always left me wanting more from her.

"*Vieni. Vieni.* Everything is ready," she said. Her blonde hair barely showed roots. She must have visited the hairdresser recently. Probably to look as good as she could for me. She knew I worried about her, which was another reason I needed to return to Italy. It wasn't fair that she was alone.

As I followed, I couldn't help but think she deserved better than this, considering she had helped Papà rise to the heights of wealth and influence in Rome. In the States, it shocked me at how fairly women were treated. In Italy, divorce meant half and half. Half for the man, and the other half for the man.

"I've prepared everything. *Prosciutto. Bresaola. Ricotta. Pasta al'forno. Insalata.*" She adjusted her glasses as she started pulling food from the fridge.

"I'm sorry, Ma. I'm not that hungry," I replied. I could see her deflate with rejection. She always expressed love with cooking, and judging by her softer waistline, she had loved herself a great deal since I last saw her.

"Tired? You must be. It was a long trip. How long was it? I keep saying you live too far away. America is on the other side of the planet. I wish your uncle lived somewhere closer. Like England. I love England."

Mamma was heading off on one of her verbose tangents again. If I didn't stop her, she would recount her entire life's story. Sometimes it felt like I was caught in the middle of a conversation with herself. I felt badly that she didn't have anyone here to talk to, so I normally would just let her ramble on, but I really wasn't in the mood right now. Exhausted, I had to think of something quickly before I was drowning in nostalgia.

"I don't know how long the trip was, Ma. I've been up for over thirty-five hours."

"What do you want to do then? It's too early to go to bed. Do you want to see your friends? How about your cousin, Alberto? He'd love to see you. Should I call him?"

The only reason to see my cousin was to remind me how snobby Romans could get. And after zero sleep for almost two days, I probably would have told him to shove his snobbery where the sun didn't shine, if he could loosen up long enough to let sunshine in. Besides, he was good friends with Giancarlo and it wouldn't take long for word to get around that I was back.

"Gelato," I blurted. "I want a gelato."

Mamma perked up. She had a thing for sugar.

"Mmm. Gelato. *Daje! Annamo!*" she exclaimed in thick Roman dialect. She rarely spoke Roman unless she was in a playful mood.

"Annamo!" I played along, thankful to have found the right distraction.

Within minutes we had left Mamma's apartment and were on the busy streets of Rome, where she asked me which *gelateria* I wanted to go to. I had to think carefully. I didn't want to run into Giancarlo. He lived in this neighbourhood, so the possibility was high.

"How about La Signora's?" I asked.

Mamma nodded in grand approval as we linked arms. Breathing in the thick Roman air, we headed in the direction of the second best gelato in Rome. Giolitti's was the best and the more likely place that I'd bump into Giancarlo.

I should be safe there. I'm pretty sure Giancarlo doesn't even know about this place.

I scratched my head to think if we had ever gone there.

No. It should be safe.

But what if I ran into him? Was I ready to face him? I needed to make sure he didn't creep back into my life.

Chapter 4
Welcome to Italy

Alex

"We need to get that will," Mum said.

Like a cat turning on a mouse, she twisted to face Maria and Francesca, who stood behind us with looks of concern. They would have looked like sisters if Francesca didn't have a few more wrinkles and a touch of grey hair. Tuscans looked a lot different from Laura, whose skin was much darker and whose waist was far more curvaceous.

"Where did the officers say we can get more information on Anne's will?" she asked bluntly.

Maria responded in broken English. "We have to go to the *Comune*." She looked to her mother uneasily.

"What is that?" I asked.

"In Italy, the *Comune* is a . . . *come si dice 'buco nero'*. . . a hole black?"

"A black hole?" I asked.

"Yes! That sounds right. A black hole."

"What do you mean?"

"Unless you know someone there, it will be very difficult to get answers."

Francesca jumped in with a string of rapid Italian. I caught a bit of what she said, but thankfully Maria clarified, her face brightening.

"My mother has a friend who is the uncle of someone who knows the father of a taxi driver who knows the mother of the director of the *Comune*!"

Mum and I looked at each other and shook our heads.

"So?" I said.

"So?! We have a connection! This is good news! The uncle of my Mum's friend owes my uncle's friend a favor. His neighbor is the mother of the director. We can ask him to introduce us."

I was coming to understand how things worked here. It sounded like you had to know someone who knows someone who owes someone in order to get to know someone who knows.

"That doesn't make any sense," I said.

"Welcome to Italy," Maria replied.

"Great. How can we meet, um . . . whoever we have to meet?"

"Don't worry. I can take you with my car. Mamma will phone her friend while we drive to the *Comune*."

"To the black hole then!" I said as we all made our way to Maria's car.

•   •   •   •   •

Francesca led us all into the drab-looking *Comune*. I didn't really know what to expect from an Italian government office, but a maelstrom of harsh language greeted us. A ranting lady stood at a marble counter with a baby dangling from her arms. Her face was as red as her rage as she leaned over the counter, screaming at a hidden secretary.

"Si, signora. We're still looking for your file," the secretary said.

"Still looking! It has been five hours. How long does it take to find a single file?"

"Si, signora. Mi scusi, signora. We're doing everything we can to get the answers you're looking for."

"Everything? My newborn child could find a file quicker than you!" The baby in her arms started to scream with her mum, adding to the pandemonium. The twenty other people in the dreary lobby fidgeted in their seats as they tried to ignore her.

"If you could please wait in the waiting area, we will do everything we can for you."

"Wait? I've been waiting for hours! What do I have to do to get these stupid files?"

"I'm sorry for the inconvenience, but we are doing the best we can . . ."

Excuses were the last thing the lady wanted to hear. The secretary's condescending tone was like fuel on the fire of her anger as she exploded into a volcano of profanity. Even the gruffest of men in the room covered their ears as not to taint the remainder of their fleeting innocence.

"Welcome to the hole black," Maria said seriously.

Francesca walked up to the counter. It took several more curses before the lady calmed down. The secretary, wanting any distraction from the explosive lady and her wailing baby, turned her attention to us.

"Si. Prego. How can I help you?" she said as though nothing was out of the ordinary and then stood. As she did, my shock over the ranting lady turned to disbelief. The secretary's beauty was dazzling. Her stunning appearance silenced the entire room — Mum, Maria, Francesca, the other patrons. Her fellow colleagues. Even the loud lady's newborn stopped crying, turning to witness the artistry of her elegance. God had a weekend project, and she was standing right in front of me.

All I could do was pretend not to stare, which made my staring even more obvious.

Francesca started. "*Buona sera. Sono* Francesca Mugnaii. I have an appointment with Mr. Battista."

The livid lady was watching us carefully.

"*Si*, Signora Mugnaii. I have your file here."

The livid lady's back stiffened, looking like a Doberman ready to pounce. I could read the question on her forehead. File? How did they get a file just by walking in off the street?

The secretary flipped her long sensual hair from one shoulder to another. Every man in the room got whiplash. My hands started to sweat. No, wait. They were sweating all along.

The livid lady couldn't contain herself. "Oh I see. I've been waiting here for hours, and these people get their file prepared for them *before* they walk in. Nice. Who do you know here?"

Francesca ignored the question. The truth was impossible to deny. I suddenly realized how important it was in Italy to know someone who knows someone who owes someone in order to get to know someone who knows.

Plucking a phone receiver to her ear, the secretary made a quick call and within minutes we were sitting in the director's office.

Direttore Battista was not a tall man, but he was modestly good-looking and had a tan that made him seem luxurious. He was adjusting his white hair as we entered.

"*Buona sera.*" He extended his hand to Francesca, who was the first to meet him at his large wooden desk. When it was my turn to shake his hand, I was surprised by how soft they were. They were well moisturized, unscathed by manual labour.

"*Salve,*" he greeted me. "It is nice to meet all of you. To what do I owe the honor?"

As we all sat down on wooden chairs, his secretary retreated to a corner to take notes. A sly look crossed between her and the director. It only flashed for a split second, but it spoke volumes, or at least an entire dirty novel. Mum gave me a less than impressed glare.

"Now, how can I help you?" Mr. Battista asked.

"My friends are trying to locate their aunt's will," Francesca said. "The *Carabinieri* said you may help us with that."

Mr. Battista looked over to the secretary, who suddenly erased her sensual expression. She produced the file and handed it to the director. He opened the file with impatience. We were obviously disturbing more important business.

"Ah, yes. Signora Watson. I knew her well," he said, stroking his chin as he leaned back in contemplation. A smile of admiration seemed to crease his lips. "She was a beautiful woman, your Aunt."

I translated for Mum, who shot me a quick glance that said "told you Anne was a hussy."

"It saddened me to hear of her death. My condolences." He placed the file down and looked at us with sympathy. "Now, in order for me to release any information, I will need you to sign a release."

"A release?" I asked.

"Yes. This is normal procedure when releasing sensitive information."

"So you can help us?"

"*Si.*"

"I just need to sign."

"*Si.*"

"Can I read it?"

"*Si.*" He handed me the form. It was all very technical, so I handed it to Maria and Francesca to look over. Once they read it, they both nodded with approval.

I looked around for a pen and noticed that the director had one nearby.

"*Posso usare la tua pene?*"

Maria barked out a laugh, Francesca choked, and the secretary suddenly looked very nervous.

"*Pene? Pene?*" I pointed at his pen.

"I think she has it?" Maria said to me in English as she motioned over to the secretary.

"What? I just want to borrow his pen."

Maria leaned over to me and whispered. "I think you mean *penna*."

"Why? What did I say?"

"You just asked the director if you could use his penis."

I felt like crawling under the desk and hiding. Laura and I hadn't discussed the difference between those two words during our lessons. Why would we?

Avoiding the director's eyes, I asked again. "*Posso usare la tua penna?*"

The director handed me his pen, after which I quickly scribbled my signature on the form.

"*Bene.* Now I am free to tell you what I know," he continued, gracefully ignoring my request of the use of his male appendage.

"Which is what?" Francesca asked.

"Nothing."

"What?" all three of us said in unison. Mum couldn't understand, so she remained nervously silent.

"That's right. I have very little information to give you. Signora Watson didn't register a will with us."

"Well, where is it then?" Francesca asked.

"You'll have to go to Roma to visit the main registrar there. If Mrs. Watson has registered her will in Italy, it will be there."

"There is no other way? We can't phone them?" I asked.

Every Italian in the room scoffed, laughed or threw their arms in the air. It took a while before their lamenting faded away to disbelieving head shaking.

"That would be a waste of time," the director said. "Phoning the Italian registrar is like phoning God. You will have to wait until you're dead to get an answer."

"Another hole black," Maria said.

"Do you have a lawyer here?" Battista asked.

"No. Why would we?"

"To deal with Italian bureaucracy. I suggest you get one, otherwise, you'll have a hard time finding out anything." The director leaned back in his wing-backed chair. It squeaked.

"You make it sound very difficult," I said.

"Welcome to Italy," he replied.

Chapter 5
To kill Alberto

Laura

As we walked, Mamma filled the time expressing every thought that came to mind, reminding me that if I returned to Rome, I would have to get my own apartment just out of earshot.

"How was America? Did you finally give up on Luke? I told you he was no good for you. After he hurt you the way he did. How are your wrists? Are they still sore? I don't know how you managed to live way in the forest like that. It's dangerous, you know. He could have hurt you far worse than he did. I always said he was crazy. I never trusted him. Did he touch you again after that first time? He better not have. I was ready to come over there and deal with him myself. If your father had found out, he would have made him disappear. I hope you find someone else. Someone who loves you. You don't deserve my fate. You deserve way better."

Mamma always talked about my father like they had just broken up, even though it had been almost twenty years. She still loved him, despite everything. I couldn't understand why she was still stuck on him. She'd only had one relationship since, a short one with a younger man named Andrea, who had shown remarkable immunity to her incessant talking.

She never allowed herself to fall completely for a younger man. I never let her. What would a younger man want with an older woman, anyway? Money? A mother? It was too weird. It was bad enough that

Papà's Polish mistress was my age. I couldn't let Mamma date a *man* my age. What if they had gotten married?

Then I would have ended up with a stepmother and a stepfather who knew the words to *Pokerface* better than I did.

Way too weird.

"Yes, Ma. I know. I'll find someone. But I'm not settling. I want a man who puts me first."

My Italian student, Alex jumped to mind. We often talked for hours after each lesson, and he really listened, so much so that sometimes I even felt like we were dating. He had a fearless receptivity that was openly teachable. And alluringly sexual. I always wondered why he was constantly single. It made no sense.

"You know . . . Giancarlo keeps calling. Can you believe it!"

My heart jumped a quick beat.

"I'm proud of you for turning your back on him. That was the *diavolo* trying to tempt you. There is an angel out there for you, I know there is. God works in mysterious ways," she said.

Mamma's wise tone didn't just come from her Catholic upbringing. While she tried to mend things with my father, she ran away to the ashrams of India to try to make sense of her life. It was there that she learned the value of tolerance. She never judged me for the men I dated, even when I made the mistake of falling for a married one. It was a surprise myself. The last thing I wanted to be was a home-wrecker, but Giancarlo told me he was going to leave his wife, anyway. I guess I was foolish enough to believe him.

"How is it going with your student?"

I stopped. My heart jumped another beat. This time, a little higher. "Alex? Why. . .why do you ask?"

"Oh, I don't know. You always seemed to talk about him over the phone."

"He's just a kid! I'm fifteen years older than him!"

"I wasn't talking romantically. What are you talking about?"

Hold on. What was I talking about? Was I actually thinking romantically about Alex? No way. I shook my head. Forget it. He probably thought *Pokerface* was an oldie.

"He's my student," I said primly. "He's a very good student. He knew he'd be coming to Italy to help settle his great-aunt's estate."

"She died? Was she Italian?"

"English, I think. She lived in Italy, though. She sounded like a real firecracker."

"Really? An English woman?"

We shared a look before bursting into laughter.

"All women have their charms, I guess. Besides, men are easily led by their less intelligent heads," Mamma continued.

We fell into a rare silence as the conversation distilled in our thoughts. The air was warm with heat as a light gust freshened our faces. Soon, La Signora's came into view. It was nestled at the base of one of Rome's little secrets: the Zodiac. This is where Romans went to admire the view of the seven hills. Tourists didn't know about it, so it was a good place to escape the crowds.

"Laura!" Elisabetta yelled from behind a counter of colorful ice creams as we walked in. "*Bella! Come stai! Ben tornata!*"

I didn't know what I loved more. Elisabetta's hospitality, or her gelato. Thankfully, I could have both. She operated the store with her husband, Giulio. I had been one of their first customers when they opened.

She ran from behind the counter of *gelati*, and gave me a big hug. Her squeeze reminded me of the warmth that I had missed back in the States.

God, it is good to be home.

"What can I get you fine ladies?" Elisabetta asked.

Mamma ordered first. "For me, strawberry, Spanish fruit and mango."

"With whipped cream?"

"Of course! Do you have to ask?"

Elisabetta smiled. Whipped cream on top of gelato was as close to orgasmic as any food could get, and after not experiencing a real orgasm for a *long* time, that gelato looked beyond good right now. "Laura?"

"I'll have my usual . . ."

"Let me guess. Pistacchio, hazelnut and chocolate with whipped cream?" Elisabetta said.

"Brava! Yes! You remember!"

Elisabetta beamed with professional pride and dug a heap of each flavor onto a cone. "*Una cialda?*"

"Grazie!"

She placed a wafer cookie on top of the whipped cream and handed me my orgasm. I waited about one second before plunging my tongue into its creamy depths. A dab of whipped cream caught the tip of my nose like I was five years old again, but I didn't care.

Mamma laughed. "You *really* missed this, didn't you?"

I nodded, licking my lips while my eyes rolled into the back of my head. Pleasure-meter: one-hundred percent. "You have no idea."

Yep. Definitely better than sex.

I took another lick. "How much do we owe you?" I asked Elisabetta.

"*Niente*. Welcome home!"

"Are you sure?"

"*Ma figurati!*" Before I could protest any longer, she had moved onto the next customer. I had forgotten how generous my people could be.

Mamma and I walked out arm-in-arm. Nothing tasted better than fresh gelato after a long flight. It was good to be home.

Just then, my cell phone rang. With the elegance of a drunken flamingo, I perched my bag on one knee, held the ice cream in one hand and rummaged for the source of the incessant ringing with the other.

Thankfully, Mamma came to the rescue and grabbed my gelato, which she promptly stole a lick from. With two hands free now, I could search through the pile of makeup, old airline tickets and sugar-free gum wrappers until I found my phone.

The number on the display was an Italian area code.

Mamma, now thoroughly enjoying two ice cream cones, asked with chocolate ice cream on her lips. "Who is it? Is it Alberto? He knew you were arriving today."

I tapped the green answer icon. "*Pronto.*"

"*Pronto.* Laura?"

"*Si.* Who is this?"

"It's Giancarlo."

I nearly tripped on one of the *sampietrini* cobblestones when I heard his voice. One thing I had liked most about Giancarlo was his exuberant confidence. By his greeting, he still had it in spades.

"Your cousin told me you were back in town. I'm sorry if I'm disturbing you. How are you keeping? How was your flight?"

I looked to Mamma who had stopped licking. She had probably seen the terror on my face. Chocolate had now crept to the outer edges of her lips. I was going to kill Alberto when I saw him.

Oh my god. This was it. It was time to turn on "snub-mode." "I'm fine." Take that, Mr. Sexy-voice. Every man knew what "fine" meant, and I wasn't afraid to use it.

I can do this. Just pretend that he's a telemarketer.

An awkward silence passed before Giancarlo cleared his throat. Ha! He wasn't expecting that, was he?

"Anyway, I'll make it quick. I've decided to run as a Member of Parliament, and I'm looking for supporters to further my cause. I remembered we always shared a similar political interest and would like to invite you to a fundraiser party. As a guest, of course."

"No, thank you. I'm not interested."

Pretend he's just a telemarketer. An annoying one…

It was hard when his smooth voice could melt chocolate. He didn't give me a chance to continue. "Don't worry. I'll be with Lucinda. This isn't a romantic invitation. Trust me, I learned to give up on that notion when you moved halfway around the world."

"That's not what Mamma tells me. She said you've been calling every week."

What are you doing? He's a telemarketer, stupid! Don't let him pull you in!

His pitch was quick. "Yes. But only to see if you wanted to get involved in the party. Do you have a job in Italy yet? I could organize a good position for you."

I knew what kind of position he was talking about. "Still not interested. Thank you."

That's it Laura. Good recovery. You can do this!

"Very well. If you change your mind, your cousin knows when and where it is. I hope you can make it. We're going to change Italy. Enough of the corruption and crooked politicians. It's time for real change."

I certainly agreed with this, but I knew any kind of affirmation would open a door I wasn't interested in walking through. "I won't be changing my mind. But good luck. Now, if you don't mind, Mamma is waiting."

"Of course.. I apologize for keeping you and welcome back. Goodbye, Laura."

"Goodbye."

I slammed my thumb on the red icon, fuming. "I'm going to kill Alberto," I said, scrolling through my contacts so I could get the homicide started. "It was Giancarlo! He invited me to a political rally. Can you believe the nerve of that guy? It sounds like he's running for office."

"He always was ambitious. Is he still with his wife?"

"Yes. She'll be there as well," I said, hating the pang of regret that followed. I knew I would always find him attractive. Whenever I looked in the mirror to see that eating an entire jar of Nutella the night before was not a good idea, I thought of how he had chosen me over so many other women. "It doesn't matter, Ma. I want someone with no baggage."

Mamma nodded and handed back my half-eaten ice cream, forcing me to put my phone away.

"Forget Giancarlo and your cousin," she said. "I want you to meet someone."

I rolled my eyes. "I'm not in the mood for Mamma's matchmaking service."

"It's just around the corner. C'mon. You need to make some new friends."

She took off down the sidewalk, a new spring in her step. She was getting older, but she wasn't old yet.

I gave my gelato a disinterested lick. After Giancarlo's call, I had lost the taste for gelato-induced orgasms. They only made me think of the ones he tried to give me. He wasn't *that* good of a lover after all.

The last thing I wanted to deal with right now was one of Mamma's blind dates. I was tired of Italian men; they were charming and handsome, but they only wanted one thing. At least American men were a little more complex, although that meant they could surprise you.

My ex-boyfriend Luke was a great example. He was like a puzzle that needed to be solved. It was fun slowly peeling back his insecurities and lack of self-esteem. It was like unwrapping a big present until I discovered what was inside. Depression. Anxiety. Mommy issues. After a year together, Luke became the gift that kept on taking. In the end, I packed my things and headed back to stay with my uncle just outside Port Angeles.

Why was it so challenging finding the right guy? I had traveled halfway around the world, and I still couldn't find him. If I moved back to Italy, I may have to get used to the idea of being a spinster. I shrugged. At least I wouldn't have to worry about how much Nutella I ate.

I gave my ice-cream another indifferent lick when my tongue found the pistachio layer. Hmm. To give up on a good gelato over men would have been a real shame; especially when there was perfectly good pistachio at stake. With renewed vigour, I kept on licking while I followed Mamma ten yards ahead, who motioned me with the nub of her cone to keep following.

Chapter 6
Piccolo Diavolo

Alex

Tapping her foot on the piazza cobbles, Mum crossed her arms dictatorially. Her aquamarine eyes were as commanding as a son would know. Pinned up like a brown cinnamon bun, white wisps streaked her hair like treacle. Maria and Francesca were standing off to one side as we all stood outside the *Comune*. The day was growing long as the sun peeked from behind the highest church steeple, blinding me with jabs of light.

"I'm not calling Laura, Mum. Not doing it. She's visiting her mother. She didn't come to Italy to be bothered by one of her students. She's got better things to do." Like hook up with hot Italian men who were far more gorgeous than me. I bet they didn't have their mothers breathing down their necks like I did.

"I'm not asking, Alexander. I'm telling. She is the only contact we have here. You don't have any other choice."

"Don't you mean "we" don't have any other choice? We are family, remember. "Family first" like you and Dad always said." Quoting the family motto did the trick as her expression loosened. A little.

"Of course. You know what I mean. Just call her. She won't mind. I get the feeling Italians are very generous."

That comment made me cringe. "So that means we should take advantage of her? I'm not calling just because we *need* something." I wondered what Anne would have done as I thumbed her photo now in my hand. Would she have endorsed our motto? Would she have used Laura to get what she needed? Looking at her smile in the picture, I couldn't imagine Anne as the "breaker of hearts" and "user of men" that Mum had described. And if Anne had been so callous, was Mum acting any differently right now?

"I'm sorry, lovey, but we don't have a choice," Mum continued.

I wanted to say that I wanted to keep it professional between Laura and I, but that would have sounded a little too much like I had a thing for her. Which I didn't. Why would I? Being a sexy teacher was one thing. Being a decade and a half older was another.

So why are you making a big deal about this? Just call her.

Now even my mind was working against me. Or maybe it was just Mum's rationale that had been bred into me since birth. Sometimes it was hard to distinguish between what I thought and what I was told. It would be nice to be allowed to feel for myself for once. Too bad Mum made sense. It was hard to fight good reasoning.

"C'mon lovey. Get a move on. We don't have all day. And make it quick. Data costs," Mum ordered, realizing my silence was a symptom of defeat.

Shaking my head, I looked down at my phone knowing that I didn't have a choice. I hated when people used me for their own interest, and now I was about to do the same with Laura. She didn't deserve to be an instrument of Mum's ambitions. In a way, I liked having Laura all to myself. She was *my* tutor. *My* friend. I didn't want Mum intruding on that.

Whenever Mum got involved with women important to me, her anti-girl super-power couldn't help but reveal itself. Suspicion of anyone foreign to the family was her natural state of being. But a woman close to her son? Well, that had to be snuffed out right away.

Turning my back on her, I walked deeper into the piazza so she couldn't hear. I didn't know why, but I wanted a little privacy for this. Scrolling through my phone for Laura's number, I wondered where she was right now. I knew her number by heart, but scrolling gave me time to think of what I would say.

She probably won't even pick up. I bet she was with that guy she talked about; the mystery man she always mentioned but never elaborated on. She always fell into a deep, rare silence whenever he came up, which was a little too often for my liking.

It's not that I minded talking about her past, but. . .well, actually I did mind. As a matter of fact, I hated talking about her past. Her experiences seemed so rich. So lush. She was so worldly, and in comparison to my life, it made me feel trapped in a nest of country circumstance.

Family first. The beating drum of an immigrant family. It had been pounded into my head all my life.

Laura gave me a glimpse into a world that I had no idea existed, and it had stretched my heart to consider new ways of thinking. New ways of being. New ways of loving.

Wait a second? Loving? What's wrong with you? Just dial the stupid number, would ya?

I gave myself a shake and tapped her number. It rang.

I bet she was with him right now. The mystery man. I bet they were tearing each others clothes as her phone rang and she ignored it, lying on his big, huge, enormous bed. I could hear their wails of delight as they laughed at the young student who was silly enough to think that—

"*Pronto?*" Her sensual voice spoke.

Just as I was about to open my mouth, a bicyclist leapt out of nowhere, catching my arm, and flinging my phone half way across the piazza. It landed with a loud crack on the cobbles. The cyclist carried on, barely aware of what he had just done.

No!

Running to within an arm's length, I could hear Laura on the other end "*Pronto? Pronto?*" just before a small lorry zoomed by, rolling right over my phone, crushing it and Laura's warm voice.

Nnnooo!

"*Piccolo Diavolo*" was painted on the truck's rear door with a red devil smiling at me. Now in pieces, I stared at the electronic carcass pulverized on the ground.

Shit!

"Now what?" I shouted back to Mum. Maybe this was a sign. Maybe fate had stepped in to stop me from making a fool of myself.

Maria pulled out her phone. "You can use my phone if you like, as long as you remember the number."

Or maybe not.

"Do you know that girl's number?" Mum asked. I hated when she called girls I knew "that girl." She did it all the time.

"You mean Laura? She has a name, you know."

"Stop being silly, Alex. You know who I mean. Do you know it? Yes or no?"

Luckily, I did. If there was anything I could remember, it was numbers. Besides, she made me memorize it during one of our lessons to practice my Italian numerology. She touched my arm whenever I got something right. And I made sure I got a lot of things right.

"Yeah, I know it." I could have lied, but I never lied to family. It just wasn't done. Family first.

Maria handed me her phone. My heart started to race again.

Here I go. Goofy, Camerican student calling his sophisticated Italian tutor from someone else's phone because he can't even avoid a simple cyclist. I'm such a loser.

Taking Maria's phone, I dialed her number. The phone rang.

Chapter 7
Cugio

Laura

Pistachio lingered on my palette with tantalizing sapor. Just as I licked the delicious demise of my gelato, my phone rang. Again. I recognized the number.

"Alberto!" I responded. It was not a greeting. It was a threat.

"*Cugia*! Welcome back!"

Alberto was like the little brother I never had. The annoying kind. We'd always had playful nicknames for each other, but today I wasn't in the mood to be playful. "*Cugio*! I'm going to kill you!"

"It's been months since we've talked to each other, and that's the greeting I get?"

"What did you expect? You gave my number to Giancarlo?"

"Are you kidding me? The man was pathetic. Every time we talked, he kept asking me where you were. He was like a broken record. What was I supposed to say?"

"Nothing. That's what. I told you not to tell him. Now he's invited me to his stupid fundraiser."

"Me too. Maybe we can go together now."

Alberto loved fundraisers. Given the chance to rub shoulders with high-society, he would show up and pretend that he wasn't the son of a butcher. There was no doubt he was successful in his own right, but no matter what, he was always ashamed of his background.

"You're an idiot. I'm not going to any fundraiser. Especially his."

"Hey? Where are you, anyway?"

I looked around. "In front of that Sicilian restaurant you always liked."

"Great. I'm right around the corner. Wait there."

Within minutes, Alberto's long legs stretched out of a black Maserati as he parked in front of us. His hair was light brown with more white than before. His work was obviously taking a toll, though he still kept a trim waistline.

"Welcome back, *Cugia*." He didn't run over to hug me; hastiness would have ruined his practiced haughtiness. Instead, he sauntered over as though time was supposed to wait for him. At least his hug wasn't as flaccid as his strut.

"Good to see you," he said, then looked at me down the length of his nose. "You've gained weight."

I smacked him.

Hard.

"Good. It'll make my punch heavier, jerk. I owe you more punches after the stunt you pulled."

"What can I say? The man's still in love with you. He even told me he was ready to leave Lucinda."

Lucinda was a bitch of a woman. When I met her at work one day, she openly pushed me into Giancarlo's arms, as though she wanted her husband to cheat. At the time, she was having an affair with a German personal trainer named Klaus. The whole thing disgusted me, but in the end, his charms were too hard to resist. I thought if she was cheating on Giancarlo, then they must have been close to divorce. It wasn't until the final stunt that forced our breakup that I realized he would never divorce her.

"Well, I'll believe it when I see it. He had plenty of opportunities to leave her. I think he likes her influence more than he liked me." Lucinda was Giancarlo's connection to high-society. She came from a very long line of blue bloods. Her prominence had grown Giancarlo's legal practice to one of the biggest in Rome. Without her, he would have been just another lawyer. "Besides, I'm over him, anyway. I'm a free woman."

I wish I believed my words.

Just then, my phone rang. Frustrated, I answered it.

"*Pronto?*" Waiting for a response, a loud crack came from the other end. Hurting my ear, I pulled my phone away before trying again. "*Pronto? Pronto?*" Another loud crack replied before the line disconnected.

"Who was it?" Alberto asked.

"I don't know. There was only a bunch of crackles."

Alberto shrugged. "Like I was saying, Giancarlo seems really motivated this time. Every time we went for coffee, he always asked about you. I tell you, if he was ever ready to leave his wife, it's now."

"I don't care…" my phone rang again, this time from a different number.

"*Che cavolo!* Who keeps calling me?" All these phone calls were making me want to throw my phone into oncoming traffic. About to ignore it, Mamma encouraged me to answer.

"Um. Hello?" the voice said in English.

"Yes, hello? Who's this?"

"Is this Laura?"

"This is she."

"It's Alex."

"Alex?" My heart jumped at the sound of his voice.

"Who's Alex?" Alberto asked inaudibly. I ignored him as I turned away to get some privacy.

"Yes. Your student. From Port Angeles. Sorry to bother you," Alex said.

"That's okay. I was wondering if you had arrived safely when I hadn't heard from you. Did you try to call me a second ago?"

"Um, yeah. Sorry. My phone broke."

"Your phone broke?"

"Yeah. It cracked on the street before a truck ran over it. What are the chances, huh?"

Mamma and Alberto were listening far too intently. Alberto spoke perfect English, so I turned on him a little more to get away from his prying ears. "Yeah. You gotta be careful. The streets are hard here. Much harder than in Port Angeles. In fact, I really miss the streets back there. They're so much . . . less soft. I like soft streets. There so much . . . you know . . . softer."

What the hell was I talking about?

C'mon. Get it together. He's just your student. Why am I so nervous?

Alberto leaned in, whispering: "Soft streets?"

"Me too. I like soft streets as well," Alex replied awkwardly.

"Yeah. Soft streets are cool," I said as I slapped Alberto away.

Okay. You're officially a complete moron. Could you please start talking normally?

"Anyway. I'm in Anghiari right now. I have to say I would've been completely lost without our lessons. That's one of the reasons I'm calling. I just wanted to thank you."

"That's . . . that's good. I'm glad the lessons worked. What are you up to?"

"Well, as I told you, my aunt passed away. It looks like we'll have to go to Rome because she may have registered her will with a law firm down there."

"Really. Didn't she have a lawyer up there?"

"It doesn't look like it. We spoke with the *Comune* director up here. It doesn't look like they have any record of her will. Things are a lot different in Italy than they are in the States. I can't even call the offices in Rome to find out. Italian bureaucracy is a mess."

"Get used to it. Nothing works."

We both chuckled, taking the edge off the tension of the call.

"You always told me it was different. Now I believe you," he laughed. "We're heading down tomorrow. Where are you?"

"Well. I'm in Rome as a matter of fact."

"Really. Cool! Maybe we can meet?"

I suddenly felt a burst of excitement. "Sure. If you like. Are you with your Mum?"

"She's here. We should be there tomorrow afternoon. Where do you wanna meet?"

I tried to think of a place that wasn't too heavy with traffic, but was popular enough that a tourist could find. "Have you heard of Piazza Cavour?"

"No. But I could find it. Without my phone, I don't have GPS. Is it on a map?"

"Probably. It's a pretty big piazza, but there are lots of places to park. Should we meet around two o'clock?"

"Cool," there was a long pause. "So, how's things with you, anyway?"

"Things are good. But I'm really sleepy. I've been up for over forty hours. I'm heading home now to get some sleep. Mamma's here with me now, and my stupid cousin." I slapped him again as he kept eavesdropping.

"Nice! Will I get to meet them?"

"I'm sure you'll meet Ma, but I don't think you'll ever want to meet my cousin."

"Sounds like a fun guy. Listen . . . I'm eating up data and it's not my phone."

"Whose phone is it?"

"It's one of my aunt's neighbours, Maria. She's right here."

"Ooo. Maria, huh? Is she cute?" My heart ached when I asked the question. "I told you you'd get a girlfriend in no time. Especially with your accent."

"She's nice. Kind of like you, only a little younger."

"Ouch. That hurt. What's a matter with older women, anyway?" What the hell was I asking? *Why* was I asking?

Alex went quiet before clearing his throat. "Um. Yeah, well. You know. Older women are nice too. You're nice, but I have to say, you're a lot prettier."

"Yeah, right. Nice try, kiddo. Maybe ten years ago." I thought my heart would leap right out of my chest.

Whoever lands this kid will be the luckiest woman in the world.

Bitch.

"Anyway. I'll see you tomorrow and you can meet Mum. Have a good night!"

"You too, Alex! Ciao!"

"Arri . . . arrivederci," he stammered.

"Arrivederci."

A strange elation fluttered through my body as I hung up. I didn't know what to think. One side of me was happy I would see him. Another was wondering why I was so happy. Mamma was looking at me with a coy expression. Alberto was bursting with curiosity.

"Why were you talking about streets?" He asked. "Is he a paver or something? You better not be interested in a construction worker."

"I'm not interested in anybody, and no, he's not a paver. Why do you care so much, anyway? What are you smiling at, Ma?" I said with my hands on my hips.

"Nothing." Mamma said.

"Nothing? What do you mean 'nothing?' Who's this guy?" Alberto asked.

"He's just a student. I'm only helping him out. He's coming to Rome tomorrow to find his aunt's will."

"Is he rich? Who does he work for?"

"He's just a kid. He barely has a job. He helps his mum in the family salon."

"Oh. So he's the son of a hairdresser," Alberto rolled his eyes in disgust. "Well, I'm glad to hear that you're not stooping to that level."

"I'm not stooping to any level! He's a good kid. And intelligent. He's smarter than you, *scemo*."

"Why are you defending him so much?"

He was right. I was defending him. I really didn't know what to say, so I relied on the best defense I could come up with. "Shut up," I huffed.

Alberto chuckled again. "Nice comeback. Anyway, you should come to the fundraiser. If you're moving back to Italy, you'll meet some important people who actually have jobs. Unless you're into low-wage construction types now. There won't be any of those there. And who knows? Maybe you'll find a decent career. You're wasted in . . . what's the name of that town you live in?"

"Port Angeles."

"Right. Port Whatever. You're wasted there. There's lots of opportunity for you here, especially with how well you speak English."

The idea of finding a high-profile job really appealed to me. The biggest problem was dealing with people like my cousin again. I hated pretense.

"We'll see," I said.

"Hey, where are you guys going now?"

I looked to Mamma for the answer. I really didn't know where she was taking me.

"To Fabio's for a coffee. Do you want to come?" Mamma asked.

I rolled my eyes. "Yeah. I think Mamma's trying to set me up with someone."

"Then I'm definitely coming. This should be fun."

Chapter 8
Handshakes

Alex

Even though it had been nearly twenty-four hours since I spoke with Laura over Maria's phone, the drive from Anghiari to Rome made it feel like a week. I'd always heard that time stood still when facing imminent death. No one told me that it involved sitting in a pool of my cold sweat as I dodged bug-eyed-sunglass wearing drivers all the while listening to Mum's shrill screams of terror as we hurtled down the highway at 120mph in the slow lane.

Welcome to Italy.

My heart was still racing as I hung up the payphone at Piazza Cavour. "She's on her way," I called over to Mum who was sitting in the car, drained. "With Fabio."

I thought "Fabios" were only found in cheesy romance novels.

"Fabio? Is that her boy-toy?" Mum joked. It surprised me she had the energy for humour as she manicured her frazzled hair.

"Just because you're called Fabio, doesn't mean you're some sort of super handsome Italian sex machine."

Does it?

Turning my back, I tried to hide my disappointment from Mum. Was this the mystery man Laura mentioned during our lessons? Maybe she had come back to Rome to be with this Fabio guy, and I was just a silly Camerican student who was ruining her plans.

"Alex?" Mum asked.

I ignored her as I tried to understand my feelings. Why was I annoyed? I shouldn't care who she was with. Latin lover. Fabio. Mystery man. It shouldn't have mattered to me. So why did it? Why was I upset? None of these feelings made sense.

"Alex!" she persisted.

"What?!" I reeled on her. "What is it?"

"Watch where you're walking."

Looking down, my feet were trampling in a puddle of brown goo. "What the heck? What is that?" When the foul odor hit my nose, I realized what I was pacing in. "Shit!" I shouted, startling a group of pigeons on the other side of the piazza.

"Literally," Mum snickered.

"This can't be happening. This isn't what I need right now. Right when I'm about to meet the girl I ..." I caught myself before saying it. The word "like" was dangerously close to the tip of my tongue.

Wait a second. Did I actually like my tutor? I couldn't tell that to Mum. Hell, I couldn't even tell that to myself. Truth always had a way of sneaking in a word or two, and right now, I didn't want to face what I was about to say. So instead, I focused on my stinky predicament. "God, it's like my shoes are painted in crap! What kind of dog leaves a puddle of poo on the ground, anyway? I've seen lumps before, but a puddle? Why don't they clean up after their dogs here?"

"Welcome to Italy," Mum said with a little too much smugness.

I was getting a little tired of hearing that.

Suddenly, a loud honk blared from behind as I looked up to see a white scooter screeching to a halt, nearly hitting me. A rotund man with a white helmet and matching white teeth looked at me from behind a visor.

Who the hell is this guy?

Sitting behind him, the most beautiful thighs I had ever seen straddled his waist. Tanned, smooth calves pressed tightly against the scooter making me wonder who on earth they belonged to.

"Ciao Alex!"

I knew that voice, but it couldn't be her. Not with those legs! When I recovered from the realization that my tutor was more than just a pretty face, my heart stopped.

"Laura?"

Her smile filled my heart with elation as angels sang from heaven.

No, wait. Those are Mum's screams still ringing in my ears from the drive down.

Laura's arms were wrapped around the driver's waist.

Tightly.

"Ciao!" She waved while the driver stabilized the scooter with his tippy-toes barely touching the ground.

I hadn't realized how much I missed her until that moment.

And how did I not notice those legs before!?

In Port Angeles, it was always too cold to wear anything but jeans, so I guessed she never wore a mini skirt.

A *really mini* mini-skirt.

Now I was really confused. Back at home, she was just a fun tutor I learned Italian with, but here, she was a sexy fox!

And I was standing in poo!!

I waved back, a little wary of the man in front. He seemed like a nice guy. It was impossible to miss his teeth as the sun gleamed off of them.

This must be Fabio. The mystery man. The lover.

Yep.

I could smell the sex on both of them. I bet they just came from tearing each others clothes off.

Mum was standing by the car now with her arms folded beneath her chest, watching carefully as Laura hopped off the scooter and bounced over to give me a hug. Before she could wrap her arms around me, she stood back, staring down at my feet.

A ridge of disgust creased her forehead as she covered her nose with her fingers. "Why are you standing in poop?"

This was not how I wanted to meet Laura on my first day in Rome. Hell, this wasn't how I would want to meet anyone in Rome. Fabio tilted his head on the scooter to stare at my shitty feet. His teeth vanished.

"This kind of sums up my time here so far," I said, staring down shamefully.

"God. Get out of there. Follow me. There are taps all over Rome. You can rinse your feet off at one of the *nasone*."

"What the heck is a *nasone*?"

"C'mon, I'll show you."

She grabbed my hand — boy, it felt good to hold her hand — pulling me over to a stand-alone tap several yards away. Mum was watching the whole scene with keen interest. Water gushed from the tap, onto the sidewalk and down a drain.

"Is that running all the time? It's just pouring water all over the street," I said.

"*Nasone* are hooked up to the aqueducts. They've run all day, every day for the past two-thousand years."

"Seems like a waste of water."

"Well, it is. But waste is an Italian thing. You'll see."

"What about the environment?"

"Environment? That's the last thing on people's minds here. That's a North American thing."

She motioned me to shove my feet under the running water. Fabio and Mum were several yards away, so they couldn't hear us. Fabio was parking his scooter beside our car. Mum was watching us vigilantly.

"Why don't people clean up after their dogs here?" I said as poo slowly melted away under the water.

Laura smiled and suggested I look across Piazza Cavour. At the center, walking under a tall statue of a portly man, another gorgeous lady — they were everywhere in Rome — was watching her little dog relieve himself on the sidewalk. "Can you imagine *that* lady with *that* mini skirt and stilettos bending down to pick up doggy doo-doo?"

Taller than most women around her, the lady would have been stunning if it wasn't for the heavy makeup layering her eyes. She walked sensually with a petite rascal on a short leash. She blew a puff of smoke from her nostrils as she readjusted her hair with her cigarette hand.

"No," I said honestly. "She'd probably fall over."

Laura laughed. "She'd *definitely* fall over. That's Rome. Romans don't clean up after their dogs. It just wouldn't look good."

"So looking good is more important than public hygiene?"

"Spoken like a true Camerican."

"Hey. You remember?" I was surprised that "Camerican" had become part of her vocabulary. I must have made a lasting impression.

"Of course I remember. You're my favorite student."

Favorite student? What does that mean? That I'm just a kid who pays the bills? That I'm the teacher's pet? That I was some kind of intellectual curiosity? A peculiarity? That I'm not worth considering as a –

I shook the remark away. "You're telling me you dress up for everything? What about if you need to run out and get some milk? You can't just throw on some sweats?"

"Oh god, no! You never know who you'll meet!" She was appalled.

"That explains why everyone dresses so well here. By the way, you look . . ." I wanted to say hot or amazing or out-of-this-world, but that would have been odd coming from her student. ". . . resuscitated."

Really?

Resuscitated?

Damn *Baywatch!* For the first time in my life, I hated Kelly Rohrbach.

She looked at me as though she could sense that my words had another meaning. "Thanks. I think," she smiled gracefully. "You look like shit. What happened to your shirt? Why are your clothes wet? And why is your hair all messy? Did you just get out of a shower?"

I looked that bad? I looked over to Fabio, who looked as polished as all the other Italians walking around.

I had to think quickly. Maybe I could get myself out of this with a little humour. "You mean you don't like my cologne? I'm wearing it just for you. It's called Eau de Caca."

Her head swayed back gently as she laughed. Her jawline shone like polished porcelain as her laugh gently filled the air with the same melody she shared during our lessons. I loved her laugh. It was the perfect blend of femininity and ease. The creases under her eyes smiled with levity. "You did? Just for me. That's so sweet. Where did you find it?"

"It's very exclusive. Personalized in your honour." As she laughed again, she touched my arm gently. Shivers tingled up my skin.

Oh man. I think I'm falling for my tutor.

Glancing over to Mum was the perfect remedy to subdue my excitement as the idea of dating my teacher quickly evaporated.

"We better join them," I said, motioning to Fabio and Mum. As we approached, I could feel Mum's girl-repulsing-superpower radiating waves of disapproval. Girls I introduced to Mum normally ran away from that repellent gaze. I wondered how an older woman would fare.

"Laura. This is Mum."

Laura extended a hand toward Mum's crossed arms, which unfolded with purposeful slowness before returning the shake.

"You can call me Mrs. Baker," she said with a cool smile as the handshake went on for a few seconds too long.

Laura seemed to note Mum's challenging tone as she squinted slightly. "Nice to meet you. How was your trip? Was it hard to find the piazza?"

"It was wonderful. No problems at all. Alex drove really well."

"Actually, there were a few times when I thought I was going to die," I said, rebuking Mum's exaggerated lie. She forced a smile in my direction. I returned the same. Laura cleared her throat. The scooter driver stepped in.

"Ciao. I'm Fabio," he said, placing his hand on the small of Laura's back. He gave me a careful inspection while extending a hairy hand.

As I took it, I stared into his eyes for a long masculine second. He did the same. In that manly moment, I understood the silent message that passed between us. It was a call of the wild. A challenge. Man against man. Or in this case, younger, taller, still rocking a six-pack man against older, hairier, slightly pudgy man. We both understood what was happening. There was no denying it. This could only mean one thing. He was vying for Laura, but had not won her hand yet.

In that defiant moment, we had officially become adversaries.

Game on.

My competitiveness kicked in. I immediately started running his strengths and weaknesses through a complex algorithm I called the "Man Rating Score."

"Mating Score" for short.

It was used to determine the strengths and weaknesses of two competing men or the compatibility of a man and a woman . It could quickly and efficiently tell me if I had a chance at winning a girl's hand against an opponent.

Question #1: Age. He was far older than me. Probably around Laura's age, and I doubted that she would be interested in someone younger.

One point for Fabio.

Question #2: Height. I stood at least ten inches taller than Fabio. As a matter of fact, I wondered how he even climbed onto his scooter. Generally, taller was better than shorter.

One point for me.

Question #3: Profession. He wore a nice white shirt, which meant that he had enough money to spend on expensive clothing. His skin had a healthy tan despite it only being May, which meant that he had been on a hot vacation recently. This led me to believe that he had employment that was better than my part-time gig at the family hair salon.

Two points for Fabio.

Question #4: Appearance. This was a tough one. He had a lazy beard which made him seem somewhat slovenly. The trouble was, my appearance wasn't that much better. As Laura had pointed out, I looked like shit. I had changed out of my gray hoodie and was wearing a Quicksilver T-shirt. The drive from Anghiari had left me damp with sweat, and my hair was frazzled from all the pollution and stress. Not to mention my sneakers were sopping with tap water and smelling of dung.

Three points for Fabio.

Question #5: Associations. It was impossible to know who he was associated with, but he certainly didn't have a brooding mother peering over his shoulder like I did.

Four points for Fabio.

There was no point going on from there. So far, I was losing. My chances didn't look good.

Wait a second! Why am I comparing myself to Fabio? Do you know what this means?

"So? Where are you staying?" Laura asked, breaking my train of thought.

I shared a gaze with Mum as I shook my head.

"I don't know. We hadn't thought of that."

"You haven't booked a hotel?" Laura asked, perplexed. "You know its tourist season. It'll be hard to find anything around here."

"Hey, what about that nunnery under your Mamma's place? They might have space," Fabio offered before frowning. I could tell that he wished he could take his words back.

"You're right, Fabio. Good idea. Not many people know about it. Let's head there now and see if they have room. If not, you're in trouble. Come on. Let's show them where it is."

Laura spun towards Fabio's scooter, snatching the helmet from the back seat. Leaning her head back, her long hair cascaded freely as she shook her wavy locks in the golden sunlight.

Time slowed. Barry White grunted as the melody of "Never, never going to give you up" played. Lifting her leg, she carefully straddled the scooter, pushing her chest forward as her breasts perked up, adding to the moment's euphoria. Barry grunted again.

Fabio and I were leaning into each other, lost in a brotherly moment of awe.

"Are you two finished?" Mum broke our trance, once again proving the strength of her girl-repulsing-super-power.

Fabio, with a victorious grin on his face, smacked me in the stomach with his hairy paw and jumped onto the front seat as Laura buckled on her helmet. Waving, she wrapped her arms around Fabio, whose grin nearly broke his visor. He must have calculated his own Mating Score. He obviously felt confident in his tally.

I didn't care though. I was happy. If I was going to be right under Laura's apartment, I could spend more time with her.

The closer, the better.

"Alex."

I ignored Mum as Laura's pearly smile flashed. She laughed sensually as Fabio pulled the scooter away like a princess on the back of a white stallion.

"Alex! You can stop staring now," Mum said crossly.

Mum's intervention was complete as the Laura-spell broke. Snapping my eyes to the ground to avoid looking at Mum, I headed to the car. If I looked at her, she would have been able to read the words written all over my face.

YOU HAVE A CRUSH.

Damn.

I opened the door for Mum and closed it behind her. As I walked to the driver's side, Laura smiled playfully while twinkling a couple of fingers in my direction. My throat clenched.

Double-damn. I'm in trouble.

I had to get to the nunnery and figure these feelings out. Sitting in the driver's seat, I slammed the door, staring at the steering wheel.

"You never told me how attractive your teacher was," Mum said. I could feel her eyes boring into me, like burning X-ray vision.

"Is she? Really? I hadn't noticed." Turning the key, the car wouldn't start. "You know me. I don't mix business with pleasure, just like you taught me." I stomped the accelerator. Damn car. Start! "Besides, she's not really a teacher. She's just a tutor. Plus, she's way older than me." Maybe if I pressed the clutch. . .idiot. The engine roared alive.

"Really? How much older?"

"Oh. I don't know. Just. . .fifteen years, I think."

"Fifteen? You've put a lot of thought into this, haven't you?"

I did a slow shoulder check to hide the truth. "Um. I don't know what you are talking about." Revving the engine as loudly as I could, I bolted in pursuit of Laura and Fabio.

I wasn't in the mood for one of Mum's girl lectures. Besides, Laura wasn't a girl.

She was a woman.

A hot, sexy, charming, fun, smooth legged, fiercely sensual woman.

I'm in real trouble.

Chapter 9
Kissy-kiss

Laura

Why did this street always smell? It was like a bad combo of dung and scooter soot. Sure, it was one of the nicer parts of Rome nestled in the *Prati* district, but sometimes I wished Romans would pick up after their dogs. Alex was right about that. Even though it was close to the center and there was a grocery store around the corner, visiting Mamma always made me think of what Papà had done to her.

I have to get her off of this street.

How? It wasn't like the States where getting a mortgage was fairly simple. Everything was harder in Italy.

One word: sugar-daddy.

I laughed at myself.

What? And give up my search for Mr. Perfect?

It wasn't like I was past my prime or anything. I was only thirty-five. Surely I could find him before I was seventy.

Forget marriage. Go for Giancarlo.

Yeah, right. If I wanted to sell my soul, I would have sold it when I was in my twenties. At least I could have been divorced by now and enjoying insincere naughtiness with stray men while pouring Botox into my morning coffee.

I looked over my shoulder at the nunnery nestled beside Mamma's apartment. Luckily for Alex, Sister Greta had space. Unluckily for me, his not-so-charming mother was closer than I liked.

Hey, you could always marry a kid like Alex. At least he's cute. And sweet.

Not with a mother like that, thank you very much.

I laughed again.

I must be desperate.

"What a cow!" I said to Fabio as I came out of the nunnery. He leaned on his bike like a "hipsterized" *Grease* character. Smokey resolve and all.

"Who? The kid's Ma?"

"Yes, the kid's bitchy Ma," I stomped my foot down on the pavement as I stopped within an arm's length of Fabio.

"Shh. She might hear you," he said, patting the air with both hands.

"I don't care. She tried to leave me a tip. Can you imagine that?"

"A tip? For what?"

"For helping them find a room. What am I? A servant?"

"Did you take it?" Fabio joked.

A smack on the arm seemed like the perfect response. Unfortunately, he seemed to like that a little too much as he leaned off of his scooter and moved a little closer.

Note to self: random hitting with Fabio makes him alarmingly perky.

That was the last thing I needed was Fabio after me. It wasn't enough having Giancarlo on my tail. Adding Fabio the Great would have been one Italian-man too many.

"You should have let Fabio Il Grande take them upstairs." Fabio puffed his chest, preening like a rooster as he declared his name for all to hear. The pigeons ignored him.

I laughed. Italian machismo had no limits. It was one of the things that I really didn't miss. At the same time, it was sweet in its juvenility, like a boy bragging to his friends in front of a girl in grade school. I could see why Mamma had wanted me to meet him. There was a simplicity to him, even if he desperately lacked self-assuredness. I had learned that any man referring to himself in the third person needed a woman willing to tolerate vast insecurity.

I also knew that I was not that woman. Any man by my side would have to be confident enough to deal with an opinionated woman. My friends often told me I was a handful, even for an Italian. It was true, though. I knew I was rambunctious, hot-headed, and sometimes downright stubborn.

All right, I was always stubborn. But I could see reason if reason was reasonable.

It was why I was still unmarried. Italian men couldn't handle me. The men I dated always wanted someone submissive. Someone passive. I was anything but. My uncle used to tease me that I would be a spinster if I didn't tie a man down soon. Women my age were usually onto their third child by now or having an affair with an Italian lover named Fabio.

Judging by the look in his eye, an affair was exactly what Fabio wanted. It was a look I had seen many times before from Italian men. It was filled with expectation for favours rendered. After all, he had driven me all around Rome today, and that meant I was in the unenviable position of owing him.

Why couldn't chivalry be free in Italy?

"That's okay. You've done enough for today. Thanks for the ride."

"No problem. You know, if you ever need a *ride* again, just let me know." He was moving closer as he emphasized the word "ride."

Oh, brother.

I needed to change topic.

"Maybe if you were Alex," I said.

Wait. What did I just say?

"What did you just say?" Fabio asked, just as surprised as I was.

Did I actually mean that? My student?

It might be kind of like riding the teacups at Disneyland. Young, but fun.

I shook my head. What the hell was I thinking?

"Nothing," I tried to play it cool. Fabio fell silent. In a heap of sulkiness, he looked at me like a whimpering puppy who had lost its bone. It would have been cute if he were a puppy, but seeing a grown man longing for attention made me feel sorry for him.

Pity is not sexy.

I had to be careful how I dealt with this situation, so I treated him as I would any friend. "*Grazie*, Fabio. You were a great *friend* today."

He pulled himself together, encouraged by my attention. If he had a tail, it would have wagged. He leaned in to give me a hug. I returned the gesture as I would with any Italian friend; with two kisses on each cheek.

Everything was going according to Italian custom until he asked me the question that sealed his fate from ever attracting my romantic interest.

"*Damme un bacino?*"

I couldn't believe what I was hearing.

A 'kissy-kiss'? He wanted a kissy-kiss?

Summoning every ounce of tolerance, I responded as politely as I could. "Gross! Not a chance!"

With that not-so-subtle comment, any remaining shred of Fabio's masculinity shriveled away like a turtle thrown in the Arctic. There was only one word to describe the next few seconds.

Awkward.

"Anyway. I've got to get going. Mamma's waiting upstairs. I'll see you later." With that, I spun and fled into Mamma's apartment building, leaving Fabio the not-so-great standing in the street. It was the first time I enjoyed the elevator ride to Mamma's. At least he couldn't fit in there with me. After I made it upstairs and closed the door to her place, I couldn't contain myself anymore.

"He asked for a kissy-kiss."

"A kissy-kiss? Who? Alex?"

"Not Alex. Fabio! It was the sorriest thing I'd ever seen."

"Why did he want it?"

"Who knows? Maybe he felt entitled because he helped me today. God! There's never a dull moment with Roman men!"

"I thought you were tired of dull moments with American men?"

I laughed bitterly. "Sure, but are there no real men anymore? I mean, c'mon! A kissy-kiss after just meeting. For crying out loud! Give me a break! Why can't they just be a good friend first? They want to jump right to it. American men might be reserved, but at least they don't ask for kissy-kisses."

"What about Alex?" Mamma changed the subject, probably knowing full well that I was about to head on an angry rant.

"Alex? He's fine. He's next door at the nunnery with Sister Greta and his mother."

"What's she like?"

"Do you remember Enzo's mother, how she used to come with us on our dates and sit in the back seat of the car?"

"How could I forget?"

"Mrs. Baker is a sneakier version of that."

"Sneakier?"

"And guess what? We're having dinner with them tonight."

"Why would you want to have dinner with that kind of person?" Mamma knew I was the type of woman who didn't spend time with people I didn't like.

"I don't know. I guess I feel for Alex. He's a really sweet kid. Those two are completely lost in Italy. They didn't even book a hotel room. If Sister Greta didn't have space, I don't know what they would have done. I certainly wasn't going to help them." I knew that was a lie, and so did Mamma, who gave me a cockeyed look. "All right, all right. I would have probably ended up driving them all over Rome."

"You know you can't help yourself. Whenever you see someone in need, you have to get involved. Besides, you've been talking about Alex ever since you met him."

"I have?"

"You didn't notice? Every time you called me from America, you'd end up talking about your "amazing student." I thought maybe you had a crush on him."

"A crush! Give me a break, Ma." I could feel my cheeks turning red. "He's a child. I'm not Macron's wife."

"No. You're not. You're my daughter and it's time you found someone to settle down with. Enough running around the world trying to find him. Sometimes the person we need is right in front of us."

"I know you're not talking about Giancarlo." That would be an odd statement coming from Mamma. She never really liked him. Ever since Papà, she was cautious around rich and powerful men. Especially married ones.

"All I'm saying is that no man is ever good enough for you, so maybe you need to change your perspective a little." Mamma was starting one of her preaches again.

"It's not my fault they're not perfect."

"I always thought your father was the perfect man. He was handsome. Charming. Funny. But then he turned into a beast. Cheating. Lying. You know how the story ended. All I'm saying is that perfect doesn't exist, and sometimes imperfections are the perfections we need."

"What are you saying Ma? That I should marry someone I don't get along with?"

"I'm saying that you need to loosen up a little and have faith. Only then can fate bring you who you *need*. Not who you *want*."

Great. Another one of Mamma's preaches when what I needed was a partner in life who wasn't crazy, or married, or asking for kissy-kisses. What I needed was my soulmate, and I would not stop looking until I found him.

Chapter 10
One

Alex

Sister Greta was a skeleton of a nun. Her habit hung over her bony body like a curtain. Although short, she exuded a painful austerity that commanded obedience. A veil covered her narrow head, and if eyes were the windows to the soul, hers were guarded by small round glasses. It was clear that crossing her would mean summoning the full wrath of God's fury.

As she led us up a long staircase, younger nuns scurried around her like frightened ants. Eyes never met as they all avoided her gaze in case she might find a trace of guilt that could merit a scolding. Once we reached the top, three hallways forked, one to the right, one to the left and one in the middle.

Tall ceilings held pale lights that dimly lit the halls to the left and right. It was the middle hall that remained lost in darkness. Stopping, something beckoned from its dark depths as I froze in a moment of analysis.

"Are you joining us?" Sister Greta broke my trance.

"Um, *si.*" I said as I shook my head at the bizarre hypnosis. Turning to join Mum and Sister Greta, I couldn't ignore the curiosity of what was down that middle hall.

"Here you are," she said, opening our door with a reaper-like hand. "Remember, men sleep on this side of the hall, and women on the other. There is to be no mixing of the virtues here. There are two bathrooms. The one at this end of the hall is for women. The one at the other end is for men."

"You don't need to worry. This is my Mum," I explained.

"I wasn't referring to you and your mother, young man. I am referring to you inviting women up to your room. It is strictly forbidden. Do you understand?"

"I'll cancel that orgy I had planned tonight then," I whispered under my breath.

"What?" Mum asked in shock.

"*Che cosa?*" Sister Greta asked.

"Nothing. Don't worry," I shook my head, surprised that Mum had taken me seriously. "One-night stands aren't my thing, anyway." Let alone one-night orgies. If I was to be with a woman, it would have to be for love and nothing else. Senses were not toys to be played with like boys. Instead, they were meant to help us find the deeper meaning of life. And right now, I needed a moment to find the deeper meaning of my life away from Mum and Sister Greta.

I usually knew if a girl was a good fit for me. In fact, my friends teased me because I rarely dated. It wasn't for a lack of trying, but after first dates, I knew whether I could get along with a girl. Most girls my age were too young in an emotional sense, spending most of our date time chatting about their favorite drinks or who they followed on Instagram. They lost interest when I told them that I didn't even have an Instagram account. After all, who wants to date someone with zero followers?

Laura was someone I could connect with. I'd spent so much time fooling myself that our connection was strictly Platonic, just the chemistry of a great student-teacher relationship. But after seeing her today, I discovered feelings I must have ignored because she was my tutor.

As Sister Greta and I spoke Italian, Mum looked at me inquisitively, but I didn't bother translating. The last thing I needed was her thinking I might invite Laura up for a "nightcap." Then I would have a nun *and* a mum watching my every move.

I dropped Mum's suitcase on the granite floor of her room, which was small, but not nearly as small as my own. All that was missing from my toadstool-like room was Smurfette, although, as Sister Greta had warned, Smurfettes were prohibited.

After Sister Greta marched away, Mum looked at me from across the hall. "What time are we meeting Laura and her mother?"

"She said in a couple of hours. I really need a shower." I turned to look down the hall just in time to see a hairy man enter the bathroom and close the door. "Or maybe the shower can wait. I guess I'll lie down for a bit. It's been a long day."

"Okay, love. I'll see you soon." Mum looked tired as she closed her door.

I looked back down the hall to see if the stocky gentleman's visit was a brief one. Anything beyond thirty seconds in the bathroom meant it would be unvisitable for a while. After a minute, I unfortunately gave up hope.

Closing my door, I carefully placed my bag on the ground, remembering that I had stashed Anne's picture inside. Too tired to take it out, I flopped on the tiny bed. It was so short that my legs hung over the end. It seemed that Italy hadn't been built for anyone over five and a half feet tall.

It didn't matter though. The discomfort of my body paled in comparison to the discomfort of my soul. Asking a teacher out would be the strangest thing I had ever done.

A lot of the guys I knew treated dating like a race. More women somehow meant they were more masculine. It always seemed like a never-ending race to me. When did a man stop? Was there a number? Were fifty women enough? A hundred. I had heard that Genghis Khan had bedded two thousand women.

I tried to do the math on that one and got tired thinking about it.

I'd always had one number in mind.

One.

That was all I needed.

As I drifted off to sleep, a big question still lingered. Did Laura like me back? Or was I just a foolish romantic who had fallen for an older woman because I found her more interesting than 'Instagirls'?

•   •   •   •   •

Loud knocking came from my door. My arms felt like the gangling appendages of a puppet as I awkwardly willed myself upright.

"Alex. Alex. It's Mum. Are you asleep?"

"No. I'm good. I'll be right there." I sounded more irritated than I wanted to. It wasn't anger towards Mum. I was just dazed from the long journey.

Her muffled words came through the door. "All right. I'll be downstairs." Her footsteps fade down the hall.

When I finally joined her outside, she was talking with Laura and an older blond lady wearing thick-rimmed glasses. "I've never seen my son like this before," Mum was telling Laura. "He seems very comfortable around you."

Was she drawing Laura into a false sense of security? I needed to keep an eye on her. She'd done this before only to sabotage my relationships by undermining me. A sharp quip about the drool on my cheek first thing the morning, or how I liked to play video games, or her tried and tested bed wetting lies were all ways she'd try to drive women out of my life. The last thing I needed was for her to treat me like a child when I needed to show Laura that I was man enough for her attention.

"Hi, Mum. Ciao, Laura."

Mum turned, a brief look of guilt sketched across her face before it became stony once again. Her arms were behind her back like she was hiding something in her hands.

"Ciao, Alex. This is my mamma, Michela."

I couldn't help but compare her to Laura. Michela was as short as her daughter with golden blond hair. Except for a few wrinkles around her mouth, her plump face was smooth and flawless, though a double chin and missing waist hinted at a love of food. When I quickly glanced down, her legs were a stark contrast to the rest of her body. It seemed God had spent too much time shaping them and then rushed to move onto the next person. Laura's genetic inheritance was obvious.

She smiled warmly. "*Salve*. Nice to meet you. Laura has told me a lot about you."

"Nice to meet you. Is it just us?" I asked.

Laura looked surprised. "Who else would there be?"

"What about Fabio?" I tested.

"Fabio? Why would he be here?"

"Oh. Sorry. I thought he was a close friend."

"No. Fabio . . ." She looked to Michela. ". . . well, Fabio is Fabio." She shrugged and laughed.

Perfect. There was only one thing that could destroy a high Mating Score: the friend zone. Even a guy with a five-out-of-five score would drop to a zero if a woman put him in this romantic limbo. If I was reading Laura's reaction correctly, Fabio had been relegated. This automatically canceled his previous score, which put me back in the lead.

I smiled. "So where are we going?"

"*Andiamo da Tesone?*" Laura asked Michela.

"*No lo so. Quello che vuoi? Volete la pizza?*" she asked Laura while shrugging her shoulders.

"Do you guys want pizza?" she said.

I looked to Mum who quickly said, "It doesn't matter. Wherever is easiest."

"We had an amazing *cinghiale* in Tuscany. Is there a place that serves that here?"

"*Cinghiale*? Not in Rome. That's a Tuscan plate. If you want a real Roman dish, then you have to try *pasta alla carbonara*."

"What's that?"

"You've never had it? C'mon. I'll show you."

Linking arms with Mum and Michela, she led them down the street. I followed behind, hoping that maybe Laura's charm could win over Mum. I liked that about Laura — she made everyone around her feel comfortable and welcome. It was the same way she made me feel during our lessons. There was never a hint of awkwardness.

Then it struck me.

Is Laura a flirt?

A flirtatious personality had misguided me in the past, leading to heartbreak when I learned it was a false flag. I had to be careful here. The only way to find out the truth was to see if she was flirtatious with other men. That should give me an idea if her teasing with me was real, or just her normal social behavior.

I scoured my thoughts, searching for tangible evidence of my theory. Had I seen her flirt with Fabio at Piazza Cavour? I reviewed every scene carefully, looking for anything that could have been remotely flirtatious. She had her arms wrapped around his waist when they first drove up on the scooter.

But she had to, or else she would've fallen off.

Just as I was thinking all of this, she turned and stuck her tongue out cheekily.

I laughed.

She was so much fun. And sexy. I loved flirts.

Damn it! Be careful! Let's see how she behaves at dinner.

A true flirt would flirt with me in front of anyone. On the other hand, if she had feelings for me, she might be careful how she behaved in front of Mum. This dinner would be important.

I lost the thought when the smell of fresh pizza caught my nose, igniting a salivary riot in my mouth. I hadn't eaten since breakfast and my stomach was doing somersaults at the sumptuous fragrances coming from Tesone's, which was full of local diners. Men and women, all beautifully dressed, sipped from tiny taster cups or small glasses of wine on an outside patio. We had to dodge plumes of cigarette smoke as we stepped around the tables on the sidewalk.

Once we were inside, Laura grabbed a table big enough for all four of us. I sat across from Laura to make sure that she was within "flirting distance." Mum sat beside me and across from Michela.

This could work. Now, I had to see what she would do.

Please don't flirt. Please don't flirt.

"So, Laura, what was it like teaching my son?" Mum asked, starting her inquisition.

Laura crossed her arms, betraying a hint of defensiveness. "Your son is an amazing student. I'd never seen someone learn so quickly.

Besides, he's very handsome, which made the lessons that much more fun."

Uh-oh. Verbal flirting. And in front of Mum! This is a disaster!

That meant she was extremely comfortable with our relationship, even when under maternal attack. The question remained, was I in the dreaded friend zone?

It was Mum's turn to cross her arms. "Well, he has many strong points."

Just then, a waiter came to our table.

"*Buona sera*," he said.

"*Buona sera*. Oh. I like your bracelet," Laura said to the waiter.

Shit. More verbal flirting. This time to a complete stranger.

This wasn't looking good.

"Thank you. My sister made it. She's a jeweler."

"She's very talented," Laura responded with no follow through. This was a neutral sign. She could have been making a simple comment. So far, nothing was conclusive.

"Can I bring you folks anything to drink?"

"How about some wine?" Laura looked to me and Mum.

"Sure. What do you recommend?" I responded.

"If we're having *carbonara*, then we have to get some wine. Red."

I watched Laura's hands carefully as the waiter left. I placed my arm within reach, praying that she wouldn't touch me.

Instead, Laura leaned forward, placing her arms on the table. "You'll love *carbonara*. It's made with cheese, eggs and bacon."

"Yum. Sounds delicious," I said.

"And fattening," Mum added.

"What do you need to worry about, Mrs. Baker? You're skinny." Another compliment, this time to my mum. I was starting to get the feeling that she was complimentary to everyone. I needed more proof. I started tapping my fingers to see if it would lure her into a touch.

"Are you okay? I've never seen you this quiet before. You're usually so talkative during our lessons," Laura asked me.

"He is? Well, that's news to me," Mum said as she gave me a long look.

"You mean he doesn't talk at home?"

"Oh no. In fact, this is the most out-going I've ever seen him. He's usually such a bore."

Great. Mum was fabricating lies. She was skipping the more embarrassing moments of my youth and going straight for the "slander-Alex method." I needed to act quickly or else she'd be telling everyone that I suffered from incontinence and wore a diaper. But I still needed to get to the bottom of Laura's flirting. This would be tricky. Maybe a compliment of my own would incite some casual flirting and keep the conversation away from my bowel movements.

"I really like you hair, Laura," I said. Hopefully, the compliment was enough to push back against Mum, and potentially trigger Laura's flirting mechanism. If she touched me after a compliment, then it was game over. Only someone completely disinterested in romance would touch a 'complimentarian.'

Please don't touch. Please don't touch.

Her hands came within an inch of my arm. My eyes widened.

"You mean you haven't noticed all the younger girls around Italy?" she asked flipping her hair back with one hand.

"There are always beautiful girls around, but no one beats you," I replied sincerely. If that compliment didn't incite at least a little touch, then nothing would.

My prayers were answered. Instead of touching me, she blushed. "You see. How could I not enjoy teaching your son?" she said to Mum. "He's so cute."

Shit.

She called me cute. Of all the compliments I wanted to hear, cute was just a little better than ugly.

I'm not cute. Tea-cup poodles are cute. Kittens playing with toilet paper are cute. Justin Bieber when he was five was cute. Me? I'm not cute.

This was definitely heading into the friend zone. I had to act fast. I had to do something sexy. Something unexpected. I had to surprise her with grace to pull myself out of this social nosedive. Just as I was losing hope, a miracle appeared.

He was short, dark and not handsome at all, but he came right up to our table, an angel walking through the mists of my desperation, and stood wearing a tuxedo and a bouquet of roses.

"A rose for your ladies?" he gestured to me.

"*No grazie*," Laura and Michela said in unison. They were obviously used to this kind of sophisticated hawker.

"How much?" I asked with a little too much zeal.

The man smiled greedily. Teeth chipped and stained. "Five euros," he replied.

"No," Laura said in English. "What are you doing? These guys rip people off. One rose for five euros? It's ridiculous."

It was just the thing I needed. It was perfect. This should send the right message. No friend zone for me. As I opened my wallet, Laura clapped her mouth in surprise. Michela smiled. Mum teetered in her seat, poised to tell everyone that I wore *Depends* and changed them every hour.

Looking down, my wallet stared up at me. Empty. I didn't have a single bill to my name. All I could find were some old receipts for those chocolate-covered cherries I bought at Fiumicino airport. I looked up to the vendor, who leaned in even closer with a beautiful rose, his breath nearly wilting their petals.

"Um, Mum, can you lend me a few bucks?" I kept my chin down hoping to hide my red face.

Mum snickered with a little too much satisfaction and dug into her purse. I took the money and handed it to the vendor, who handed the rose to Laura. I wasn't sure how this affected my score, but it definitely helped. She blushed as she looked to Mum, who was smiling victoriously, but I didn't care. I'd done it. The friend zone was slowly pulling away. Now she knew. I had made my intentions clear, but I still had to see if she felt the same way towards me.

Chapter 11
Ketchup?

Laura

Just when I thought Mrs. Baker couldn't detest me anymore after refusing her tip at the nunnery, her son gave me a rose with *her* money. And I thought this evening would be boring.

Sniffing the rose, I didn't try to hide my smile of satisfaction. Your son just declared himself to me, right in front of you.

How does it feel to have your son crushing on his teacher?

Ha. I bet she didn't see that coming. What mother would ever expect her son to have a thing for his tutor? My guess was the rose completely floored her, and she was panicking right now. I could see it in her eyes. Yep. She was losing her mind.

Wait.

Hold on a second.

Back up.

My student just gave *me* a rose. My cute, sweet, gorgeously dimpled, *younger* student just gave "not-that-fat-but-definitely-fatter-than-I-was-at-twenty" me a rose! What did this mean?

You know exactly what this means, Laura.

I had received many roses before, and they always meant the same thing: affection.

Which led to dating.

Which led to dinners.

Then dessert.

Then taking me home.

Then a first kiss.

Then—.

This isn't happening.

Looking up from my rose, anxiety wiped away my smile. What was I going to do? I couldn't date my student. No way. This was just a friendship rose, that was all. He probably enjoyed giving gifts to everyone. Just the way I did.

This is just a gift, that's all.

"I bet he does this for every girl?" I asked Mrs. Baker, holding the rose up to cover my panic.

She laughed, leaning on the table with her elbows. Fingers knit together with the careful English pomp of a *John Smedley* sweater. "All the time."

I exhaled in relief.

You see. He doesn't have a crush on you. He's just being nice.

Mrs. Baker continued. "You have no idea how many times he's asked me for money. It gets tiring providing for three sons, but you wouldn't know anything about that, would you? You're still single at—how old are you? Forty?" She leaned back in her chair with a smug mug as Alex's expression tightened.

All right. I get it. It's bitch time. Bring it on, lady.

I looked over to Mamma, who didn't know whether to giggle or frown. She knew the level of man I had dated. Some were movie stars. Others were politicians. I grew up in Eur and lived in a home with a garden in the living room. My personal maid, Graziella, gave me foot massages on demand.

I had lived the life of a princess, until Papà took it all away, forcing Mamma and I to live in a dingy little apartment as I went to work at the age of fifteen. I scrubbed concrete entrances outside retail stores to get by. I could still feel the acidic cleaner burning through my hands, stripping away years of manicures and paraffin treatments.

I quickly learned the value of hard work as I lugged heavy clothes up and down stairs at my next job. For five years I slaved away before getting a coveted promotion to sell fashion on the floor at *Gente*. I worked my tail off to get by. So did Mamma, and this woman was lecturing me on responsibility.

I wasn't going to take it.

Just as I was about to open my mouth and lash out, Alex intervened. "Stop being mean, Mum. She doesn't look forty. I think you look great. When I first met you, I thought you were my age."

The red from my anger quickly turned to a blush of embarrassment. "Really? Your age? C'mon." From another man, this would have sounded like empty flattery. But from Alex, it felt different. It felt real. Usually men gave me compliments to get me on my back, which ended with them flat on their backs after I kicked them. Alex was saying what he felt, not what he thought I wanted to hear. It was refreshing.

"No seriously. When we first met at the coffee shop, I thought there was no way you were a tutor. I always expected someone like— well like Mum." He motioned to Mrs. Baker who straightened in her chair.

Ha. Take that. And from your own son.

In that moment, I no longer saw my student, nor his youthful age. Instead, I saw a man who was confident enough in his feelings to ask his mother for money to buy me a rose.

A super-sweet rose.

Not only that, but he was actually standing up to his mother. This was something I rarely saw in a man. Especially at twenty. Hell, I had friends who were in their fifties who still couldn't stand up to their mothers. And he was doing it right in front of me.

Who was this kid? And why had I never noticed him before?

Um. Because he's fifteen years younger, Laura!

I shook myself.

Stop it! I can't date him. Even if he is more man than most I knew.

As the thoughts came, a deep pit in my stomach opened. I looked to Alex with his perfect complexion and broad shoulders and felt jealousy for the woman who would get him.

"Thank you, Alex," I said with more feeling. "You're very sweet."

"You're welcome. I mean it. The rose as well. I wouldn't be able to speak Italian the way I do if it wasn't for you."

"You did the work. I was just there to help," I responded.

"Exactly, you helped me out. So here's a rose for you."

God, his eyes are amazing. Are they blue or gray? I could swim in those eyes.

"So, Laura, do you have a boyfriend?" Mrs. Baker took the reins of the conversation. She was obviously mortified at her son's compliments towards me. Her question caught me by surprise. Alex seemed interested as he cocked his head to one side.

"Not right now, no," I said, thumbing my rose.

"But you must have had some serious men in your life?" she prodded.

"Sure. I wouldn't be very well adjusted if I had remained single until now." *Where was she going with this?*

"What were their names?"

Oh, I get it. Dredge up the past to make me look bad. A little slut-shaming, huh? What a bag.

"There were too many to remember," I joked. *That should shut her up.*

Alex shifted in his seat. "Mum," he said.

"Well, I'm just trying to get to know Laura a little better." She continued her assault. "Were you ever engaged?"

Alex looked down at his empty plate. He didn't seem very impressed. Mamma shifted in her seat as she tried to understand the building tension and why Mrs. Baker was leaning in like a wolf cornering a rabbit.

She didn't understand that I wasn't a rabbit.

"No. I haven't found love like you have, Mrs. Baker. Were there any men before your husband?" It was time to go on the offensive. Alex grew visibly nervous as he squirmed in his seat; I doubted any son would want to hear that his mother had been "easy" with other men. I didn't want to do this to him, but I had to defend myself.

She parried quickly. "Who me? Goodness, no. I married the love of my life and bore three beautiful boys. Alex is the pickiest, though. He doesn't date just anyone."

"Well, he is a special kid. He deserves someone just as special," I said.

"My sentiments exactly," Mrs. Baker said as she sat back. "You must want to find the right person before time runs out."

Real bag.

"So far, no man has shown me what I want to see."

"That's surprising. I mean, you're beautiful. Intelligent. Not short of personality." Sarcasm stained her tone. "And yet you've had a hard time finding what you're looking for."

"Well, a good man is worth waiting for," I replied. The idea of Alex and I together was melting like ice on a summer sidewalk; Alex would have to do *way* more than buy me a rose to inspire me to put up with Mrs. Baker. He was a special guy, there was no doubt, but so was she. Just a little too special for my taste.

Luckily, our waiter turned up with our food.

"*Eccolo.*" He placed the food down in front of us. The only one who said a word was Alex. He must have wanted to change topics. Smart kid. I was about to eat his mother for dinner.

"What's this?" How could inquisitiveness make someone so sexy? "Is it spaghetti?"

My anger towards his mother suddenly softened when I looked at his sweet face. And what a beautiful face it was. I sniffed the rose before putting it down beside my plate. Ignoring Mrs. Baker, I reached out and touched his arm.

He tightened.

Strange. Why was he so tense? He never reacted that way during our lessons when I touched him. He always seemed to like it. "*Pasta alla carbonara.* You wanted a Roman dish, this is as Roman as it gets."

"It smells amazing! What's in it?"

Mrs. Baker pretended not to care as she slowly leaned forward, curling her nose with distaste. "It looks heavy. Is this why Italians are so big-boned?"

"Mum. Cut it out," Alex said shooting her a sharp look.

I ignored her. This was going to be the last meal with this cow, anyway. "It's made with eggs and *guanciale.*"

"Pig cheeks?" He asked.

"Good job. You remembered." I touched him again to see if he would tighten.

He didn't this time, but his mother did.

Everyone picked up their forks, with Mrs. Baker being the last.

Alex looked around the table, a little lost. What was he looking for? Did he want to pour me more wine? Or offer me some salt? Was he trying to ensure my happiness before his own? No-strings-attached chivalry, perhaps?

"Where's the ketchup?" he asked.

I dropped my fork as it clattered on the floor. All the other patrons looked over to us.

"Ketchup?"

"Yeah. It looks like it could use some ketchup."

"But, you haven't even tasted it yet," I gasped.

Mrs. Baker smiled. Satisfaction smeared her features. She must have known her son would do something like this.

"What? I like ketchup," Alex said, confused by my reaction. "Don't Italians use ketchup?"

"This dish is perfect. Why would you ruin it with sugary-tomato gravy?"

That was it. Crazy mother. Fifteen years age deficit. Bad dresser. Now ketchup and carbonara?

No way. Not going to happen. I could never date a man who wanted to put ketchup on his carbonara. It just wouldn't work. What other strange things would he want? Raspberry sauce on his tiramisu? Parmesan on his mussels? Not to mention his attire. A T-shirt to dinner? Sneakers? He had way too much to learn. We were far too different.

Like Nonna used to say: *mogli e buoi dei paesi tuoi.* Stick to your own people.

I didn't care how sweet he was, Alex and his cooky mother were so far off of my radar now that they may as well be on the moon. I would *never* date a Camerican kid. End of story.

Chapter 12
Who Is This Guy?

Alex

The carbonara looked delicious, but ketchup would have made it that much better. I just knew it. Obviously, Laura thought otherwise.

"I had no idea condiments were so controversial in Italy," I said meekly.

Laura stared at me in disbelief. "I can't believe you want ketchup!" She was half laughing, half serious. "Just so you know, you won't find ketchup in any Italian restaurants."

To think a condiment could be the end of our relationship even before it began.

I glanced over to Mum, who had a strange smirk. She had been more belligerent than ever tonight.

Sensing the tension, Michela leaned over and put a hand on Laura's arm. She spoke so quickly that I couldn't understand most of it. Laura sat back in her chair, nodding.

"What did she say?" I asked.

Laura flashed her shiny brown eyes up to me. Puddles of warmth. "Mamma has traveled a lot. She has been all over the world, and the one thing she learned is that each country has its own culture. She said I should be a little more accepting."

"No, you shouldn't," I said immediately.

"What?" She asked in surprise. "Why not?"

"This is your country. I'm here to learn. If I wanted ketchup, I should have packed it in my suitcase. I didn't think it was a big deal, but obviously it is. If anyone needs to learn to accept, it's me. I'm the guest here. I came here to find Italy. And in Italy, I just learned, there's no ketchup."

Laura translated for her Mamma. Michela gave me a smile of approval. "*É intelligente, questo.*"

Taking my fork, I rolled a mound of carbonara and popped it into my mouth, making exaggerated sounds of enjoyment. Everyone laughed. Even Mum. The tension seemed to dissolve, until a voice called over from behind me.

"Laura? Is that you?"

Laura looked over my shoulder and froze, the color leaving her face.

When I turned, I understood why. I had never been star-struck before, but the gentleman walking towards us had the air of a movie star. It was as though Pierce Brosnan had given the world his only begotten son to lead all men down the righteous path to manhood. Every woman in the room turned to watch this fine figure as he walked up to us, jealousy and lust in their eyes.

"Giancarlo. What are you doing here?" Laura asked.

It was the first time I had seen her flustered.

"I'm here with some friends. It's nice to see you. You look wonderful." His voice made Andrea Bocelli sound like a *castrato*.

"Ciao, Giancarlo. *Comè stai?*" Michela broke in.

"I'm well. Very well. How are you both?"

Laura seemed to shake herself back to reality. "Giancarlo. We are good. Very good. What . . . um, these are my friends, Alex and Mrs. Baker."

Mum laughed nervously. "Oh now, Laura. Please call me Angela." She threw her hand out to shake his.

He grasped it delicately. "Very nice to meet you," he proclaimed in perfect English.

Is Mum fluttering her eyes?!

He turned his virile gaze to mine. I wiped my sweaty hand on my napkin. His skin was smooth and dry as I clasped it.

"I'm Alex," I said feebly.

"Very nice to meet you, Alex."

"How do you know each other?" Mum asked, leaning on her elbows.

Laura and Giancarlo shared a glance of familiarity as they each tried to find the words to the question.

"We were good friends," Laura said, looking back at me with something that almost seemed like embarrassment. Then it struck me. Could this be the mystery man she mentioned during our lesson? And all this time I thought it was Fabio.

You wish it was Fabio now, don't you?

"Hmm. Very good friends by the looks of it," Mum said.

"Giancarlo was my lawyer," Laura offered.

"A lawyer? How wonderful! We're looking for a lawyer," Mum said. "We're trying to locate my aunt's will. Can you help us with that?"

"I don't think that is such a good idea," Laura interjected.

"Why not?" Mum asked.

"Giancarlo doesn't deal with wills."

"But I can certainly point her in the right direction. Especially if you are friends with Laura and Michela," he said far too smoothly. "What kind of problem are you having?"

"We're trying to locate a will that was registered here in Rome. My aunt passed away and apparently she didn't trust the lawyers in Anghiari."

"Oh? I'm sorry for your loss. I can certainly see what I can do. Laura? You still have my number?"

"No," Laura protested. "I lost it."

"Well, here's my card, Angela. Feel free to call me whenever you like."

"Thank you. I will. I most certainly will." Mum took the card with both hands, like she was being handed a golden flower.

Giancarlo turned to Laura. "Did you give some thought to my invitation? The dinner is Thursday night. I hope you can come."

"I won't be *coming* anywhere," Laura said with suppressed frustration.

"What dinner?" Mum asked.

"I invited Laura to a fundraiser for my political campaign. Would you like to join us? Everyone here is invited."

"Oh, you're running for office. How wonderful. Thank you. We will keep that in mind, won't we, Alex?"

I shrugged and looked at Laura, who seemed flattered and annoyed at the same time. She was tight and nervous. I'd never seen her like this before.

This had to be the mystery man which meant I didn't stand a chance. This guy's Mating Score was through the roof! I was nowhere near his level.

A lady came up behind him and touched him on the shoulder. She was a little older than Laura, but not as beautiful.

"Oh, hello Laura. It's nice to see you again," the lady said.

"Hi Lucinda." Laura's reply seemed almost resentful.

Weird.

"Are you coming, darling? Our friends are waiting," Lucinda said to Giancarlo.

He turned and gave her a knowing nod. "*Si, si. Arrivo,*" he murmured.

"Anyway. I won't disturb you any longer. My friends are waiting. Hopefully, I will see you Saturday night. Nice to meet you, Angela." He shook Mum's hand again. "Alex." He nodded in my direction. "*Arrivederci,* Michela."

"*Arrivederci,*" Michela said.

Laura looked like Mount Vesuvius before it erupted. Shaky and red-hot. She said nothing though, remaining oddly quiet. Once again, it was Mum who was the talker.

"You two were an item once?" She directed the question to Laura, but I think it was asked to make me wonder. Laura looked up at me and then back down at her rose. Strange. I wondered what on earth she could be ashamed of?

"Just friends. More wine anyone?" Laura changed the subject as she reached for the bottle on the table.

"*Very* good friends by the look of it," Mum said. I shot her a dirty look. She pretended not to notice. "Hmm. You're right, Alex. This pasta could use a little ketchup," Mum said.

A frigid gaze passed between Mum and Laura.

This was not going to be easy.

Chapter 13
The Zodiac

Laura

I couldn't wait to leave the restaurant. Giancarlo's eyes had been trailing me all evening, and Mrs. Baker's venom was worse than her bite. If it wasn't for Alex's sweetness, the entire dinner would have been a complete waste of time.

"Well, I guess we should call it a night," I said once we were outside the restaurant.

"And go to bed on a full stomach. How about a walk?" Alex suggested.

I just wanted to go home, but didn't want to be rude, especially to Alex. I sniffed his rose.

"*Volete andare allo Zodiaco?*" Mamma asked.

"The Zodiac? What's that?" Alex asked.

"It's up the hill from here. It has a beautiful view of Rome, but it's a bit of a drive."

"That's okay. I have a car. I can drive."

He was eager to continue the night. At least up there, I could get some time away from his mother. I looked over to Mamma, who seemed to encourage the situation for some reason.

"All right." I grabbed his arm and led the way back to the nunnery. Even though they knew little of one another's language, I let Mamma talk to Mrs. Baker. God forbid I had to be her designated translator all night.

In no time, we had jumped into Alex's car, heading for the top of Rome.

•   •   •   •   •

The Italian stars always found a way to twinkle through the smog. Whenever I felt at my loneliest, the view from the Zodiac made my problems seem so small. It was where a lot of Romans came to see their city, away from the tourists and traffic that made Rome so unlivable at times. Alex and I leaned on a balustrade and watched the lights of the eternal city flicker and gleam as I sniffed his rose.

"Thanks for dinner tonight," Alex said while looking over the city. A spiff of wind flicked his dark hair onto his forehead. I wanted to trip over his dimpled chin and fall into his deep eyes.

Damn, he's cute.

"You're welcome. I hoped you liked it. Carbonara is my favorite."

"Of course, ketchup would have brought it to another level," he said.

I slapped him on the back. "I still can't believe you asked for ketchup!"

"I can't believe you didn't reach across the table and strangle me. I seriously thought you were going to."

"Well? What did you expect!?"

"I dunno. Maybe Heinz. There are no other kinds."

I slapped him playfully again, even though I partly meant it.

"Sorry about Mum. 'Family first' is her mantra. She takes it a little too seriously sometimes."

"I'd say. But you've never met Italian mothers. They can be worse."

"Where are our mothers, anyway?"

We both looked around. He was the first to spot them as he pointed. "There, by the ice cream stand. They seem to get along. I wonder how they communicate?"

"You underestimate Mamma. She finds a way to talk no matter what. You can say a lot with your hands. It looks like they're getting *gelati*."

"Do you want one?" he asked.

"No. I'm stuffed. Thanks, though. Besides, I need to lose some weight."

"What are you talking about? You look great."

"Nice try, young buck. I'm at least ten pounds overweight. I'm a size eight right now. I used to be a size two."

"Who cares? Men don't care. We love you gals for who you are."

"Maybe in Camerica land, but not here."

"What? I see tons of full-bodied women with men here."

"So now I'm full-bodied?"

"You're perfect. Curves are nice," he said, sounding genuine and honest rather than glib and practiced.

I didn't think he could tell a lie if he tried.

"Well, those full-bodied women you speak of were probably skinny at one point in their lives. Then life got a hold of them. Kids. Working. We run out of time to stay skinny. Before you know it, men are looking for some other skinny chick to play with."

"It wouldn't matter to me. If the woman I loved gained a few extra pounds, I would always love her. What about you? What would you do if we got married and all I did was sit around and watch TV and get fat?"

"That would never happen."

"What? Get married or me getting fat?"

"Get married."

Alex looked away. He seemed to be searching for something as he looked out over the twinkling lights of Rome. I must have poked a soft spot. I hoped I hadn't hurt his feelings.

He recovered quickly. "Oh yeah? Why not?"

"You're too young for one thing."

"Are you kidding me? Who cares about age? Besides, what if I was your soulmate?"

"Too young," I said, not even considering the idea. I needed a man that adored me, not a youngster who wanted to experience an older woman.

"So if I was the only one you could ever find happiness with, you wouldn't, because of age."

"That's right."

He nodded slowly. "You're right, then. We aren't soulmates. I could never be with someone so shallow."

"Shallow?!"

"If you won't see love because of an age difference."

"No, I'm being practical. When I'm older and fatter, you'll be in the prime of your life. When I'm fifty and getting old, you'll be thirty-five and sexy. Men age better than women."

"Oh, so I'm not sexy now?"

"Shut up." I smacked him again. "I can't believe I'm having this conversation anyway."

"Well, I wouldn't *not* love someone because they were too old. I don't care about age. And anyway, girls my age are boring. All they want to do is party. I'm more interested in finding someone who wants to build a life together. I want to experience life. There is so much to see and do. I want a woman, not a girl."

I couldn't believe I was listening to a twenty-year-old. There was fire in his eyes, a passion and determination that I didn't even see in men my age.

"And what is a woman to you?" I had to ask, even though I was a little afraid of what he would say. Why? I didn't know. Maybe I was worried that he might describe someone that might exclude me?

"A woman is my reflection. Opposite, but complementary. She supports my weaknesses, and I support hers. It's someone who wants the same things and is not afraid to go after them. I'm looking for my soulmate, and I won't stop looking until I find her."

Funny. I agreed with everything he said, but it hadn't worked out that well for me so far. It was like listening to a younger version of myself, full of optimistic idealism. It made me want to be his age again, so that we could fall in love together.

"That sounds nice, but there are millions of women out there. How will you know when you find her?"

"I'll know."

"Yeah, but how?"

"I'll listen to my heart." He tapped his chest as he looked into my eyes.

"That's funny. I never married for that reason," I said.

"What reason?"

"My heart. It never felt right with other men. I always knew there was someone else out there. Someone better."

"What about Giancarlo?" he asked. "Was he one of them?"

Great. This was the last thing I wanted to talk about. I didn't want him to know that I had been the "other woman." I always felt ashamed of that. My father had betrayed Mamma and I more times than I could count with other women, so becoming one myself never sat well with me.

"No. He was one of my biggest regrets. I don't regret many things in my life, but he is one of them."

"Why? What happened?"

I paused. "Let's just say he wasn't ready to commit."

"Got it. He wasn't a real man." He must have read confusion on my face, because he continued. "A real man commits. He does what he needs to do to take care of the woman he loves."

Where the heck did this guy come from? The eighteenth century? "You're pretty old-fashioned, aren't you?"

"You think? I don't know. I don't believe a woman should be in the kitchen, barefoot and pregnant. In fact, kids don't really interest me that much."

How could this be? Why was God teasing me with a guy who shared my goals, but in a man who was a kid? If only I was fifteen years younger. It might have been perfect. Except the ketchup thing, of course.

"Really? Me neither. I never wanted children."

He cocked his eyebrow. "We seem to have a lot in common, especially for two people who will never get married."

"Right! I'm too old," I said, stubbornly.

"I thought you said I was too young? Get your story straight," he joked.

I laughed, somewhat stunned by his maturity. I could see why he would have had a hard time with girls his age. He would probably scare most of them away.

"So . . ." he said, "do you have a younger sister?"

"What! You cheeky thing!" I stuck my tongue out at him. "Do you have an older brother?"

It was then that I realized the rose he had given me was not just for friendship. I still held it in my hand and was sniffing it while we were talking. That insubordinate question left me no doubt. He was interested in me.

"Yeah, but he's fat. You wouldn't like him."

We both laughed. He waved to Mamma and his Mum. They both seemed to be happy doing sign language.

"I forgot to ask, what's going on with your aunt?"

"I'm not sure. We have to find this will. Apparently we have to go to some registrar in the center. Aunt Anne may have registered it there. Maybe Giancarlo could help us out with that?"

I really didn't want Alex learning about Giancarlo and me.

"Did she have any friends she trusted back in Anghiari?"

"There were her good friends, Maria and Francesca. They were really helpful."

"And there was no one else? No other friends? Boyfriends?"

"Well, I found a picture of her with this guy. There were several photos of them together scattered throughout her apartment. I wish I knew who he was. I sure would like to talk to him, or anyone for that matter. Even just to understand Anne a little better. Mum and Dad never really talked about her, but she seemed like a real character. She kind of reminds me of you."

"Me? Why?"

"I don't know. She seemed like a free spirit that didn't let anything hold her back."

Once again, his praise felt far too sincere to be mistaken as flattery. I was starting to like his compliments. "Was she single?"

"As a matter of fact, she was. But I don't really know for sure."

"Maybe she had been disappointed by people far too many times to put her faith in anyone. Everyone eventually disappoints you, one way or another."

"Is that how you feel?" He asked.

"Sometimes, yes."

"Well, I hope that you'll find someone who won't let you down."

Alex kept surprising me tonight. He was really a sweet guy. I hoped his prayer was answered, and I would find someone who wouldn't let me down. So far, aside from Mamma, I hadn't found a single person who honored their word. Maybe I needed someone a little more old-fashioned. I just wasn't willing to make that someone a kid, no matter how tender he was.

Chapter 14
My Frozen Heart

Alex

By the time we returned to the nunnery, I was pooped. It had been one helluva night, and despite my best efforts to understand what Laura thought of me, I was more confused than ever. I couldn't get a clear sign from her that she was interested in me. It was obvious that our age difference was a big problem for her, but I didn't see why. Sure, I understood the practical things she mentioned, but was that any reason to simply deny what my heart was telling me? Why should I let conventional thinking decide for me?

After trudging up the stairs, I walked past the strange middle hallway that beckoned to be explored. With my thoughts brooding on Laura, I said goodnight to Mum, closed the door of my tiny room, and flipped on the dull, murky fluorescent light. My bag lie slumped on the floor, reminding me that I had tucked Anne's photo inside.

I wondered what Anne would have done.

Pulling it free from my clothes, I blew off any bits of dust that still clogged the edges of the frame. Staring up at me, Anne and her mysterious partner were the silent company I needed as I lay down to bed.

Inspecting Anne's face closely revealed happy wrinkles around her eyes, unforced and sincere. Her smile radiated genuinely as her beau stood beside her, his chest inflated with macho guile. Smiling an equally contagious grin, they both glowed with the light that only love could bring.

If they couldn't make it last, how could I when Laura wouldn't take me seriously?

Why would she when she was used to guys like Giancarlo? Staring at the hope in my great-aunt's face made mine slowly fade to nothing.

I wondered why their relationship hadn't worked out. Was it just the age difference? Or was there more to it? Maybe it was the cultural barrier. Anne was English, and he was Italian. Maybe the divide had been too great. Maybe it would never work out between Laura and I because we were from two completely different worlds. Was it even worth asking her out? I didn't even have my career sorted out yet. Hell, I was still living at home. I wasn't ready for a woman like her. I was too young. Too immature.

The questions floated in my head like a restless lullaby, until finally, with the sounds of fading Roman traffic coming in through the open bedroom window, I drifted to sleep.

•   •   •   •   •

It was early when chirping birds outside my window woke me up. I looked at my Timex.

6:45.

Immediately, my mind picked up where it had left off last night, racing like a wild stallion in a crowded city. Instead of lying with a restless mind, I set out for an early morning walk to clear my head. Without thinking, I shoved Anne's photo into my pocket as my sole companion. I wanted someone by my side, even if it was a figment of a past I never knew. A naïve part of me hoped that somehow her picture would transmit some kind of otherworldly wisdom in my time of need.

Stepping outside, it was hard to believe that Rome could be so peaceful. Even the scooter screams that normally soiled the day's silence had taken a break, allowing a subtle breeze to sing its whisper across my face. Soot and baked bread reminded me of how far away

Port Angeles was, where mornings smelt of seaweed and mountain air.

We were meeting Laura and Michela for lunch. Laura had seemed unsure, but Michela insisted that they take us to a beach nearby. At least one of the two mothers was on my side.

Deciding which way to walk brought my gaze to a slender form disappearing around a street corner.

Is that Laura?

About to call out her name, I bit my tongue as not to shatter the stillness of the neighbourhood and wake everyone. Instead, I followed after her with quick steps.

I need to get closer to see if it's her.

Rounding the corner, I glimpsed her bare legs as she disappeared down another street.

There she is. Yep. It's her. I recognize those legs even from a block away.

Hurrying now, I picked up the pace. Parked cars along either side of the boulevard made for tricky obstacles as I tried to close the distance between us.

I hoped she was thinking of me. Maybe she was clearing her head as she fought her own feelings towards me? Maybe she was just as confused as I was?

Dodging the occasional pedestrian, I passed the block, darting down the street she had chosen only to miss her disappearing around another corner.

She's moving quickly. I can barely catch up to her.

Forgetting about walking, I moved into a slight jog, the sound of my footsteps vanishing as traffic grew louder. Coming to the next avenue found myself thrown into oncoming pedestrians, cluttering the distance between Laura and myself.

Where is she?

Just when I thought I had lost her, she appeared standing in front of a coffee shop. Smiling, I moved closer before slowing my pace.

What is she doing?

Staring into the shop's window, Laura stood fluffing her hair and checking her makeup.

Is she primping?

Curiosity took hold as I hid behind a large delivery van parked to the side. Laura looked nervous, almost angry at herself as she puckered her lips before nodding at her reflection and disappearing into the coffee shop.

Who is she primping for?

I looked around to see if Fabio's scooter was anywhere in view. If it wasn't him, then that could leave only one other person.

Snoopiness got the better of me as I approached the coffee shop, keeping my presence concealed in case she mistook me for a creepy Camerican stalker.

It was hard to see through the reflective window from my angle, but I thought I could see—

My heart froze.

It can't be.

When I realized who she was meeting, my heart no longer froze.

It died.

Chapter 15
Tired Of Men

Laura

Stuffing my feet into *Zanotti* sandals, I slammed each foot down in frustration.

"I can't believe he was there last night! What are the odds?" I ranted in Mamma's kitchen as she stood by the stove, her little Bialetti bubbling a fresh brew of espresso. The smell of gas and coffee was unforgettable. "Giancarlo was the last person I wanted to see, but fate just keeps pushing him back into my life."

Every time I wanted to move past his charms, he just seemed to be there to tempt me. This was why I ran away to the States in the first place. I thought time would have helped me forget my attraction to him, but seeing him again only reignited my confusion.

"Remember that folly is as meddling as fate. It's up to you to figure out which one is which," Mamma said. "Do you want a coffee?" she asked as she poured a short espresso for herself.

"No, thanks. I'm heading to Antonini's." After drinking stove-top coffee for the past several months in the States, I wanted to have a good cappuccino from my favorite bar. "I know, but I just can't seem to get away from him. I mean, since when does he eat at Tesone's anyway? He never used to go there."

"I've never seen him there either. It was definitely strange." She sat down at the small kitchen table. "He's still as good-looking as ever though, isn't he?"

"Ma, I'm trying to find reasons not to go to the fundraiser. I have Alberto bugging me to go, everywhere I turn there's Giancarlo, and now you're joining his fan club. You're not making this any easier."

"Good looks doesn't mean he's a good man. Besides, I'll give you the biggest reason not to go: he's still married. Just look at your father. Women would trip over themselves to get to him, and in the end, he couldn't keep his hands off of them, and his fists off me."

"I know that, but Alberto said that he was ready to leave his wife."

"And you believe your cousin? Think about it. If he gets elected, he'll be more tied to Lucinda than ever. They'll never get divorced after that."

"Yeah, but maybe I'm supposed to be with him. I have had no luck anywhere else. Either that or I'll have to marry some beaver-hat-wearing yokel from Port Angeles,"

"You know what you need to do? You need to stop listening to your head and look at other possibilities. Look at how sweet Alex was last night."

"And how bitchy his mother was. God, it was as though she wanted me to crush her son's hopes! What kind of mother does that?"

"I'm not sure, but it sure looks like he has a thing for you."

"He is sweet, isn't he? But he's very old-fashioned. He's like a ninety-year-old stuck in a twenty-year-old's body."

"Youth and wisdom all wrapped into one. Doesn't sound that bad to me," Mamma replied.

"That's because you're older."

Mamma balked. "You're no spring chick either. In case you hadn't noticed, you're five years from forty. Maybe it's time you thought outside the box before you run out of time."

"Out of the box, maybe. But not out of the cradle."

"C'mon. At least he seems stable. Relationships aren't what they used to be. Maybe an old-fashioned man is exactly what you need."

"Really, Ma. He's not even a man yet. If he at least looked older than his age, then I could fathom the idea. But he doesn't. He doesn't know how to dress, he doesn't have a job, and his hands sweat. . . oh, and not to mention that he still lives with his parents!"

"Since when were you so conventional?" Mamma gave me a sarcastic look.

"I know, Ma, but I get the feeling he's barely dated anyone. Maybe he just wants to date a cougar and see what it's like with an older woman. I don't have time for that! I don't want to be his adventure. I'm looking for stability and security."

The thought of being some kid's "cougar notch" really turned me off. I had often heard of young men going after older women to "see what it was like." That wasn't me at all. I wasn't going to be a notch on anyone's belt.

"He doesn't seem to be that kind of guy," Mamma said.

"Yeah, but how do I know?"

"I guess you'll just have to have faith in fate."

"Faith in fate? I used to have faith. I had faith when Giancarlo came into my life. That ended up with me being his mistress. Then I had faith with Luke, and he turned out to be crazy. Now you want me to have faith in a twenty-year-old student who hasn't even left home yet? I've had it up to here with faith *and* fate. I'm making my own choices now, and at this moment, I'm going for coffee at Antonini's."

I spun on my heels and left the kitchen, completely fed up with everyone, even Mamma and her words of wisdom. I just wanted to be alone.

The road to Antonini's was one I had walked a thousand times before. I knew everyone in the neighborhood, and everyone knew me. I normally waved to Mario, the butcher who always liked to whistle at me, but today I was too furious to be flirtatious. Then there was Federico, who made the best pizza this side of Rome; it was too early for him to be open, so I didn't have to worry about seeing him. The last neighbor was Luigi. He served Rome's worst coffee and was another married loser who had tried to get me in the sack. Luckily, he was inside taking care of some clients.

I didn't want to see any men right now. I was tired of men, even sweet ones like Alex. I knew that he didn't deserve my wrath, but I didn't really care anymore. Who did he think he was, anyway? Did he think a rose would make me fall in love with him? I wasn't in the mood of playing games. My life wasn't a joke. I didn't care how well we got along. He was too damn young!

By the time Antonini's came into view, the brisk walk had only incited my frustration. It would be nice to enjoy a cappuccino with no distractions. I might recognize the odd person here and there, but luckily, Antonini's had quiet corners where I could be alone. I couldn't wait. I was imagining the creaminess trickling over my tongue as I stepped onto the red-carpeted entrance.

This is what I need. Simplicity. Enough drama!

Just before I could get through the doorway, I froze.

His black hair was unmistakable. It had the perfect amount of wave and volume, making me want to run my fingers through it and give it a racy tug.

What the heck is he doing here?

Holding my breath, I hid behind a tall, potted shrub. I needed to make a game plan. I looked to see if he was alone, or if Lucinda was with him. It took several minutes before I realized that he was by himself.

Maybe he came here on purpose. He knows this is my favorite bar.

The idea of him waiting to see if I would show up at my prized spot was a big ego boost.

Maybe he's ready to leave Lucinda. Maybe fate was working with me this time. This is what you always wanted, wasn't it? But what about Alex?

What about Alex? Why was I even thinking about Alex? I needed a man, not a boy. Giancarlo was definitely a man, but he was standing between me and the only thing I really wanted right now: one damn cappuccino—alone! Was that too much to ask?

Enough was enough. I stepped from behind the bush and checked my hair in the reflection of the bar window. It wasn't perfect, but at least I had put on a nice dress. My sandals showed my legs really well. I only had coloured lip balm on, but at least I had some mascara.

I took a deep breath, and entered Antonini's bar. The front door slid open automatically. Without a single hesitation, I walked right up to him, and tapped him on the shoulder.

Chapter 16
Kissing a Nun

Alex

Tearing myself away from the sight of Laura with Giancarlo, I pushed blindly through the streets of Rome, angry with myself for being so foolish. Of course she was with Giancarlo. He was perfect. I was just a kid with no future, no money and nothing to offer.

The streets were growing busier now as I ran as fast as I could. Only when my heart pulsed in my ears did I screech to a halt, feeling Anne's photo poking me in the side of my leg.

Ripping it out with fury, Romans funneled around me as I scowled at my great-aunt's picture, pleading with her for answers. When they didn't come, I threw the photo on the ground, shattering it to pieces.

Why try? It was hopeless. I would just have to surrender to the idea that I'd be stuck in Port Angeles the rest of my life, dating Instagirls and talking about citrus-melon Bellinis. Or else I'd become a hermit and live in the woods all by myself. That sounded somewhat attractive right now. At least I could forget the idea of ever finding my soulmate.

Kicking the remains of Anne's photo sent it skittering into the heels of a lone nun who startled with a squeak.

"I'm so sorry," I apologized.

Now you're attacking nuns. Calm down!

The nun, taking my apology in her stride, bent down and picked up the photo that was now free from the broken frame. Somehow, not a single shard of glass cut her skin. Lifting it up, she looked at the back.

"Margotti," she said.

"No, that's my aunt and her boyfriend years ago. I'm sorry to have bothered you."

"No, it says it here on the back. Pierluigi Margotti." Her habit hung over her head as her youthful eyes read the back of the photo.

"What? Where?"

"Here. Look." Handing me the photo, I snapped it up, flipping it over impatiently.

Pierluigi Margotti. 1972. Parioli. Roma.

Not believing my eyes, I jumped on the spot with joy. "This is it!"

"This is what?" She asked.

"This is the answer I've been looking for! Thank you, Sister, thank you. If you weren't a nun, I'd kiss you!"

"Don't let that stop you," she flashed a coy smile.

What the hell.

Not caring anymore about anything, I laid a smooch on her cheek, wondering what to do next. If I had my phone, I could have googled Pierluigi right away.

"I know where that photo was taken."

"You do?"

"Oh yes. Have a look." She carefully relieved me of the photo. "See this sign."

The frame must have hidden a business sign hanging above their heads because I hadn't noticed it until now.

"*Bar Arcangelo Michele,*" she said.

Archangel Michael.

This isn't the first time you've seen him.

Wasn't there a picture of Archangel Michael hanging in Anne's bedroom?

Just a coincidence.

"Do you know how I can find it?"

Giving me the directions I needed, I gave the nun another kiss to which she blushed brightly.

Before I could say "*Andiamo*," I flew down the street, following the nun's directions. But first, I needed to find an internet cafe to google Pierluigi's name.

Within minutes, I found what I was looking for. It was awkward trying to communicate with the owner, who spoke little Italian and even less English. Most of the computers were available, but a few red eyed Russians were fighting over one of them. I felt like telling them that there were plenty of other ones, but thought better of it.

After a quick game of charades with the owner, I was soon in front of a computer of my own. Within minutes, I had searched Pierluigi Margotti and found one living in the Parioli area. I laughed when I saw his address: *Via di San Valentino.*

The same street where the bar is.

This was far too serendipitous. Was the hand of luck intervening?

A quick search again pulled up a map of Rome. Before long, I was marching down the streets in search of Anne's enigmatic lover.

Questions ran through my head. Would he look the same as in the picture? How old was he now? Would he remember Anne? Would he even be willing to talk to some unknown Camerican relative, wandering off the streets with an old picture of him and Anne?

After thirty minutes of dodging traffic, I was standing in front of a large palazzo. It was hard to tell a posh neighborhood from a poor one in Rome, but the building was clean and bright and had a beautiful gate around it. I stepped up to a large door with an interphone recessed into the yellow stucco beside it.

My heart was racing now. I didn't know what to expect. It was showtime. The only thing standing between me and solving the mystery of Anne's past was a panel of single enamel colored buttons. Each had a name beside it. I searched for Pierluigi's.

Sig. Margotti, P. - 33

I checked my watch. It was almost nine o'clock. The timid sounds of a waking neighborhood yawned alive: windows groaning open (squeak), cars shivering awake (vroom), cats seeking shelter (meow), business owners shuffling to work (grumble). Was it too early to buzz?

Just then, the main entrance door opened, and a young man came out. He was wearing a charcoal suit and carrying a red, white and green scooter helmet.

"*Mi scusi?*" I said.

He took a guarded step back. "*Prego?*"

"*Conosce quest'uomo?*" I said, showing him the picture. He leaned in just close enough to get a good look, but just far enough to be out of arm's reach.

I get it. He didn't know me.

When he saw the photo, his posture loosened. Squinting, he cocked his head to better understand who he was looking at. "Is that— Pierluigi?"

"So you know him?"

"If that's Pierluigi, then yes. But he looks different here. Fitter. And who is that with him? She's beautiful."

"That's my great-aunt." My heart skipped in excitement.

"*Molto bella.* But what do you want with him?"

"I'd like to talk to him."

"Well, he's rarely home. I usually see him in the bar across the street. That'll be your best bet."

Following his tanned finger, he pointed to the same bar from Anne's photo. With serendipity as my guide, I thanked him and crossed the street, making sure traffic didn't end my enthusiasm.

Coming to a pensive pause outside, Bar Arcangelo Michele wasn't like the bars back home where alcohol stench soured the air. Instead, the strong aroma of coffee and baked bread pulled me further inside with tempting allure. Rumbling voices mulled over the start of the day as cups and croissants were thrown around with exact precision.

By now I was used to being scanned by Italians with distaste, but invisibility was a new level of discomfort. For a quick second, clouds of doubt formed shade over the idea of finding Anne's enigmatic past as any sight of Pierluigi was not to be had. But before I could leave, the bartender called over.

"*Buongiorno,*" he said.

"*Buongiorno,*" I replied nervously.

My accent must have been off as some patrons turned to see who was butchering their language. Their gazes flicked over my shoes, my pants, and my hair as my appearance was thoroughly judged. Laura had warned me. "If you dress like that in Italy, you're going to stand out. And not in a good way," she'd said after one of our lessons. I should have listened to her.

Then, without a second thought, my scrutineers returned to their conversations. One second, I was the main exhibit of a freak show. The next, I was the red patch of skin that had been scratched and forgotten.

"*Un caffè?*" the bartender asked.

Never having tasted Italian coffee, I couldn't help but wonder what it was like.

"*Si, per favore,*" I replied.

I needed to blend in if I was going to find any information on Pierluigi. Maybe the bartender could help. Stepping up to the bar, I leaned against the counter as I scanned the crowd while waiting for my service.

"*Eccolo,*" the bartender placed a cup smaller than a Tequila shooter in front of me.

A scant amount of black liquid made me wonder if this was a sample of some kind, like that time I went to that fancy restaurant in Seattle. They served a miniature soup before my meal to "cleanse my palate." Maybe this was a little taster before my real coffee. It definitely wasn't *Tim Horton's.* Looking around to see what others were doing, an elderly man with more wrinkles on his tanned face than hair on his head sipped from his sampler, delicately.

Feeling like an elephant picking up a cooked pea, I pinched the microscopic cup handle between my index finger and thumb. Sipping felt more like slurping as my elephant imitation continued. But it was the taste of burnt molasses that made me recoil quickly.

Placing the empty taster down, I sucked my numbed tongue which felt cauterized, not cleansed. Maybe that was the point: give me something so horrible that anything would taste better.

While puckering my mouth, I continued scanning the audience before settling on three men sitting in the deepest corner of the bar. Being plainer than plain, they were nearly invisible. If everyone else in the bar looked cut from a glossy magazine, these three looked like an old black-and-white photo, crumpled at the bottom of a newspaper pile. One looked like Humpty-Dumpty with a weathered ball-cap. The second like his face was melting. It was the third who caught my eye.

Not wanting to embarrass myself by accusing a random stranger of having an affair with my dead great-aunt, I showed the bartender Pierluigi's photo. Showing similar surprise as the witness outside with the scooter helmet, the bartender confirmed that one of the plain gentlemen was indeed Pierluigi.

Thanking and paying, I thought twice about my approach before the thought of Laura with Giancarlo quelled further doubt. I needed help to win Laura's heart, and hopefully, Pierluigi would be my saviour.

Chapter 17
A Proposition

Laura

"What are you doing here?" I asked.

Giancarlo's perfect features turned with surprise.

"Oh, Laura! What a surprise!"

Even when he lied, he was sexy.

Damn it!

"Surprise, my ass. You know perfectly well that this is my bar."
My hands on my hips meant I was really pissed.

His false shock quickly evaporated. "All right. You caught me. I
was actually hoping to bump into you."

Oh my god. I was right. "Bump into me? Why?"

"Why do you think? After seeing you last night, I couldn't get you
out of my mind. I needed to see you again. I had forgotten how
beautiful you are."

His compliment felt sincere enough, but it lacked Alex's sweetness.
Alex again?

"But how did you know I was going to be here?"

"I didn't. But as you said, I remembered that this was your bar, so
I took a leap of faith. And lo and behold, fate brought you here."

Faith and fate. Maybe Mamma was right and I needed to have faith
in fate. After all, fate was standing right in front of me and he was
sexier than ever.

"Here. Let me order you a cappuccino just the way you like it. Short and skinny." He gestured to the barista, who nodded in affirmation.

"Listen, Giancarlo. I don't know what you want from me, but as long as you're married, I'm not interested in you."

He laughed. A deep, sensual laugh that made me forget I was clothed.

"You never were one to beat around the bush, were you? That's what I always liked about you. Your blunt honesty."

"Most men call it bitchy."

"Ha! You see. That's the spirit. Pure, brutal honesty. So I'll I extend you the same courtesy."

The barista placed a perfectly creamy cappuccino in front of me. I didn't want him to believe that he could satisfy me in any way, so I ignored it. My gaze was firmly fixed on Giancarlo's eyes. His dark, sultry brown eyes.

Damn it, Laura. Focus! Pretend he's a Dyson salesman. Remember: you hate vacuuming.

"So. Spit it out. What do you want?"

The smile from his face disappeared. "You. I want you."

I couldn't let him see my shock; it would have only encouraged him. So instead I let him see my anger.

"You have some nerve. I should slap you, but I don't want to make a scene. You haven't seen me for years, and after I just got back from the U.S., you tell me this! Sorry Giancarlo, but I refuse to be your mistress ever again."

"Who said anything about being my mistress?" He interrupted. "I never thought of you that way. You were always so much more to me."

"Yeah right. If I was so much more to you, why didn't you leave your wife? Especially since you knew that she was cheating on you."

Giancarlo flinched. "I never meant to hurt you, Laura," he said with a steady sadness. "You're the only woman I have ever truly loved."

Emotion stuck in my throat. "Loved? Be very careful, Giancarlo. I'm in no mood to be toyed with. If you're talking about the 'L' word, then you better be serious." I hadn't seen him in over four years, and he was talking about love? In all the time we were together, he never once mentioned "love" to me.

"I know this is a lot to take, but I want to ask you for a fresh start. I believe fate has given us a second chance. Will you take that chance with me?"

"You've got to be kidding me. I'm not giving us a second chance. As long as you're married, there is no us." I motioned to leave.

"I understand, but just let me explain. I'm ready to leave her. She keeps cheating, and I can't take it anymore. After you left for America, I realized just how important you were to me. I realized that I can live without you, but I don't want to."

"Then leave her. Now. Leave her and be done with it."

"It's not that easy. It means changing my entire life. It means walking away from our kids. Our plans. It means giving up on the election. It means a lot of things."

"You see! That's precisely what I mean. You'll always find an excuse not to leave her. If you want to be with me, then that's what you'll have to do. You'll have to prove it to me."

I pushed the cappuccino away (and boy, did I want that cappuccino — damn him!) and made my way to the exit. I had enough of his empty promises. I'd rather be alone than deal with these lies. But before I could leave, he grabbed my arm.

"Wait! I'll prove it to you. Come to the fundraiser, and I'll show you. I'll leave her right there and then." He was nodding. "I'll end it all for you."

This was shaping up to be one hell of a trip. First Fabio, then Alex, and now this. Was it possible that a few pounds wasn't the only thing I had gained in the States? Had I somehow turned into a man-magnet? The question was: had I turned into a husband-magnet, a jerk-magnet or a boy-magnet? I needed to get the hell out of here and figure things out.

"Listen, Giancarlo. This is too much. I haven't seen you in years, and all of a sudden, I've seen you twice in less than a day. And now you're telling me that you're willing to give up on your wife and kids for me. I need some time. Alone." I pulled my arm from his grasp.

"I understand. I'll leave it up to you. But if you come to the fundraiser, I'll take it as a sign, and do as I promised."

"Listen. I have to go. I'm meeting a friend for lunch."

"It's not the kid from last night, is it?"

"Watch who you're calling kid." There was only one person who could call Alex that, and it was me. "He's more of a man than you've ever been."

What did I just say? Did I call Alex a man?

Giancarlo remained as graceful as he always did under pressure; a lawyer to the bone. "Of course. I'm sure he has a lot to offer you. Security. Prestige—"

"Honor. Honesty. Sweetness. Things of which you might not be aware."

"I deserve that, and those are all nice things, but can he give you what you need? Can he secure your future? Buy you a home? Vacations to exotic destinations? All the fashion trips to Milan you could want. I will."

It was time to shut him up. What did he know about giving me what I needed? "Alex bought me a rose."

Take that, jerk. I'll show you.

"A rose?" Giancarlo nearly laughed.

"Yeah. With his mother's money." That sounded better in my head.

"His mother's money? And that's what you need?"

"Yeah. It's called being genuine. You should try it some time."

"I am being genuine. Can't you see that I'm suffering without you?"

"You're suffering!?" tears were pushing my eyelids. I pushed back. "I need more than money, Giancarlo. I need what you were never willing to give me."

Like your undivided admiration!

"If I failed you in the past, I'm truly sorry. I was a fool, but I've learned from my mistakes and I'm being honest with you now. I'm ready to give you what you need. And if it means I have to buy you a flower shop full of roses, then I will." His eyes were moist around the edges, as the spring of tears welled up in my own. "But the decision is yours. If you don't come to the fundraiser, then you'll never see or hear from me again. Please think about it. I really miss you."

With his words, I tore myself from his presence so that he couldn't see the tears that finally burst free. Why was this happening? I had thought that escaping to the U.S. would deaden my desire for him, but I'd had no idea it would strengthen his desire for me. The possibility that he would give everything up for me was almost too good to be true. It was what I had always wanted when we first started our affair.

Maybe fate was finally working for me.

So why was I crying?

Chapter 18
Pierluigi Margotti

Alex

"Signor Margotti?" I asked.

Humpty looked up at me, his hat barely perched on his round head. "Who's this, Pierluigi? One of your long lost sons?"

"What's in your hand, kid?" asked Mr. Melt, his cheeks flapping like loose mozzarella.

"I think it's a photo of you." I showed Anne's picture to Pierluigi. For a split second, the rims of his eyes softened before his entire body became rigid. His paralysis became contagious as Humpty and Mr. Melt froze.

"What is it, Gigi?" Humpty finally asked. When he didn't answer, Mr. Melt snatched the photo from his hand.

"Hey, Gigi. Is this you? Looking good. Who's the blonde?" he asked.

"Blonde? What blonde? Let me see that!" Humpty grabbed the photo. "Wow. Gigi! Way to go! *Bella gnocca!* And look at you! You actually look good. So what does that make you, kid? Gigi Junior?"

As his friends laughed and taunted him, Pierluigi looked down at the cards in his hands, blushing.

"Don't worry. We're not related. That's my great-aunt Anne in the photo," I offered the answer Pierluigi couldn't. He looked up with astonishment, lips trembling as he tried to find words he must have buried long ago. His friends were oblivious to his anxiety.

"Anna," Humpty whistled loudly. "How did you lose that one?"

"Don't let your wife see her. She'll kill you for just being in the same photo," said Mr. Melt.

"Quiet," Pierluigi said under his breath.

"Whoa. *Che biondona!* How far did you get with this one?"

"I bet she was fun. Was that one of your famous flings?"

This last remark sparked something in his eyes that was distinctly familiar. In that instant, I saw the Pierluigi of the photo. Strong. Bold. Daring. And in love.

"*Zitto!* Anna was never a fling!" Their laughter quickly died down as they realized this wasn't a joke. It took him several long breaths to calm down before he looked to me. "What do you want?"

I cleared my throat. My moment of discovery had arrived. "I just wanted to see if you could tell me a little more about her."

"Why?" he snapped.

"I'm trying to learn more about my aunt. I found this photo of the two of you at her place when we were looking for her will, and I thought maybe you could help me out?"

"How the heck should I know? I stopped seeing Anna years ago."

"You were serious with this hottie?" Humpty was stunned. "And you let her get away?"

Pierluigi's face tightened even more. "I don't know anything about a will, anyway. Now beat it, would ya?" He turned and started shuffling the tiny cards, aggressively.

I wasn't about to give up. I hadn't come all this way to be given a cold shoulder. It was time to bear my heart for whatever ridicule could come.

"Actually, there is something else," I continued.

"C'mon, Gigi. There's something else," Mr. Melt said, delighted. This was probably the most excitement they'd seen in a long time.

Pierluigi rolled his eyes and continued shuffling the cards. "What is it now?"

"Well, I know this is weird, but could you tell me why it didn't work out between you and my aunt?"

"C'mon, kid. Don't you have anyone else to bother? Can't you tell I'm busy." He tapped the cards on the table as though they were pressing documents of the utmost importance.

"Tell us!" Humpty encouraged.

"Can't a man regret his life in quiet misery anymore?" Pierluigi asked. "Now I have to tell some strange kid and my two idiot friends about my biggest failure?"

"Wait a second. Is this the girl you keep referring to?" Humpty asked.

"Yeah, the one you whine about after too much grappa? The one that got away?" Mr. Melt said.

With the compassion only best friends could have, Humpty and Mr. Melt did what any good friends would have done.

They taunted him.

"Gigi! Gigi! Gigi!" they jeered and banged the table with their hands like a drum. The sophisticates in the bar turned to see what all the commotion was as the plainest people in the establishment suddenly became the loudest. Before his face could turn red, Pierluigi hushed his friends.

"All right! I'll tell you. But you can't tell my wife, okay?" he warned, pointing his index finger like a dagger. After they zipped their lips, Pierluigi huffed and began.

"That picture was taken a long time ago, sometime back in the seventies." He smoothed his gray hair, which was still as thick as it was in the photo. He spoke with a charm that I could see would have been alluring to Anne. His smooth voice even hypnotized me as he spoke.

"Anna and I were kindred spirits. Dare I say, soulmates."

"If you were soulmates, why didn't it work?" I asked. I could tell he'd reached the limit of what he was willing to share while under his friends' predatory gazes. "Come here, kid—let's go over there away from these two pariahs."

His friends complained loudly as we left to sit on the opposite side of the bar, picking a corner where not even the longest ear could hear.

"So, you really want to know what happened?" He looked around to double-check we were alone. "The answer is simple. I screwed up."

His lips quivered as he closed his eyes, trying to bottle the emotions threatening to escape. Touching his shoulder for comfort, I felt the tremble of regret shaking the core of his being. Fighting to regain his composure, he struggled to control his breathing. "I was a fool who let the love of his life slip away. I just didn't have the strength to stand up…"

He fell silent again. I could see why he wouldn't have wanted his friends to see him like this.

"Stand up against what?" I encouraged.

"Stand up against convention. Anna was the opposite kind of woman my family wanted me to be with. She was English. Protestant. Free-spirited. But mostly, she was older."

"How much older?" I hoped the difference of age was at least as vast as the one between Laura and me.

"Twelve years."

"That's not a lot," I said, dismayed to hear that I was more impaired than he had been.

"Maybe in the face of love, you're right. But to my family, it was a chasm too far to cross. They threw everything against us. Guilt. Shame. Pride. Jealousy. They couldn't stand to see their son being with an older woman. In the end, they drove us apart."

"How could family ever do that to one another?" I asked. The family motto etched in my consciousness echoed questioningly.

Family first?

"You'd be surprised what family will do to protect itself. Family supports the familiar. Anything different is seen as a threat. That was how they saw Anna."

"A threat? How? What on earth could Anna have done to them?"

He was calmer now. Pensive. "I don't know. But after she finally left me, I spent the rest of my life wondering why I let her go."

"She left you?" That sounded like the Anne of Mum's description. The hussy. "Did she give up easily?"

"Easily? What gave you that impression? Anna fought harder than anyone to keep us together. I wished I had her strength."

"That's not how she was described to me." I hesitated, remembering his reaction when his friends criticized her. "To put it gently, I was told that she was a floozy and a narcissist."

Pierluigi straightened. "Whoever told you that didn't know Anna at all. She was the most loving, generous woman I had ever had the pleasure of knowing. She fought for us until she couldn't fight anymore. In the end, my weakness was too much to bear."

His explanation either meant love had blinded Pierluigi to what Anne was, or Mum had lied to me.

"But what would you have done differently?"

He answered without hesitation as he pounded the table with a fist. "I should have spat in the eye of convention and listened to my heart!"

Hearing about the past was one thing. Encountering it was another. In that quiet corner in Bar Arcangelo Michele, the sounds of Rome passed by unnoticed as Pierluigi's words became my raison d'être. Over the next hour or so, Pierluigi recounted the trials and triumphs of their relationship. He flushed with pride when telling how people would tease them about their age difference, and in defiance she'd kissed him with such passion and length that all naysayers fell silent.

Pierluigi frowned when he told me of Anne's many confrontations with his family. They had tried everything to separate them, causing Anne to become more obstinate about their relationship. Unperturbed, she had told them that love had no age, and that nothing would separate them.

These were not the workings of a hussy like I had been told by Mum. The things he described about my aunt made me laugh, cringe and cheer. By the end of our conversation, I had slowly fallen in love with the spirit of the woman that I was proud to call my aunt.

He wasn't the only one to share his tale. In between reflections of Anne, I told him of Laura and the difficulties I was having with her past. Giancarlo became a topic of interest for him, as he nodded with understanding of what I was going through.

As the time came for us to part, we had become the best of companions sharing in a mutual struggle with the optimism that I could succeed where he had failed. Before I left to return to the nunnery, he had one final piece of advice for me.

"Love conquers all, but first, you must conquer love. You must defeat your beliefs if you want to win Laura's hand. Don't be threatened by this Giancarlo character. I know his type; they're not as flawless as you think. Listen to your heart and take charge."

I gave him an understanding nod before embracing Anne's soulmate and heading back to face my next big decision: was I going to tell Mum about Pierluigi?

I had learned that Anne hadn't abandoned Mum's family. Instead, she'd run away from an impossible situation, one where her sister was so lost in mental illness that Anne couldn't reach her. Every time Anne tried to intervene, her sister would become a raving lunatic, calling her horrible names and accusing Anne of trying to break up her family.

Grandma became so paranoid that she started telling everyone that Anne was a floozy trying to steal her husband. In the end, she had to make a choice: watch her sister destroy her life, or preserve her own. Finally, Anne chose to distance herself from the family, hoping her absence would help them grow. That was when she came to Italy, and shortly after, met Pierluigi.

As I made my way through the throng of Romans and tourists, I thought of what to tell Mum. It was nearing ten-thirty, and we were to meet Laura at eleven. After two hours of absence, Mum would be wondering why I had left her alone. I needed to get moving, but first, I needed an alibi.

Chapter 19
What To Do

Laura

I never cried. I was never allowed to. Papà used to slap me harder if I did, which made me more determined to never show sadness to anyone. Especially a man.

Giancarlo had a knack of getting me to do things I vowed I never would. Becoming his mistress was just as surprising as the tears that rolled down my face.

Why was I crying?

I'm a strong woman, dammit. Don't cry.

Trying to stop something that surprised me was as hard as admitting that I truly wanted it. I wanted the relief. I wanted the ease. Life had been so hard up until now. There had been so much drama. Pain. Beatings.

Why couldn't life just be easy?

Now it can be.

No!

Not this way. I needed Giancarlo to leave Lucinda without further proof from me. If he truly loved me, then it was the least he could do.

But this is what you always wanted. Don't be a fool.

I wasn't going to the fundraiser to prove myself to him. He had to prove himself to me. It was up to him to show me how much he loved me, not the other way around.

Pushing through the crowded morning, thoughts haunted me with tempting fantasies. I could have it all. The man. The life. It could all be mine. But would it be what I needed?

What do I need?

Sweetness.

Purity.

The "L" word.

Like any of those things existed.

There's always Alex. Think of the rose.

He'd change. They all did. Once they got a taste of Italy and *la dolce vita*, they all become slime balls. Alex was too naive for this country. Too naive for me. He couldn't handle me. I've been through too much. I knew too much about the world. I would be the ruin of his gentle kindness. I wouldn't want to be the one who took that away from him. He deserved someone just as sweet as he was.

Would you stop thinking about him!

I wasn't going to teach him fifteen years of life's experiences. He needed to live his own life. Make his own mistakes. Do things that twenty-year-olds were supposed to do.

You mean like have their hearts broken by the world just as it broke yours.

The tears started again. This time, like one of the *nasone* pouring onto the streets, washing the past down ancient drains.

"Aoo! Laura!"

The voice caught me by surprise. Though my eyes were bleary, my ears knew exactly who called my name. Turning, I found myself standing right in front of —

"Fabio's Bar."

Great. How did I end up here?

"Are you all right?" Fabio appeared out of the enclave of his business.

Fabio's sweet.

Shut up!

My crying turned into a sarcastic laugh as I turned away from him to hide my tears.

Don't let anyone see you cry. You're better than that!

I could feel Papà's hand thrash my bare wet cheek as I stifled the tears for disobeying him. It was hard not being able to cry when I was five years old, but if I could do it then, I could do it now.

Sucking in a deep breath, I pulled a tissue from my Gucci and blotted my weakness away.

"What happened?"

What was I going to tell him? That I was confused. That the reason for my outburst was a complete mystery. That Giancarlo was doing what he always did: commit without committing.

"Nothing." Except that my ex-mister just asked me to be his lawfully wedded mistress. "It's just the pollution. My eyes aren't used to it anymore."

Fabio wrapped an arm over my shoulder which felt better than it should have. No matter what, touching felt good, even if it was Fabio's hairy arm.

"Do you want a cappuccino?"

"Yes!" I said, relieved that someone finally offered what I really wanted. One-damned cappuccino. The very thing that was too much to ask for was being offered by the most annoying person in Rome.

And I was going to take it.

Walking into his bar brought back the feeling of belonging that I missed in the States. No matter how lonely I felt, Italians always opened their arms to me.

Hopefully he wouldn't ask for another kissy-kiss.

He was behaving a little more awkwardly than before as the stale mistletoe from yesterday wilted over his mood.

So much for the macho bravado.

"So...How's it going?" He was standing behind the bar, fiddling with his coffee *macchinetta*. Thankfully, he was avoiding direct eye contact which meant he hadn't noticed my red eyes. The kissy-kiss that had embarrassed Fabio yesterday was saving *me* from embarrassment today.

I could kiss the kissy-kiss right now.

"Good." Terrible answer. Everyone knew that nothing good ever came from saying "good."

Fabio still hadn't looked up from the *macchinetta*. "How's the kid?"

"Alex? Good." I was full of conversation today. What was I going to tell him? Oh, by the way Fabio, after your kissy-kiss attempt, my student bought me a rose and told me that if I got fat that he would still love me. And then Giancarlo proposed his hand in marriage, but only if I went to a fundraiser where I could earn the "biggest-homewrecker-in-the-world" award by publicly destroying his marriage in front of all the Roman paparazzi.

"He seems like a nice kid. Have you been seeing him for a long time?"

Was he asking me if I was dating my student? The punches just kept on coming. "What's with everyone these days? Do I have a "cougar-for-hire" tattoo somewhere on my forehead? He's just my student! We've been doing lessons for three months. Yes, he's cute. Yes, he has an amazing ass. Yes, his deep blue eyes made me feel like I was swimming in the Maldives. Yes, he bought me a rose and said he was only looking for his soulmate. But he's my student! That's all!"

Like a pounding drum through the silence, my espresso dripped into my cup as everyone in the bar turned to witness the crazy *pariolina* ranting at the top of her lungs.

Fabio's eyes had widened as round as the saucer under my espresso cup as he finished pouring. Handing me my drink, for the first time since I met him, he had no words.

"I'm — I'm sorry. I guess I'm just tired from the jet-lag. Alex is fine." Taking a heapful of sugar, I sweetened the only thing I could right now and sipped my coffee.

"It's okay. Fabio understands. Whenever he travels, he gets grumpy as well.. 'Grumpy Fabio' my friends called me," Fabio's referral to himself in the third person meant that he was getting back to normal.

"I can't imagine you ever being grumpy. You've always had a smile around me."

Fabio enjoyed the compliment as he smiled even wider than usual. He did have a nice smile. He reached over and touched my arm reassuringly. "Don't worry. Fabio will make you feel right at home. Would you like a *cornetto*?"

"Is Fabio truly great?" He puffed up even more with renewed encouragement before plopping a fresh croissant on a plate in front of me. A cappuccino and cornetto was the perfect remedy right now.

God bless Italian breakfasts.

Biting down into my fresh warm pastry made all my problems fade away as the issues of life dissolved in Italian simplicity. For the next hour, Fabio and I laughed and talked as glimpses of ease peeked through my restless mind.

This was what I needed. Forget about men. Forget about fundraisers or roses or kissy-kisses. All I needed was to laugh and let life pass by.

The problem was, in between laughs and sips, Giancarlo kept popping in my mind. Life would be easier with him, there was no doubt. Perhaps I just needed to have faith in what fate was bringing me. And a proposal of love from Giancarlo was hanging right in front of me, waiting to be plucked.

Looking down at my Cartier watch, eleven o'clock was drawing near.

Time for lunch with Mrs. Baker and her son.

I hoped lunch at Fregene would distract my thoughts, but if Mrs. Baker tried anymore low-blows, I'd make her namesake a reality . . . never mind how sweet her son was.

Chapter 20
Fregene

Alex

The bouquet of roses drooped as I stood outside the nunnery. I had decided to keep my conversation with Pierluigi a secret; there were too many inconsistencies between what he had said about Anne and what Mum had described. I knew Mum. Confronting her would only inflame her defensiveness. It was best if I kept everything to myself for now. Instead, I hoped the bouquet of flowers would be a diversion from any questions.

A little sucking up certainly couldn't hurt.

After I ran up the stairs of the nunnery, and knocked on Mum's bedroom door, she flung it open with a look of disappointment. "Where have you been?"

I stepped back. "I ran out to do some errands," I replied.

"What kind of errands could make you leave your own mother stranded in Rome by herself?"

"I went to get you some flowers." I pulled out the bouquet of roses from behind my back.

"Flowers. Is this supposed to make up for last night?"

"What do you mean?"

"Well, you bought your girlfriend a rose but nothing for your own mother."

"Sorry, Mum. Besides. She's not my girlfriend. The rose for Laura was spontaneous."

"Yeah, yeah. Nice try, lovey." She sniffed the fresh flowers. My ploy had worked.

"Let's get going," I said. "It's almost eleven."

After putting her bribe in a glass of water, we left the nunnery. It still bothered me that she wouldn't say Laura's name. Was this what Pierluigi had to go through? I needed to be careful with Mum from here on out.

Downstairs, Laura stood outside, her back to me as she talked with Michela. I caught the last words of her conversation. I wish I hadn't.

"Giancarlo told me himself. He's ready to leave his wife. I don't know what to do…"

Those abysmal words were a stab to my heart. If what I heard was correct, I needed to act quickly, and take charge, or I could lose her.

"Good morning, gals," I said lightly. Maybe if I was cheery enough, she would forget him. Instead, she smiled a little less effervescently than normal. Something was wrong. She was distracted. I guess I would have been as well if I was considering running away with Superman.

"How did you sleep?" I asked.

"Not the greatest," she said. "I've gotten so used to quiet Port Angeles nights."

"You mean the smashing sounds of garbage trucks at four o'clock in the morning doesn't soothe you to sleep? Well, if it makes you feel any better, I slept poorly as well. But I'm ready for a good lunch. Where are we going?"

Laura straightened, regaining some of her bubbliness.

"I was thinking of taking you guys to Fregene. It's a great beach town, with even better food. I remembered that you'd only had fish sticks in the States. How would like to try some really good seafood?"

She remembered *that* about me from our lessons. I needed to raise my game if I was going to impress her.

"Fish is good." I hated fish.

"Good. Let's get going then."

Mum sidled up to Michela and they started hand-talking again as they squeezed into the back of the rental car.

"Where are your keys?" Laura asked.

"I'll drive," I replied. I needed to start acting like a man in charge if I was going to win her heart. Move over, Giancarlo. Here I come.

"Is that such a good idea, lovey?" Mum asked.

Great. Nothing made a man feel more like a man than his mother nagging him in front of the woman he was trying to impress.

"I can do it. No problem. Just show me where to go," I said stubbornly.

"Are you sure?" Laura asked. "The way there is pretty complicated. Maybe I should drive?"

"I got this. Just sit back and relax. Captain Alex at your service."

"All right," Laura said. She didn't seem convinced.

Pierluigi said I needed to take charge, so that was what I was going to do.

When everyone was settled, I readjusted the rear-view mirror.

"Does everyone have their seat belt on?"

Laura and Michela nodded. Mum shook her head as she whispered over the head rest.

"Are you sure you don't want her to drive? She knows the way. It'll be easier."

"I'm sure, Mum," I said through tight lips. I didn't want Laura to see that I was being lectured by my mother. "I did this yesterday, remember? It was fine."

Mum sat back and embraced her bag like a giant pillow.

"Everyone ready? Let's go!"

I put the car into reverse and stomped on the accelerator. The next calamitous second involved a car honking, dogs barking, Italians yelling, a scooter veering and every woman in the car screaming the first note of the Canadian national anthem. My brief escapade into male authoritarianism had come to an abrupt halt, ending up with me sitting in an emasculated heap on the passenger side of the car, staring out the window, wondering how I was ever going to recover my lost manhood.

•　　　•　　　•　　　•　　　•

Fregene was warmer than Rome, even after a rare Mediterranean mist cooled the perspiration on my damp neck. We were all sitting under the shade of a large umbrella. The table looked like a pescatarian murder scene with all manner of fish bodies strewn and flayed on silver platters. It looked like Jack the Flipper was practicing for his big night.

My current victim stared up at me from my plate, pleading with me not to eat it.

"I can't eat this. It looks like it's still alive. It keeps staring at me."

"Don't worry. It only died a few minutes ago."

"Oh great. Next you're going to tell me that it was boiled alive."

Laura looked at me with sweet astonishment. "You really don't know anything about seafood, do you?"

I shook my head. "We never really ate seafood at home. Dad's idea of fish was throwing battered halibut in the deep fryer, and then covering it with mayo."

"Well, I'll save you the painful explanation of this poor scampi's death, then. Just give it a try," she replied.

"Go on, lovey. It can't be that bad," Mum said.

"*Dai. Forza*," Michela waved her fork in the air.

I took a deep breath before I drove my fork into the scampi's belly. It crunched and cracked as the shell splintered into red pieces. I must have had an expression of abject misery on my face because Laura was in tears, laughing.

"Am I doing this right?" I asked.

Michela came to my rescue. With two smooth, chubby hands, she reached over and ripped open its frail body with pulverizing force. I leapt back in my seat as the scampi spat juice in my eye, its final death curse.

"That's how you do it," Laura chuckled.

I looked down in horror at the exposed white flesh.

Michela pointed with her finger. "*Buono. Assaggiala. E' buona*," she encouraged.

Timidly, I plucked a few flakes with my fork. Saying one last prayer for the emaciated corpse on my plate, I closed my eyes and ate. Laura, Michela and Mum waited for my reaction as I chewed slowly.

"It tastes sweet!" I proclaimed. "This is amazing!"

I lunged for more like a starving vulture as everyone else did the same to their meals. Within minutes, I was looking around the table for my next victim. A bloodlust for Italian fish had consumed me. I wanted more, and by the end of the meal, my hatred of seafood had turned into a revelation. For the first time in my life, I understood what all the fuss was about. No more Hyliner for me. Forget the mayo. I had become a seafood convert, and all it took was a moment on the shores of Rome.

After all the dishes had been emptied, a large man with more hair on his arms than on his head appeared from the shadows of the beach-side restaurant. I had learned his name was Mimmo, and kindness shone from his clear aquamarine eyes. It was the first time I had seen blue eyes on an Italian. Years of cooking and wrestling fish had shaped his forearms into chiseled masses of muscle. He placed his stocky hands on his hips.

"I guess it was disgusting?" he joked as he stared at all four of us lying back in our chairs with soft bellies.

"You did it again, Mimmo!" Laura called out.

"*Stupendo! Ottimo!*" Michela added. She kissed her pinched fingers and thumb. This was a sign I was getting used to seeing. I liked it. It was a nonverbal way of showing culinary excellence.

Mimmo grinned as he cleared the plates and left for the kitchen. The silence that came from everyone being full and relaxed reminded me that there was a more pressing matter at hand: Mr. Perfect with Bonus Points was still in the picture, and I needed to know why. It was time to investigate.

"So, what did you get up to this morning?" I asked Laura.

Her neck tightened. I had poked a soft spot.

"Nothing really. I just went for a coffee. How about you?"

Damn. I wasn't ready for that question. I couldn't let the entire table know that I had my own secret to hide.

"Same thing. I went for a walk," I replied awkwardly. I wanted to tell Laura about Pierluigi, but I wouldn't want her to think that my enthusiasm for her was because of what he had told me. When the time came, she would have to believe that the strength to ask her out came from me, not from Pierluigi's encouragement. Besides, I couldn't talk about him now anyway. Mum was here.

So instead, I stared blankly at the center of the table, trying to avoid any further discussion of this morning's events. Laura was doing the same. To no surprise, Mum continued her new-found talkativeness as she came to the rescue.

"Alex bought me a bouquet of roses. They were so beautiful. They were a little bit bigger than yours, Laura, and there were at least a dozen," she said somewhat defiantly.

Great. Mum was being Mum again. Operation "Kill-Girl" was in full effect.

A forced smile was the best Laura could come up with as her own look of death flashed quickly. "Well, I love my rose. It's one of the most precious gifts I've ever received. I'll never forget it," she said, definitely defiantly.

Things were getting bitchier by the moment. I needed to get us out of here. It was time to move ahead with my plan. I had to push aside my curiosity about Mr. Perfect and take charge.

"How about a walk . . ." I started.

"That's a lovey idea," Mum replied.

". . . Laura?" I finished.

Laura's eyes widened. Mum's eyes narrowed. The line had been drawn.

This time, Michela came to the rescue.

"We talk? Yes?" she said to Mum in broken English.

"We won't be long. I'll bring back some sand for you," I joked to Mum. "What do you say, Laura?"

"Sounds good. I could use a walk," Laura replied.

As I left, Michela was trying to make conversation in English. From a quick glimpse, I could tell Mum's attention was only on one thing: me.

Chapter 21
I've Lost My Mind

Laura

A walk? Anything to keep me from gouging Mrs. Baker's eyes out with a fork. Besides, a little fresh air along Fregene's warm sand might be just the thing to help me decide what to do about Giancarlo's not-so-little proposal.

When Giancarlo and I had first met, I had a tough choice to make: continue to be a Miss or become a mistress. Back then, I knew he was married, and I also knew that Lucinda's romantic proclivities were well renowned. I hadn't the faintest idea why Lucinda was cheating on her husband, but when she first laid eyes on me, it was cheat at first sight.

"Oh my. Well, aren't you a pretty thing? You and my husband would make a handsome couple," she said while I prepared a fitting room for her.

Strange comment. What did that mean?

It didn't take long for me to find out. As soon as Giancarlo sat down to wait while she tried on clothes, Lucinda pushed me into his lap like I was some kind of cheap whore.

Now, falling into Giancarlo's lap would have made most girls lose their minds. And their clothes. Hell, when he grabbed me with his strong arms and I caught a whiff of *Bulgari* Cologne, I felt a button pop off my blouse all by itself. But I wasn't falling for any of it.

I knew how this worked after watching Papà in action. A little tease here. A little joke there. Then before his victim would have known, Papà would have moved onto the next twinkling tart.

If Giancarlo had been that obvious, it would have been easy to ignore him. But he was good. Subtle. Slowly, over time, he gained my affection, and after saying no for the hundredth time, and watching Lucinda slink off with the latest Klaus of the week, I gave him a chance.

That was how it started. If Lucinda had wanted me to be with her husband that badly, then their marriage must have been over. Why not go with the flow? Why not surrender to fate? After all, I had seen women take advantage of wealthy men all my life. They usually ended up with more money than they knew what to do with.

I had always been the good girl. The virtuous girl. The honest girl. Where the hell had that gotten me?

Alone *and* lonely.

So I gave in. I surrendered to fate and let Giancarlo take me as his mistress. I had uncorked the bottle of passion and was willing to let the bubbles fall where they may.

He dazzled me with gifts. Brought me to the finest restaurants. Introduced me to the highest of society. With Giancarlo, I wasn't the princess at the ball; I was the queen. There wasn't anyone he didn't know. There wasn't anything I couldn't have. I was the center of his affection and his attention. For four sensual months, I was Cupid's spoiled lover.

Until reality sank in.

The biggest problem with Cupid was that he had wings, and could fly away with the softest of breezes. I still remembered the feeling of getting Giancarlo's call that day. I was shopping for lingerie along Viale Angelico. I was excited to show off my new tan that I had been working on all summer, especially since he was hinting at proposing. He said far too many times: "Make sure your weekend is clear. I have something special planned for you."

Maybe my expectations were too high, but he made it sound like it was the most important weekend to come. When Friday came, he called. "Ciao, Laura. I can't make it this weekend," he said.

"What do you mean? I've been waiting for this weekend for weeks. I kept it clear just as you asked. What happened? Are you all right?"

"I'm fine. It's Lucinda. She wants me with her this weekend for a family function."

"You're kidding me, right? She's been cheating on you for years, and you're dropping me for her?"

"What can I say? Family first."

After all the lashings from Papà and nights listening to Mamma cry, I barely knew what "family first" meant. "Family? What does that make me?"

"Don't say that. You know you're special to me. You're my *amore*."

"I don't think so. I'll tell you exactly what this makes me: the other woman!"

"No. You're so much more than that. I care for you so much."

Care for me? What was I? A pet? Hell, even a pet gets more than caring. "I don't care about caring. I'm looking for love."

He said nothing, which said everything.

"Listen, Giancarlo, enjoy your wife and your life."

I hung up with a strong thumb. I wanted to throw my phone into the Tiber as I realized one thing: a mistress would always miss. I never answered his calls after that, even though he tried incessantly to reach me. I vowed never to be a man's second thought ever again. Within weeks, I had packed my bags and had arrived in Port Angeles to live with my Uncle Davide.

My exile had begun, as well as my penance. Not only was I pissed off that I had been dumped as the other woman, I was also angry that I agreed to give myself to a married man in the first place. But more importantly, I still had feelings for him.

As my toes sank into the warm sand of Fregene's beach, I thought about what the past had held, and what the future could hold. Would Giancarlo actually leave his wife for me this time? Was this my last chance at happiness? If I didn't attend the fundraiser, would I be a spinster forever? The way he had tracked me down at Antonini's felt too good to be true. All I ever wanted was to be with a man that adored me, and perhaps now that could happen.

Normally, I wouldn't even contemplate the slightest notion of inviting Giancarlo back into my life. But maybe it was time to be unconventional. Mamma had encouraged me to think outside the box and to have faith in fate. Maybe this was fate knocking on my door for the last time?

"May I court you?"

My thoughts evaporated instantly as I realized Alex was looking deeply into my eyes. The wind tousled his hair and his long eyelashes. We had somehow walked halfway down the beach as the waters of the Mediterranean lapped against our feet.

Did he just say court?

"Sorry, what?" I asked.

"I know I can't offer you what you deserve, but I would like to court you?"

Uh-oh. What had Mimmo put in the scampi today? I had to end this right away. I couldn't court my student. A rose was one thing, courting was another. I couldn't court anyone who even said "court." Who the heck says that, anyway? Was I in a Jane Austen novel? And how did he even know what I deserved in life when I didn't even know? I had to put my foot down. I had to make the right decision. Wasting time with a young kid wasn't an option. I was thirty-five going on seventy! Enough was enough!

"Okay."

Wait, what? Moment of insanity. Let me try that again. It must be the jet-lag.

"I would like that."

Okay. It's official. You've lost your mind.

He released a long breath, beaming a gigantic smile.

I looked down and noticed that he was holding both of my hands. They were soft and sweaty with youth. Shocked that I was staring into my student's eyes, I looked around the beach to see if anyone had noticed that I was holding the hands of a toddler. There were a few sunbathers scattered along the shore, but most were more interested in sun-worshiping than looking at us. Then I looked back to see if

Mamma was watching. She saluted an encouraging wave. No one seemed to care that an infant had just declared his love to me.

Just then, my phone rang. Alex graciously released my hands so I could answer it. I would have normally ignored it during such an intensely emotional moment, but I had obviously lost my mind, so hey, anything goes.

"*Pronto*?" I answered.

"Ciao, Laura. It's Fabio."

Great. That's just what I needed. Maybe he was going to propose over the phone. The way my day was going, I would be married with five children by the end of the night.

"How are you doing?" he asked.

I wanted to tell him I had just agreed to go out with my student and that I would no longer be accepting offers from men older than twelve. Hell, if I was going to rob a cradle, I shouldn't limit myself.

"I'm good. I'm here with Alex at Fregene."

I could hear his heart crack over the phone.

"Oh. You should have told me. I would have joined you."

"I wish I had," I replied, thinking maybe his presence would have prevented me from forgetting my brain at the lunch table.

"Really?" he said hopefully. "Do you mean that?"

Me and my big mouth. I should just shut up today.

"Did you have something to ask me?"

"Well, I forgot to ask you this morning if you were going to the fundraiser on Thursday night."

I could see it now. Me. Fabio. Alex. All three of us entering the fundraiser, when all the while Giancarlo hoping I would choose him. Hell, it actually sounded fun. Perhaps I'd get them all fighting over me and then I could hide somewhere in the Alps with the sheep. Maybe I would find my lost mind up there.

"I don't really know right now," I replied.

"Well, let me know if you need a ride. I can pick you up if you don't."

"Okay, thanks. I'll let you know."

"All right. I'll wait for your call then. Ciao."

After I hung up, I had a hard time looking up to Alex who was having a hard time not looking at me. I didn't know what to say. I was completely confused. I should have told him I had made a mistake, but when I saw the sweet sincerity in his eyes, I chickened out. So instead, I let him take me by the hand as we walked back to our mothers.

Chapter 22
Seed of Doubt

Alex

After Laura said "yes," a new found confidence coursed through my veins. Virility. Strength. A sense of purpose. Suddenly, all those years of "family first" and denying my feelings were lifted from my spirits, buoying my soul to new heights. Everything was great; even Mum's scowl couldn't bring me down.

Pierluigi had been right: spitting in the eye of convention was worth every discomfort. It was too soon to say that I was in love with Laura, but I was starting to feel a sense of freedom I had never felt before. I was changing. I was nervous about it, but I was ready for the challenge.

I knew how Mum was going to react. She'd question my decision — she always did when it came to my romantic choices. Like that time when I dated this beautiful Asian named Naomi. Mum kept telling me that she was too short and too quiet for me. I couldn't blame her when she was right, but this time, she'd better back off.

Laura was unusually silent as she dropped us off at the nunnery, probably because I hadn't mentioned that we were officially dating to anyone. It was my duty as a gentleman to break the news to Mum.

When we were all outside the nunnery, I needed to prove to everyone that I was cultured enough to merit Laura's hand.

What would Giancarlo do? I know!

As Laura came close, I put my plan into action. "Well, thanks for lunch." I moved in to give her a sophisticated double-kiss, one on each cheek.

That's what a Roman would do, right?

When my nose ended up in her eyeball, Laura recoiled.

"Ouch! What are you doing?" she said as she covered her eye.

Mum, who had been an iceberg the entire drive home, scoffed as Michela gracefully ignored my failed attempt at refinery. Frozen with disgrace, the most Camerican words came out of my mouth.

"Sorry."

Polite sorries were obviously not Laura's taste as she gave me a look that was less than impressed. Water trickled from her eye as she rubbed it.

"Here, let me help you," I pulled a Kleenex from my pocket, and shaking away the lint, went to blot her eye. Just as I was near, she pulled away causing my finger to poke her in the other.

"Ouch! What are you trying to do? Blind me?"

Mum snickered again with a satisfied scoff.

"Just be Camerican, okay. You're better at that," Laura said as both eyes teared up.

Don't say it. Please don't say it!

"Sorry."

I said it.

Laura shook her head, rolling her red eyes at me. Great. It hadn't even been an hour and I was already getting the eye roll. How was I going to work my way out of this one?

I know!

"Here. Let me help you with your bag," I reached down and pulled her bag, which was attached to arm.

Which was attached to her hand. And her fingers.

Which were rubbing her eyes.

Which were promptly thrust back into her eyeball.

She recoiled again. "*Cavolo!* Stop trying to help, would ya? I can carry my own bag."

Don't say it...oh, I give up. Just say it.

"Sorry."

She rolled her eyes again. "I'll see you later," she said as she tottered into their apartment building. Michela gave me a look of sympathy as she guided her newly blinded daughter.

With my confidence suddenly shaken, I waved goodbye awkwardly.

Not a good start.

Looking over to Mum, I knew it was time to tell her. She would accept my decision. Right?

Before I could recount my noble pursuit, she rolled her eyes and walked into the nunnery. Great. Now I had two women rolling their eyes at me. This was going to be harder than I thought.

Once we were in the hallway of the nunnery and Mum was opening the door to her room, I laid it on her.

"Mum, I have to tell you something."

She turned. Significantly shorter than me, she somehow always made me feel small. "Yes, love. What is it?"

I looked around the hallway for a way out. No luck. "I've asked Laura if she wants to date." There. I said it, albeit with the confidence of a used car salesman selling an engineless car.

Her answer shocked me.

"Oh, I know."

"What? What do you mean you know?"

"Do you think I'm blind? I know when my son is interested in a woman. I've never seen you act this way with anyone. You will make a lovely couple."

I couldn't believe my ears. This had never happened before. This was unchartered territory. What was I supposed to do? It was too soon to be cautiously optimistic, so I settled for caution instead.

"What do you mean? You don't care?" I asked.

"No. Of course not. She's lovely."

"You don't care about the age difference?"

"Care? Why would I? It's your life."

Weird.

"I don't know. I thought maybe you would want me to date someone my own age."

"That's up to you, love."

I had been expecting a big lecture, so to receive a blessing instead left me without words.

"Just remember..."

Here we go.

"...she does have fifteen more years of experience than you."

I knew it. Too good to be true. "I'm aware of that. That's why I had a hard time telling you."

"I know you *think* you understand the difference, but do you really know what that means? Think about it. How many other relationships could she have had in fifteen years? Half a dozen? A dozen? Maybe more."

"Geez. You make her sound like a slut. Anyway, even if she had . . . who cares? It's not important to me, Mum. She was in serious relationships, but it's not like she's been jumping around from guy to guy."

"How do you know?"

"Because she..." I thought about what I was about to say; I really had no idea what her past was like. "Well, I trust her."

"Trust her all you like, but that doesn't change the fact that she is far more familiar with men than you are with women."

"How do you know?"

"You're my son. A mother knows."

"You seem to know a lot about me all of a sudden." Here was the mother I knew all too well. "A son knows his my mother just as well, and right now, you're being jealous."

She ignored me. "You may not care now, but when you get closer, things might change. Intimacy brings jealousy."

"It still doesn't matter to me. Love conquers all."

She scoffed. "Stop being naive." She crossed her arms the way she did before a lecture. "Let's say you get married . . ."

Here we go again.

"It's way too soon for that."

"I know. But let's just pretend that you ask this girl to marry you. How would you like it if several other men knew your wife intimately?"

This was the first time I stopped to think. "Um. I guess I don't really like the idea."

"Right. So will you be able to love a woman that has been around."

"Shit, Mum! You make it sound so vulgar."

"Well, I'm just saying. It's something to think about. And don't forget her feelings either. How will she feel when she gets older, and you are in the prime of your life? Don't you think that's a little unfair on her? Shouldn't you consider that she might feel intimidated later on in life. That's a lot of stress for a woman."

My brain was back on as convention knocked on my door. "Laura mentioned that last night." Mum's plan was sucking me in. She was prodding to find the button that worked and she had found it.

"How are you going to feel when she is getting old and older-looking, and you are still young and strong? Fifteen years is a lot, especially for us women. Time is not kind to us. She looks good now, but how will she look when she's forty-five and you're thirty? What about when she's fifty-five and you're forty? Are you okay with the physical and energy differences? You don't know this now in your twenties, but once you hit thirty, you'll see a change. Will she have the energy that you have? I doubt it."

These were all things I hadn't thought of.

"Besides. Look who she's dated before. Did you see Giancarlo? I love you, son, but you're no Giancarlo. She's accustomed to another class. We're working class from England. Do you really think she'll fit in with us? Do you really think she'll fit in with the family?"

The "family first" umpire had stepped on the court. Game. Set. Match.

With just a few simple minutes of rationalizing, she had carefully planted seeds of doubt. I wish I had the answers to her questions. I wished I could look into the future and see how things would work out.

Love conquers all, but first you'll have to conquer love.

Pierluigi's words rang in the back of my mind. His family had stood in his way with Anne. When we had talked about the obstacles he had to face, they sounded easy enough to overcome. But now, as Mum rationalized reality for me, those obstacles felt like giant concrete walls.

Spitting in the eye of convention was going to be harder than I thought.

Chapter 23
First Date

Laura

"How do I look?" I asked Mamma who sat on the edge of her bed, mouth twitching.

Truthfully, I didn't need her answer—I knew how I looked. The tall mirror in Mamma's bedroom hadn't lied to me in over thirty years. Even though I was two sizes bigger, I looked hot. The red, sleeveless Alexander McQueen dress covered my décolletage with a halter neckline. It clung perfectly to my body, only showing sensual curves, not senseless bumps. This would set any man on fire.

"Isn't that a bit much? You're going to intimidate the guy," she replied.

"Weren't you the one who encouraged me to think outside the box? Besides, if he can't handle me as I am, then this will be a quick date." And I was hoping I might run into Giancarlo. "I'm not holding back for anyone. He needs to know what he's getting himself into. I'm a Roman girl and proud of it."

My callous tone made me twinge. I didn't want to bulldoze Alex. He was too nice for that, but I needed to see if he had what it took to be with me. I knew Giancarlo did, but what about Alex? Could sweetness tame my savage beast?

Besides, this dress looked really hot. My strapped Prada heels weren't bad either.

"You're right. But be nice. And try to keep an open mind," she said.

"Open mind about what? This is just a date, Ma."

"Why did you agree to go out with him in the first place, if this is how you feel?" Mamma asked.

"I really don't know. It just came out of me. It was like listening to someone else's voice. It was almost like a…" The feeling I had was juvenile. Childish, really.

"Like what?" Mamma asked.

"I was going to say like an angel, but that's just silly." I shook away the idea as I smoothed the dress over my waist, making sure no fabric wrinkles could be mistaken as fat rolls. I didn't want any extra showing down there.

"It's not that silly. You know how I feel about that."

"Yeah, yeah. You think angels are everywhere. Does that mean they are inside me then?"

"All it means is that something higher is telling you to give this kid. . .I mean 'young man' a try. It's called faith. Remember?"

"The only thing that I have faith in tonight is that Alex won't know what hit him when he sees me." I turned in the mirror to check the curve of my *culo*.

Yep. Still got it. Life in the States may have flattened my spirits, but as least it hadn't flattened my butt.

"I'll just think of it as one of our lessons. Yeah. That's it. It's just a romantic lesson." I cocked my head at myself in the mirror. "Does that sound weird?"

"Really weird," Mamma shook her head. "Maybe you should try to see him more as a date than a student."

I huffed. "I'll try, but it's really hard. I'm not used to this. I'm used to men with hair on their chests. Alex barely has hair on his arms."

"Some women find smooth men attractive."

I looked over to Mamma, who was trying to hide a coy expression. "Gross, Ma! We're talking about Alex here, not some cheap underwear model. He's too sophisticated for that."

"Oh, he is, is he? Just a second ago, you said he was just your student."

"Well—he's a sophisticated student. He's a guy who is ready to be a man, but his humility gets in the way."

"Doesn't that make him more sophisticated? I thought you were tired of arrogant men. Now that you've found one who's modest, you're saying he's too modest?"

I hated when Mamma was right.

"Fine," I said, sulkily. "He's somewhat sophisticated, in a backwater kind of way. Even though he poked my eyes out today, at least he's trying. Let's just see what he wears tonight, then I'll let you know. If he's going to be with me, he can't wear flannel all the time. Even if it's nice flannel." I paused, thinking about my words. "That sounded really shallow, didn't it?"

Mamma nodded.

"Fine. I'm shallow. But what do you expect? I grew up in Rome."

Mamma grew serious. "Just try to keep an open mind. Remember, love is found in the strangest of places."

"Who said anything about 'love'?" I asked. "This is just a date. Nothing else."

I looked in the mirror and said the words again. "This is just a date."

•   •   •   •   •

Alex walked out of the nunnery like the fresh-faced, Camerican kid he was. There was no mistaking that he was from another land where simple sweetness hadn't yet been tarnished by Italy's disdain for naïveté.

He waved, like a goofy Prince Farming.

"Ciao, Laura." His eyes widened and his step slowed as he approached. "Wow. You look . . ."

"Hot. Yeah. I know."

"Actually, I was going to say 'like a Christmas tree,' but hot will do."

"What? A Christmas tree? Well, at least I'm not wearing flannel."

"Hey. This is grade A, 100% Canadian blue flannel. It matches my jeans. I'm glad you noticed. I spent hours trying to decide what to wear."

"Hours, huh? Well, at least you're coordinated." That was the least I could tolerate. "So, where are we going?"

"I don't know. What do you want to do?"

"What do you mean you don't know? *You* asked *me* out. You're the one who's supposed to organize this."

"Oh. I hadn't thought of that."

Instant turn-off. A man without a plan was a man without a direction. Even depressed Luke could organize a date. "What do you mean? You're the 'dater,' and I'm the 'datee.' It's the dater's responsibility to organize the date for the 'datee,'" I said.

His eyes darted from side to side. "Oh." He cleared his throat. "Well, there's a nice restaurant just down the street." He pointed in several vague directions.

"Good. Which one?" I knew he hadn't any idea, but I wanted to see how he'd react. It was time to see if this Camerican could keep up with me.

"It's a surprise," he said, barely flinching.

He was quick. That was one thing going for him.

"I like surprises," I said.

"Good. There's going to be a few of those tonight, starting with this." He pulled a wrapped gift from his back pocket, and handed it to me.

Okay. This showed promise. What was it? A bottle of prosecco? Perfume? A strangely shaped jewellery box, perhaps?

"Just a little something in case of emergencies. Go ahead. Open it."

My curiosity piqued. I carefully unwrapped the paper to reveal a red bottle. I laughed out loud. "Ketchup?"

"Ta-da. Just in case you need any tonight," he said. "I know you miss American food."

"Where are you thinking of taking me? McDonald's?"

"Is there one around here?" he asked.

"No!" I screamed.

While we were both laughing, he'd managed to slip his hand into mine, just like he had on the beach. How did he keep doing that without me noticing?

"You're pretty good at this, aren't you?" I said.

He smiled confidently.

I liked that as well. At least he hadn't poked my eyes out again.

As we walked down the street, people looked at us in a way that wasn't the usual Italian curiosity. I looked down to see if there was something awry. Had my dress unzipped? Or was my makeup smudged? It wasn't until we walked past a couple of elderly ladies and overheard their whispers that I clued in.

"Look at that. That's just disgusting," one of the ladies said.

"She's a grown woman. What's she doing with a teenager?" whispered the other.

I looked over to Alex, who had the air of someone who'd never had a dirty thought in his entire life. He was the embodiment of youthful energy, reminding me of myself when I was his age. Optimistic. Brave. Passionate. Things that had been dulled by the disillusionment of experience, like a silver chalice tarnished by time.

When I had dated older men, youth had always been my advantage. Youth meant beauty, and beauty meant control. Come to think of it, most of the men of my past were far less attractive than I was beautiful. In a way, it made me feel safe. If I was the better looking of the two, then they would never leave me.

No man ever leaves a woman who is more beautiful.

Right?

Was that why I broke it off with Giancarlo? Had I felt like I lacked control because he was more handsome? Was that what was bugging me with Alex? Maybe it wasn't just his age that bothered me. Perhaps it was something else.

As we walked by more people, I grew more self-conscious with each passing step. My imagination ran wild as I envisioned what they saw when they looked at us. I could see the glaring contrast that made those two ladies protest. I saw a handsome, strong young man holding the hands of an aging beauty who was at the tail end of her attractiveness. A woman who would never be able to keep up.

In a way, I felt less powerful. I saw how young girls looked at him. Hell, I even heard how Mamma liked "smooth men." The whole relationship would be a power shift for me. I would have to keep Alex enticed with more than just my beauty, and that scared me to death.

"Why do the men here keep staring at you?" he said as we walked down the street.

"Who's staring at me?" I asked. In my paranoia, I hadn't noticed that men were staring at me.

"Yeah. They stare at you like I'm not even here. I feel like the invisible man. If they're not careful, they're going to get an invisible fist. It's disrespectful."

"You mean you don't stare at girls?" I asked.

"Notice, yes. Stare, no. They're two different things. Staring is obvious and unflattering. It renders someone to being an object of desire rather than a person of interest. Noticing is interest without desire."

These didn't sound like the words of a twenty-year-old.

"Who taught you that? Your Dad?"

"My Dad? God, no. You don't want to know what he taught me."

"Now you've got my interest," I said. "C'mon. What did he say? I want to know how a kid your age gets these ideas."

He rolled his eyes. "My Dad was famous with my brothers and I for the three F's of women."

"The three F's? What's that? Some kind of gentleman's code of conduct?"

"Not quite."

"Now I really want to know." Did it mean: faithfulness, focus and fortitude? Feminine fancies and forget-me-nots? Fabulous fabrics and facials? Flowers, foot massages and family? What could his dad have possibly said that influenced him so?

"All right. Here goes. But brace yourself; they're not very nice." A look of distaste tainted his face with lemony sourness. I was almost sorry to have asked him, but this was too big of a detail to skip over, especially if it had shaped his thinking.

"Find 'em," he started.

"Okay," I nodded, waiting in anticipation.

"Fuck 'em."

"What!"

"And forget get 'em."

I nearly slapped him.

"That's awful!" I said. "No. That's worse than awful. That's downright filthy. In what possible way could that have shaped your thinking?"

"I don't know. In a strange way, it made me not want to be my father. To search for more meaning than his thoughtless advice. It became my motivation to do exactly the opposite."

"Thank God. So does that mean that you never used the three F's in your life?"

"No. Even though I would be lying if I said I didn't have the opportunity. But something made me choose not to."

"What made you choose not to?" I asked. I wondered how anyone could find the strength to overcome such a horrible education. What kind of mental fortitude would Alex had to have had to disregard such ill advice and form his own perspective?

"I don't know really. Faith."

"Faith? In what?"

"In something better. Faith in fate, I guess."

I stopped in my tracks.

"Have you been talking to Mamma?" I asked.

"Michela? About what?"

For a split second, I saw him much older than his years showed. There was definitely more to Alex than just being a good student. I could sense a sleeping geyser beneath his youthful exterior. I wondered what would set it free.

"For what it's worth, you don't sound like a twenty-year-old."

"Well, in a way I'm not. I might physically be twenty, but really, I'm as old as time."

We started walking again.

"Well that makes me feel better," I said.

"Why?"

"If you're as old as time, then that makes me the youngest here," I joked.

He squeezed my hand. "Ha! I guess you're right."

When we laughed, I forgot all about our age difference. I didn't even care that people were staring at us. I only cared that time seemed to slow down when we talked. It reminded me of our lessons.

"Are you going to keep studying Italian when you get back to the U.S.?" I asked.

"Only if you're there. I couldn't imagine studying with anyone else. I would feel like I was betraying you."

A lump caught in my throat. Should I tell him that I was planning on staying in Italy?

"Alex, I need to tell you something."

He turned to face me. "Sure. What is it?"

My heart stuck in my throat. I wanted to tell him, but I was afraid that the news might hurt him, so I decided to wait and see how the night went. Hopefully the date sucked, giving me an easy exit.

"Where are you taking me?" I asked instead.

"Right here."

He pointed to a restaurant I knew all too well. Alluring fragrances that could only come from a Sicilian restaurant wafted by. The aromas of fish and peppers teased my taste buds.

"This one? This is my cousin's favorite. He might even be here."

"Then the food is good?"

"Yeah, but it's a bit expensive. And fancy. Are you sure? Why don't we go to the pizzeria next door?"

"Well, the way I see, I've been uncomfortable ever since I landed in Italy, so the way I look at it, how could it get worse?"

"I don't know. But are you sure you want to find out?"

My warning sank in. He looked like a fish about to jump into a desert.

"Yeah. Why not? I've come this far. *Prego, signorina*," he said with a bow.

"Signorina?" This was a term applied to young girls, not mature women, especially when the person saying it was younger than me. "You know I'm older, right?" At least he didn't say signora. Then I would have felt really old.

"Really? You could have fooled me."

"You're way too flattering for your own good, you know that?"

"And you're way too pretty for my own good. Besides, flattery is nearly as bad as staring."

"Let me guess. Another anti-lesson from your dad?" I asked.

"Nope. That one's mine. There's one thing you can always count on with me: I will always tell you the truth."

"Even if I don't like it?"

"Especially if you don't like it."

Honesty and integrity. I could get used to this old-young man. Maybe Mamma was right. Maybe Alex was just what I needed. But there was no sense in wasting time, so I put him to the test.

"Then answer this: does this dress make me look fat?" I giggled at my own silliness as I twirled a pirouette.

He stared me straight in the eyes. "No," he said, then held my gaze with such strength that made my breathing stop. It was the most honest thing I had ever heard. It was so far from a lie that truth could never be so honest again. In that moment I knew that Alex would never, ever tell a fib.

I *really* liked that.

A maitre d' with a black suit and tie stood ready to greet us as we walked in. When he saw Alex, his nose twisted upward before coming back down upon seeing me.

"Good evening." he said.

Alex caught up to me, and was about to speak when…

"A table for you and your son, Signora?" the maitre d' asked.

Alex froze, not knowing what to say. The maitre d' looked between us for an answer leaving me with a big decision to make: should I strangle him with his necktie, or kick him in the shins with my Pradas?

"He's not my son," I said. I didn't know what else to say. I'd never been called anyone's mother before.

It was hard to recover from such a gaffe, so the maitre d' began a chorus of apologies. His face turned red as beads of sweat popped up on his forehead. It was so painful to watch him suffer that I should have reassured him.

I should have.

But I didn't.

Let him burn.

"*Mi scusi, Signora. Mi scusi.*" The redness of his face became more vibrant with each uttered syllable. He looked everywhere for a place to hide. He was mortified.

"Excuse him for what?"

It wasn't Alex who asked the question. It came from a voice smeared with the kind of slyness that could only come from one person. I turned to face my cousin.

"Alberto. What are you doing here?" I asked him.

"Dining? What are you doing? Embarrassing waiters?"

I gave him a quick peck on each cheek as the maitre d' slunk away.

"Are you here alone?" He asked, either oblivious to Alex standing beside me, or purposefully ignoring the kid in blue flannel. My guess was the latter.

"No. I'm here with Alex. Remember the student I told you about?"

He feigned surprise at Alex's presence, hand on his heart. "Ah, yes. The mysterious paver. . .I mean 'phone caller.' Nice to meet you."

Alex shook his hand without hesitation. It was nice to see that he wasn't intimidated by my cousin's priggishness.

"Alex, can you excuse Laura and I for one second? I need a private word with my cousin." Alberto grabbed my arm and pulled me aside before Alex could even nod.

"What do you want?" I asked. I knew full well he was up to no good.

"You're dating *that*?"

I knew it.

"Yeah. So what?" I asked. He better not say anything stupid, or else my Pradas would end up somewhere softer than the waiter's shins.

"He's a *carciofo*."

"Did you just call him an artichoke?" I looked over to Alex, who stood stiffly. Like a *carciofo*. "Well, he kinda is. But he's a good kid. Leave him alone."

"All right. But just don't do anything stupid. Remember: you could've had Giancarlo wrapped around your little finger, and instead you're settling for this."

I could have told him that Giancarlo had used the 'L' word this morning at Antonini's. I could have, but I didn't.

"Just stay out of my business."

"All right." He looked down at the bottle in my hand. "What's that?"

"Ketchup," I said. I couldn't let him know that Alex had bought it for me, so I told a tale. "I needed some for home. I miss it."

"You use ketchup? Since when?"

"Since I lived in the States."

He cocked an eyebrow before he looked over to Alex. "You're not bringing it in here, are you?" He could tell by the look on my face that we were about to. "Do me a favour then, if you leave the bottle at the door, you can join us. I have some friends arriving soon," he said.

Seeing Alex with his flannel shirt and blue jeans made my heart twang with tenderness. I couldn't subject him to my cousin's pompous friends.

"That's all right. We're going to McDonald's. I need to put this ketchup to use."

"McDonald's? What are you talking about? Since when do you eat there?" Alberto asked.

I straightened my back defiantly. "Since I discovered Big Macs."

Alberto looked puzzled. "You really have changed. The Laura I knew would never eat at McDonald's."

"Well, sometimes you just feel like a Big Mac. C'mon, Alex." I grabbed his hand. "I can only handle a few minutes of my cousin's snobbery."

"Hey!" Alberto protested. "Having good taste doesn't make me a snob."

"No. Having bad manners does." I stuck my tongue out at him. He always hated when I did that. "Enjoy your dinner," I said.

"Suit yourself. I'll see soon anyway. You're coming to the fundraiser, right?" he asked.

"I'm not sure yet. I'll let you know."

I gave Alberto a couple of farewell kisses, even if he didn't deserve them. I may have objected to his *carciofo* comment, but I wasn't rude.

"Okay. Because I can pick you up if you want. Remember, it's going to be a big night."

How could I forget? Everywhere I turned, someone was reminding me of the choice I had to make. But for now, all I wanted to do was see my city. For now, I wanted to get away from the Albertos of this world, and spend time with someone much sweeter.

Chapter 24
Juliette and Romeo

Alex

I wondered if Romeo had to put up with garlic breath from a mouth-breather while standing in line at the ice-cream store with Juliette? If he had, what would he have said?

"Mine pungent friend. Wouldst thou closeth thine whiff lest mine wrath wail a tempest?"

That's what I felt like saying as I stood in line at Giolitti's Gelateria. Masses of drooling patrons pressed up against us at the counter as flavours of all colours blinded me with indecision.

Laura and I had both agreed that a gelato would be a good substitute for dinner, especially since I would not usually eat dessert for supper, and since I was getting in the habit of trying new things, like dating my teacher, what the hell.

"Do they have bubblegum-ice-cream?" I asked my server who stared blankly at me with a flat, metal spatula in his hand, ready to plunge.

"They don't have bubblegum-ice-cream in Italy," Laura drummed her fingers anxiously against the marble counter as she glared at some kids who were pushing their luck by pushing against her.

"What about tiger-ice-cream? Chocolate mint? Rocky-road?"

Laura shook again.

"Tutti-frutti? That sounds Italian."

Laura was losing her patience and the server was about to move onto the next starving patron, a young Italian with hair gelled as hard as my decision. It looked like his eyebrows had been waxed. I wanted to tell him that his breath was going to curdle the ice-cream, but he looked like he was ready for a fight. "*Annamo*," he muttered impatiently. His girlfriend had matching fingernails and makeup more colorful than the gelato. She looked at me about as unimpressed as Laura did.

"C'mon. They don't have those kinds of flavors here. They have real flavors, like mango, pistacchio, chocolate, vanilla. What's your favorite fruit?"

"Apple."

She rolled her eyes. "That's about the only one they don't have. Do you want me to choose for you?"

After meeting Laura's cousin, I was feeling more out of place than ever, and having my date choose ice-cream for me was nearly as emasculating as poking her eye with my nose. The pressure was on. I couldn't give-up, Waxed-eyebrows couldn't give-a-darn, so I gave-in.

"Go ahead," I shrugged.

Within seconds, three decadent slices of ice-cream we slashed on top of a cone, with a swirl of whipping cream on top. Unlike Amercian ice-cream, where flavors were pilled one on top of the other, Italian gelato was arranged side-by-side.

Once we had both escaped the fray inside Giolitti's, I asked her. "Why are the ice-creams not on top of each other?"

"Simple. You can taste all three flavors at the same time. It's about combinations. Do you like yours?"

"It's definitely not tutti-frutti, but it'll do," I winked. "Hey, I feel badly that you have to carry that ketchup around with you all night. Do you want me to carry it for you?" I was used to dates pretending to be tough, as though accepting chivalry meant weakness. I once offered my jacket to a girl because she was shivering. She outright refused, saying that she was "fine." Well, she shivered "finely" into a terrible cold for the next two weeks.

So much for gallantry.

"It was about time you asked. Here," she said as she handed me the bottle. Surprised, I grabbed it immediately, and stuffed it into my back-jeans-pocket.

At last. A place for my chivalry.

With our backs against an untextured, stuccoed wall, we stood off to one side, licking our gelati with satisfaction, watching the onslaught of the gelateria continue, feeling the cool sweet melt the day away. Romans and tourists attacked the business with ferocious focus, only to saunter out casually with colorful tongues, lapping and licking.

Among the happy lickers, beautiful girls sashayed by sensually, their sweat moistened blouses barely fluttering from a breeze, eyeshadow smeared after a day of tiring and wiping, relieved to be indulging in the perfect Roman reward of frozen, refreshing ice-cream.

"Lots of cute girls, huh?" Laura asked. "Are you noticing or staring?"

Hmm. A test. No problem. I got this.

"I *noticed* that none are as cute as you," I replied.

Take that. I may be younger, but I'm not falling for that one.

"I really like that girl's dress." She pointed to the most attractive of all of them.

"That would look great on you," I replied.

Too easy.

"She has great legs, don't you think?"

"Truth or dare?" I asked.

"I thought you only told the truth."

"Then, yeah, she does have nice legs."

Laura licked her ice-cream, evaluating me carefully with a sideways stare.

"Is this a lesson, a date or an interrogation?" I asked, slurping a lick of my own.

"An interrogation." She wiped her mouth with a napkin, smudging her lipstick. "So — how many girls have you dated?"

Not the question I was expecting. I wondered if Juliette had asked Romeo these kind of questions on their first date

Romeo, Romeo. How many wenches hath thou bed, Romeo?

Romantic.

"Enough," I answered. In a world that prized conquests rather than virtue, I always felt like Romeo's toothless brother.

"What does that mean?"

"It means that I've dated enough girls to know what I want."

"That's vague."

"Well, what do you want? Specifics? Hair color? Height? Bust measurements? Foreplay duration?" I was more abrupt than I wanted to be.

Why do girls always want to talk about my past girlfriends?

"Well, no. But it would be nice to know what kind of experiences you had just so I know what I'm up against. You already know about two of my past relationships. I don't know anything about yours. I feel disadvantaged." She looked over in glances, making sure she kept her attention closely on the drips melting off of her gelato. "For instance, you've done *that* with a woman, haven't you?"

Oh boy. Here we go.

"That's a weird question for a first date? Why do you ask?"

"Because I'm not going to be with someone who has never done *that*, that's why. Men need their experiences before settling down. Otherwise, they want it later."

"Is that what life has taught you? That's a pretty dim view on men," I said.

"Actually, yes. Men can't settle down until . . ."

". . . they've sown their wild oats?" I finished her sentence, annoyed with where the conversation was going.

"Exactly," she agreed.

"You know who you sound like? My dad. That's precisely the kind of thing he would say. 'Get out there, son, and sow your wild oats.' Do I look like a wild oats kind of guy?" I asked.

There was a major problem developing here. I'd had this conversation with women before; it always ended up in one of two ways, and neither of them were good. I was wondering which way it was going to end up with Laura.

"Well, you have the confidence of a guy that has done *that*," she said.

"But?"

"But you don't have it in your eyes. Men with experience have a certain look about them when they look at a woman. I see it all the time. In Italian, we call it *l'occhio di triglia*. Sleazy eyes."

"Is that what you're looking for in a man? Sleazy eyes?"

"God, no. I've had enough of that in my life. But when a man never shows that tell-tale look, then it usually means that they've never done *that*."

"So basically you're saying once a man has done *that*, then they automatically become sleazy?"

"No. I'm not saying that. I'm just saying that a woman can tell when a man wants *that*, and you don't seem to want *that*. Which means that you're either very good at hiding that you want *that*, or you've never done *that*."

"Couldn't it also mean that he may not be looking for *that*?"

"It could, but that would make him a rare exception," she said. "So if you don't want *that*, then that tells me you've never experienced *that*. Because if you had, then you would be like every other man, and want *that* all the time."

"Just to clarify, we are talking about kissing, right?"

"No! *Scemo*. I'm talking about sex," she said.

"Oh, I see. You want to know what my 'number' is. My notch-count. My swag-o-meter." With my free hand, I "air-quoted" my annoyance.

"Yes, you idiot. How many girls have you been with?" she asked bluntly.

Romeo, Romeo. How many fields hath though ploughed, Romeo?
Really romantic.

"You don't beat around the bush, do you?"

"Well I was trying to avoid 'the bush,' but you thought I was talking about kissing," she replied.

"I usually wait until after the first kiss before I sleep and tell," I answered.

"C'mon, I don't have any time to waste. You wanted to date an older woman, this is what you're going to get. Think of it as a 'speed date,'" Laura replied as we slowly wandered away from Giolitti's and down Rome's narrow streets. It was strange having a date surrounded by ancient history while talking about my ancient history.

Why is she asking me all of this now?

"We have more than just one night to get to know each other, you know. Or do you want to get into the nitty-gritties right away?"

"If you're leaving for home in a couple of days, I'd like to know where we stand before you take off."

"Why? I'll see you in the U.S. when you come back."

She paused for a split second, which left me wondering if she had something more to say.

"Hey. I'm older. You better get used to this," she said, breezily.

"All right, but I have to warn you. My number intimidates a lot of girls. Most can't handle it," I said.

"That many, huh? Are we talking ten? Twenty?" she asked.

I stayed silent.

"More?"

I continued to say nothing, her curiosity bursting while I kept licking.

"Hundreds?"

"Tell you what. I'll make you a deal. I'll tell you my number if you tell me yours," I proposed.

"My number?" She asked. "Now you're making me feel nervous. I don't know if I want to tell you."

"Hey. Fair's fair," I replied, although I was hoping that she would refuse. Most women didn't like to share their number with me. I wasn't lying when I said my number intimidated them. We walked into an open piazza with an ornately carved column that stretched as high as the buildings surrounding it. The long stone monument left me hoping that my experience could stand as tall as Laura was used to. Having met Mr. Perfect, I had a feeling I was going to fall short.

"All right. If you give me your number, I'll think about giving you mine," she said at last.

"No deal. I may be younger, but I'm not stupid. You have to *promise* to give me your number," I replied. I wasn't going to let her pull a fast one on me.

"Okay, but you go first," she said.

"Are you sure? I'm warning you. This is no joke. You may not like the answer," I warned.

She thought a little longer, pausing from her gelato, before agreeing. "I'm sure."

"All right. Here goes." The soft breeze whistled by like a cheering crowd. The only thing lacking was a drum roll. Juliette stared longingly into Romeo's eyes, waiting with baited breath to hear from her hero. The bubble of hope floated suspensefully between us waiting to burst.

"Zero."

Pop.

I wondered if Juliette looked as pale as Laura did when Romeo revealed his number. Maybe that was why ladies back then wore ceruse. By looking constantly pale, they could hide their shock that their date was a virgin.

She walked in silent stupefaction, processing. "Zero . . . like 'you're a virgin' zero? How is that possible? I mean, look at you. You've never had anyone come on to you?"

"There were opportunities, I just never felt strongly enough to go through with it."

"Well, then how many girls have you dated?" she asked.

I was used to these kinds of inquiries after I revealed my number. The world expected men to be players and layers as opposed to gentlemen of valor. I had always held firm in my belief that sex was the culmination of love, which needed room to grow and develop.

"A handful."

"So you weren't kidding up at the Zodiac. You really don't date much," she asked.

"Like I told you earlier, I've dated enough to know that I haven't found the right girl yet."

She dawdled beside me, giving her gelato absentminded licks. The column behind us shrank from sight as we turned down a busier street. The world of Rome became a blur of streaking headlights, traffic pushing through the throng of red faces burnt from too much touristing, a symphony of honks, exhaust and exclamations as I waited for Laura to say something.

Anything.

"So now I guess you want my number?" she finally asked.

"Actually, no," I said. I knew her number would intimidate me as well. Would Romeo have asked Juliette for her number? I doubted it.

"What? After all that, you don't want to know?"

"It's none of my business. All of your experiences have brought you to this point in your life, and I like who you are."

"Did you say just say that you 'like' me?" she asked, flustered.

It took me a while to answer as we made our way back to the car. The silence of the walk seemed to grow ears as it waited for my reply."Yeah," I said with trepidation, feeling vulnerable. "What about you?"

I had the feeling that Laura wouldn't lie to me. If I'd learned anything by now, it was to expect her opinion no matter how brutal it may be. It was the thing I liked most about her, and though my question was a simple one, I knew the answer was not. Especially since she now knew my number.

"Of course I like you . . . you're a good kid."

A loud thud fell in the distance.

Romeo had just fallen from the balcony.

"You'll always be a young buck to me."

Yep. And his neck cracked.

The dreaded friend zone was approaching. I wondered if Juliette had ever put Romeo in the friend zone. Would I have to risk my life, like he had, to win Laura's hand? Was that what it would take to capture her heart? It would be tough to climb her Mamma's building to get to her fifth storey balcony. I would probably end up with more than a cracked neck. At that point, death would have been the better ending anyway.

I had to do something, and it couldn't be another rose. A gesture maybe. Anything to bridge the friend zone gap. We were approaching our car, so I ran to the driver side, and opened her door. When she was about to get in, she paused awkwardly, and looked up to me. I knew that look well. It was the "I wonder what kind of kisser he is" look. As a rule, I never kissed on the first date.

What would Romeo do?

Staring into her brown eyes, I gently took her hand, and laid a kiss that would have made Romeo proud. Laura blushed.

Romeo wheeled past on a wheelchair, giving me a thumbs up.

Chapter 25
Il Gianicolo

Laura

My first instinct was to run as fast as I could. A virgin? I knew I was his tutor, but I wasn't going to teach him *that*. No way. Not on my life. It was already a stretch to look past our age difference. A BIG stretch.

But a virgin?

What would it even be like? Would he even know what to do? For most guys, it took practice, years of training, copious experience, and even then most couldn't get it right.

No one ever got it right.

Even though the hand kiss was sweet, I had a feeling this whole dating-my-student-thing was quickly coming to an end. At least it made my decision a little easier.

Giancarlo, here I come.

"So. Where do you want to go?" he asked as he sat in the passenger seat. I told him I was going to drive tonight; Rome wasn't designed for Camerican drivers. It was already tough enough for a veteran Roman like myself.

"Alex—," it was time to lay it on him.

Listen kid. I'm not dating a twenty-year-old, hand-kissing virgin who uses the word 'court.' Got it!

That was what I wanted to say, until he looked me in the eyes.

God, he really did have amazing eyes.

Forget the kid. Go for Giancarlo. At least he's not a virgin.

But there was something sweet behind those eyes. Tenderness. Compassionate. There wasn't any —

Sleaze? C'mon. Give me a break. He's a kid! Move on.

"Have you been to the Gianicolo?" I asked.

Of course he hasn't been there. What's wrong with you?

"You know I haven't," he replied. "What's that?"

You see. Now you gotta show him.

"I'll take you there. But be prepared. It's the make out spot of Rome, but it doesn't mean I want to make out."

"Then why are you taking me there?"

Good question.

Why was I taking him there? Did I want to see what he was capable of? Did I want to see if his old-world manners would crack under the pressure of seeing what most people got up to under the dark Roman skies? Or did I want to see what it would be like to have a virgin try to make a move on me?

Whatever it was, I started the car with a renewed sense of adventure. "Most Romans go there to smooch, but I went there for an entirely different reason. Wanna find out?"

"How could I say no?"

Clipping in his seat belt, I saw the same sparkle in his eyes he had during our lessons.

What is that sparkle? And why am I attracted to it?

●　　　●　　　●　　　●　　　●

When I was a little girl, between Papà's beatings and Mamma's crying, we all used to head to the Gianicolo as a family. It was one of the few times I felt like a real kid. No drama. No lashings. No scoldings. Just me, Mamma and Papà .

Alex always mentioned his family first policy during our lessons, and whenever he did, my mind was transported here. I was sure he was going to like it.

"What do you think?" His rental car chirped as I armed the alarm with the key fob.

"About the steamy windows on some of these cars? Or about the newspaper on the others?" He pointed to the parked cars beside ours. Some had newspaper taped to hide what was going on behind them. Soft moans could be heard as they rocked back and forth.

"Forget that. What do you think of the view?" An orange rim glowed behind Rome as day said goodnight. Cathedral domes humped along the horizon, round shadows in the twilight.

"Amazing. It's better than the Zodiac."

"C'mon. I want to show you something," I said as I grabbed his hand.

You know you're holding your students hand, right?

Pulling him along the stone path that ran along the Gianicolo's fortress wall, I couldn't help myself from laughing.

Really? Giggling now?

Yeah. So what? This was fun. Alex was laughing as well as we dodged around the various marble busts that dotted the garden. As a little girl, I always wondered who they were, but with too many to name, I just called them all "Papà." He liked that. It was one of the few times we ever laughed together.

I missed that.

Finally, as my breath started to run out, I skidded to a stop in front of what I was looking for.

La burattinaia del Gianicolo.

And we weren't alone. Standing on sand-coloured gravel between two rows of pine trees, a group of children were gathered in front of a small theatre. They were screaming with excitement just as I had when I was a little girl. The show was about to start, so we stood behind them with all the parents.

"Thank God. We haven't missed it."

"What is it?" Alex asked, the blue of his eyes lit up under the fading sunset as they widened with wonder.

"This is where I used to come with my parents when I was a girl. It's a puppet show."

Seeing Alex smile stirred something inside of me I hadn't felt in many years. Quickly, before it overwhelmed me, I steered my focus to the tiny theatre, pushing the feeling down.

You can't be serious. You're not actually falling for this guy.

A whir came from behind the theatre as an old music box wound alive. Children fell silent as they watched breathlessly. The crimson curtain raised, and out popped —

"Pulcinella!" Everyone screamed in unison.

Alex brightened with expectation as I reached down, cradling his hand in mine. He squeezed it tightly, giving me a smile that warmed a part of me that had been cold for a long time.

The play continued: a ballad of forgotten fatherly-beatings and remembered childhood laughter where I was allowed to be a little girl, if only for a short while.

Bravely, Pulcinella fought the devil, a duel of steel and wit. Chink. Clink. Their swords met. Gasp. Rasp. The children couldn't last. Slap. Baff. Fists flew past. Run! Hide! Pulcinella nearly shied. Oh. No. The devil screamed with fear. Pulcinella! Pulcinella! The end was growing near. As laughter and fright sang throughout the night, the lullaby of nostalgia soothed my might.

Until finally, under the purple sky of forgotten time and twinkling stars, I laid my head against Alex's shoulder, sensing for the first time in a long time what it was like to be me again.

What are you doing?

I didn't know. All I knew was that Alex gave me a sense of myself I had long forgotten. Or ignored. I wasn't sure, but with him, I didn't feel like I had to prove myself. Or behave a certain way, or be strong, or sexy, or stubborn. With Alex, all the walls I usually put up with a man dissolved, and for the first time since I was a child, I felt the comfort of peace.

Chapter 26
Hands

Alex

That was the second time Laura had grabbed my hand tonight. This could mean only one thing: the "friend zone" was getting its butt kicked. Holding her hand as we watched the play finally gave me a chance to enjoy being with her without the nagging insecurities that had plagued me all day.

It was official. I was moving into boyfriend territory.

Surprised?

You bet I was. This was the first time a woman reacted this way to my virginity. Most would either want to relieve me of it, making them annoying gropers. Or they would run away as fast as they could.

I was expecting the latter from Laura. I could tell she wasn't a groper. She was far too classy for that, which only left the last option.

I didn't know what I would have done if she had ran.

She might still. Don't get cocky. She's just holding your hand.

Right. I needed to be cautious here. Remember how she flirted with everyone in the restaurant.

Don't fall for her yet.

I had to make sure first.

How was I going to do that? Maybe it was my turn to test her.

Yeah. Good idea.

The problem was, I wasn't very good at testing girls. Women were always better at that than me. What was the best way to see if a woman really liked me? I could have just asked, but that felt inorganic.

There was always the trusted "high-school" approach: ignore her. But at this point, that was pretty much impossible. Besides, it felt a little juvenile.

Then it came to me. Something that was used against me all the time.

Are you sure?

Sure, I was sure. It had to work. After all, she had done it to me. As a matter fact, girls had always done this to me many times before. Why couldn't I do it to them?

I don't know about this. Seems risky.

I ignored the thought. Up until now, my mind had been my worst enemy. It was time to change that and spit in the eye of convention by challenging my ideas about life. It was time to live on the edge. Take a risk. With a nod, I was ready.

All right. But I'm not liking this.

Quiet. I knew what I was doing. I hoped.

As soon as the play ended, and all the kids were clapping with glee, Laura lifted her head from my shoulder, facing me. Her eyes were dewy for some reason.

"What did you think?"

"It was fun." *Here goes.* "Is this where you brought Giancarlo?"

Why didn't that sound right. Her face went flat.

Uh-oh.

"What brought *him* into this?"

Quick! Bailout! Abort! Abort!

"Um. I don't know. I thought maybe this was where you brought all your boyfriends."

"What do you mean, "all" my boyfriends?" Her tone was getting defensive. She pulled her hand away from mine, crossing her arms across her chest. Happy children streamed around us as they rejoined their parents. The gravel crunched under their feet as they left us alone.

"I find it hard to believe that you never shared this with anyone else."

She looked away, a frown on her forehead. "This is a special place for me. I wanted to show it to you. I thought you would have understood."

"Yeah. It was fun, but I find it hard to believe that I'm the only person you've ever brought up here."

Shut up! Stop talking!

"Why is that so hard to believe? I thought someone who was a *virgin* would get it." She stabbed the "virgin" part. Now I was in trouble. How was I going to get myself out of this one?

Run!

I couldn't run.

Try groping. That might work.

To reduce the growing distance between us, I moved closer, only to have her take a step back.

Quick. Buy her another rose!

My mind was full of dumb ideas tonight. It was time for plan B.

I swallowed hard before initiating my exit strategy. It wasn't a complicated plan, but it did require a certain amount of finesse, especially when dealing with someone who looked ready to punch me in the throat. I had to use the utmost delicacy and sincerity, otherwise it could come off as phoney. It was a plan every man resorted to in times of relational distress.

The "B" in Plan B stood for "begging."

"I'm so sorry. Please forgive me. I didn't mean what I said. I was just trying to understand where we were at, that was all. This is so new to me. And I care for you. I guess I'm just a little nervous, that's all."

Way to go. Now if she didn't hate you, she'd pity you . Pity isn't sexy, in case you didn't know.

She just rolled her eyes, scoffed, and turned towards the fading, purple sunset, and away from me.

Go after her you idiot.

I jumped in behind her. "I'm sorry, Laura. But you have to admit this is a bit unusual."

This made her stop. "Do you think this is easy for me? Think about it. I'm fifteen years *older* than you. You're my *student*. Everyone looks at me like I'm some kind of child molester. The waiter practically called me your Mum. Oh, and speaking of Mums—you're mother hates me. This is hard enough without you reminding me that I have a bigger history than yours."

"Look. I'm sorry. I didn't know what I was saying. I was just trying to find out if you actually liked me, or if you were just holding my hand because—"

I stopped.

Don't say it.

"Because what?" Damn. Her arms were crossed again and she was tapping her toe.

"Because you're a flirt," I winced as I said it, ready for a fist.

You just don't want to make this easy on yourself, do you knucklehead?

"A flirt? What's that supposed to mean? That I'm *easy*?"

"No. No. I didn't mean it like that. I just noticed that you have a way with men—people, I mean—that is socially easy to get along with, that's all. And I didn't want to fall for you if you didn't feel the same way about me."

Okay. Decent recovery.

"And how do you feel about me?" She asked. Her toe stopped tapping.

What should I say? Something sexy. No. No. Something complimentary. Wait. How about something flattering?

Just tell her the truth!

"I don't say this to many girls—I mean—well, in this case, women. But I think I'm falling for you, and I just feel so out of my league that I kind of wonder if you're feeling the same way towards me?"

Silence. A long one.

Was that good?

I don't know. Don't ask me the hard questions? I'm just your stupid mind, remember.

"Alex..."

Oh no. She started with my name. It was starting to sound like a "Dear John" letter. Was this it? Was this over before it even began? Did this mean that I would have to trudge back to Port Angeles knowing that I missed the chance to win the heart of the first woman to intrigue me in my entire dating life?

"...why don't we just take it step-by-step and see what happens." And with that, she walked up to me, and grabbed my hand for the third time tonight.

Walking back along the balustrade, the cars with newspapers continued their rocking back and forth. Wondering if she had been one of them, I decided to keep my thoughts to myself, and shut my mouth for the rest of the night.

That's the best idea you've had all night.

Chapter 27
Me and My Big Heart

Laura

How I woke up after a date always gave me a good idea of my true feelings for someone. If I woke up with no feeling at all, then it meant that something had gone horribly wrong. If I woke up with butterflies in my stomach, then things had gone well. After last night's excursion with Alex, the feeling I had was a strange concoction of calm and confusion.

Mamma popped her head into my room like a kid on Christmas morning, leaping onto my bed — as much as Mamma could leap. "Are you awake?" she asked. Then, without waiting for an answer, "How did it go?"

Mamma-interrogation time.

Sliding up, I rested my back against the wall. Headboards weren't as common as they were in America. Sunlight streamed through the half-closed shutter. Dots of light pinpricked the room.

"I don't know. It was . . . strange."

"What did you guys do? Did you go for dinner? Did he kiss you?"

"We tried to go for dinner, but we met Alberto, and the last thing I wanted to do was have him eat Alex for dessert. So we had a quick gelato at Giolitti's, then went for a stroll at the Gianicolo."

"The Gianicolo? You haven't been there in years. Why there? Did you make out?" She gave me a sly look.

Recapping last night's events paled in comparison to what I had learned about Alex, so I cut to the chase. "Ma. He's a virgin."

Watching an Italian mother process the unfathomable was like Michelangelo forgetting how to draw. "How? I mean, look at him. Surely girls have tried with him."

"That's exactly what I said. But it's true. He's a virgin. He told me himself." I grabbed my pillow, strangling it with my arms.

"Well, I guess that explains why he doesn't have *occhi di triglia*. How do you feel about it?" Mamma sat up a little more straightly, cupping her hands together.

"Terrible! I'm not a mentor for virgins. I know I was his teacher, but I'm not teaching *that!* C'mon. It's weird. Besides, what if he doesn't like it?"

Mamma gave me a look. "Have you ever met a man that doesn't like it?"

"Well, no." I hadn't been with so many men to know how all men reacted to sex. I knew I liked it, although I had never really found a man that I could openly express myself with; there was a part of me that wanted to save my true sexual expression for my husband, whoever he was. "Maybe he's a virgin because he can't function properly. How does he know if his plumbing is working or not? I mean, this could be a big problem. Maybe he's a virgin because he's afraid of sex. Or worse, afraid of intimacy."

"What did he say about it?"

"He said he was waiting for the right woman. That he never felt strongly enough to sleep with anyone."

"Aw. That's sweet. What's wrong with that? Don't you believe him?"

"I don't think Alex could lie if he tried. But even if he does function, what happens if he likes it *too* much? Is he going to want to try with other women? I know I was curious after my first time about what it would be like with other men. I don't want to be his first. Maybe his last, but definitely not his first."

"Does he look at other women now? A wandering eye is a wandering heart."

"I tested him a little last night. I'll have to keep a closer eye on him from now on."

"This only matters if you feel something for him, you know that, don't you?"

She's right. Mamma is always right.

I wouldn't even be trying to understand his abstinence if I wasn't interested in him. It could only mean one thing and the idea scared me. If I was falling for him, what possible outcome would be in store for me? And what was I going to do with Giancarlo? I really didn't know what do to. The fundraiser was tomorrow night, so I had to make a decision by then.

"What time is it?"

"Almost ten."

"Shoot. I'm meeting them downstairs in half an hour. We're going to try and track down the missing will."

•　　•　　•　　•　　•

Stepping onto the sidewalk, Mrs. Baker stood between Alex and myself with a sour smile. Rome was heating up already, but thankfully, Mrs. Baker was cold enough to keep the temperature down.

"Can I borrow your phone, lovey?" She asked. No greeting. Or "good morning." Not even: "you better not have slept with my son, you slut!"

If she had said that, then at least I could have fought with her. That would have been better than Mrs. Frosty.

"Sure. Who do you need to call?" I smiled. Maybe she needed to call the "dial-a-bitch" hotline for pointers.

Be nice. Remember Alex.

Standing quietly behind his annoying mother, Alex seemed a little awkward. Almost like he was afraid to be himself. I couldn't blame him. How could anyone know how to behave around Mrs. Baker?

Unless he's going to ask you about Giancarlo again. He better not.

"I need to see if Giancarlo can meet us about Anne's will. I would have phoned him last night, but I lost his business card," Mrs. Baker said.

Nope. It's Mrs. Baker's turn to flog that horse.

"You lost his business card," I repeated dryly. Two nights ago, she'd held it like it was her last chance at an orgasm, now she'd somehow misplaced the only thing that could help with her aunt's will. Odd. "How are you going to call him if you don't have his number?"

"Surely you must have it?" she asked.

Okay. You can say it now. She's a bitch.

Alex shifted uneasily, and not just because it was a hot morning. I had to choose my words carefully if I didn't want to send the wrong message.

"Too bad. I deleted his number when I moved to the U.S." I wanted to stick my tongue out at her, but thought it would be best to behave like a thirty-five year old.

Alex's back relaxed. Mrs. Baker persisted. A scooter zipped by.

"Oh, c'mon lovey. Surely you still have it. You are friends, right? You don't just throw away a close friend's number for no reason. Unless—Oh my. I'm so sorry. Were you more than just friends? Then that would make sense if you deleted his number. I'm so sorry. I didn't mean to dig up old wounds."

This woman was getting on my nerves. How on earth did Alex ever come from such a cow and a father that used the three F's? My respect for him was growing.

She kept prying. "Didn't he say that he called you? Maybe you have it in your call history."

For Alex's sake, I bit my tongue, and pulled out my phone. Why was I doing this? Why was I helping this shrew of a woman when I should really tell her to fu—

I scrolled through my call history. Sure enough, there was Giancarlo's number. "Here it is," I said.

After I handed her my phone, Mrs. Baker wandered off out of earshot to make the call. Giancarlo was going to get a big surprise when he answered his phone and thought it was me.

"How are you doing?" I asked Alex now that we were alone. I stepped closer, hoping he would loosen up with his Mum further away.

"Good. Though I had a hard time sleeping. I couldn't stop thinking about you," he replied.

"Really? Last night was so boring, I couldn't wait to fall asleep." It was important to test his sense of humor after a date. If there was any kind of awkwardness, game over.

"Yeah. Me too. I was just trying to be nice. I slept like a stone." He kept a straight face, which broke my straight face, making us both burst into a spat of giggling like we had at the Gianicolo. "Thanks for the tour last night. Rome by night is something else. It was even better with you. It makes me wonder why you left in the first place."

"Now you know why I want to stay."

Wait. What did you just say?

His smile faltered. "What do you mean? You're staying?"

You're not supposed to tell him unless you want to break up with him. That was your excuse, remember?

"What I meant to say was that I stay in Rome when I come to Italy. There is no need to travel anywhere else. Rome has it all," I rushed to cover. "That's what I meant. There's no point in going anywhere else. Rome's perfect." I looked away to hide my fib. Hopefully he hadn't caught it.

An awkward moment passed as we both looked across the empty street at Mrs. Baker who was so far out of earshot, that I was starting to wonder why. It was ten-thirty and Mamma's neighbourhood was one of the last ones to wake up in the area. The sound of scraping steel window shutters told me that businesses were finally opening.

"So when did Giancarlo call you? Was it recently?" Alex asked.

That bitch. She knew her son would ask about Giancarlo.

Just tell him the truth. He needs to hear it.

"It was when I first arrived," I replied.

"And you haven't talked to him since?"

He was prying, or at least trying to. To be fair, that was something I would have done, but being the recipient of nosey questions always put me on guard.

"Nope," I lied. It wasn't any of his business that Giancarlo had tracked me down at Antonini's, though I didn't like lying to Alex. It felt dirty. Luckily, Mrs. Baker was off the phone and heading back. She looked disappointed.

"He said he is fully booked this week."

"That's too bad." I breathed a sigh of relief. I really didn't want to be tempted to see him again. Maybe fate was trying to show me another path.

"He said the only time he could meet us is at the fundraiser tomorrow night."

Or maybe not.

Alex scratched his head — the day's heat was obviously wearing on him. "I don't think Laura wants to go."

How did he know that? Is he a mind-reader?

"Why not? You two can have a nice night together while I talk with Giancarlo," Mrs. Baker asserted.

"Let me guess, he wanted me to come as well," I interrupted.

"Not at all. He didn't mention you. I just thought that maybe you would want to join my son."

There was something odd about this story. Giancarlo wanted me to come, I knew that for a fact. Unless he didn't mention it to Mrs. Baker in the hopes I would feel neglected. That would be something he would do. He was very good at manipulation. Mrs. Baker looked over to Alex, pushing him with her gaze to say something. He cleared his throat.

"Well. It could be a nice night together. I've never been to an Italian fundraiser before. Besides. How else are we going to deal with Aunt Anne's will? Unless we go to the *Tribunale* by ourselves?"

"No, no, no. You don't want to do that without a lawyer," I interjected — these two were going to be eaten alive in Italy if I didn't help them out. "The *Tribunale* is the heart of Italian bureaucracy. You need a lawyer to deal with them."

"What if we called another lawyer?" Alex posed.

"Alex," Mrs. Baker said firmly. "We leave on Friday. We don't have a lot of time. Plus, he speaks English very well. I can't imagine there are a lot of lawyers who both speak English and are willing to help us in the eleventh hour."

Mrs. Baker was pushing her point. Either she had a crush on Giancarlo — not out of the question, given the circumstances — or there was an ulterior motive. Still, as I looked at them standing in front of me like abandoned children, I knew this was their best chance at finishing their business in Italy. One of my biggest downfalls in life had always been my excessive generosity and my need for justice.

Me and my big heart.

"Your Mum is right. I don't know any lawyers who speak English, and you don't have a lot of time." Another scooter screamed by obnoxiously. "I hate to admit it, but Giancarlo is your best bet. He's a very good lawyer, and knows how to navigate the bureaucracy. And trust me, you need someone to help you out with that. But if you're going to an Italian fundraiser, you need some better clothes."

"What's wrong with what I'm wearing?" Alex asked.

"You can't be serious. Do you have a suit? Dress pants at least? A dress shirt?"

"I have the flannel shirt from last night."

"My point exactly." I rolled my eyes and grabbed his arm. "You're coming with me. If there is anything I know, it's fashion. Are you coming too, Angela?"

I used her first name intentionally.

Mrs. Baker looked a little too pleased with herself.

"I wouldn't miss this for the world," she said.

Chapter 28
Shopping

Alex

A gentle mist sprayed our faces as we passed the turquoise pool that was Trevi Fountain. Tourists lounged on the balustrade, trying to escape the sweltering heat. Some stuck their feet in the water before carabinieri told them otherwise. Everyone's phones were out as they took snapshots, vainly trying to capture a digital memory of this Roman masterpiece.

I didn't even try. My heart was unsettled. Laura was hiding something about Giancarlo, and secrets made me nervous. One big reason I had never shared myself with anyone was trust. I needed that above anything else. If she was holding something back from me, I needed to know what it was, and why.

"Where are you taking us?" I shouted over the turmoil. Tourist chatter and falling water made civil conversation impossible, so I leaned in closer to hear her answer, getting the scent of her perfume as I did: roses in a citrus garden.

Anyone who smells that good has to be trustworthy.

"The first thing any man needs is a good pair of shoes," she said.

"But I have good shoes."

"Those aren't shoes. Those are feet covers."

"Feet covers?"

"The things nurses wear in hospitals."

"You mean booties?"

"Yeah. You may as well be wearing hospital booties. Actually, that might be an improvement."

"Thanks a lot. So, if I'm not wearing nice shoes" — I wanted to say "like Giancarlo," but thought better of it — "then I'm less of a man?" I snarked.

My pettiness surprised me.

What are you doing? Why are you being so snappy?

"No, I never said that. I'm only doing this to help you out. If you want to go to the fundraiser looking like a lumber-nurse, be my guest," she replied coolly before her voice softened. "It's right around the corner. You'll like it. It has amazing shoes, and they're inexpensive."

We pushed our way through the crowd of camera-snapping tourists. Slowly, pedestrians changed from sightseers to sights to see as locals became more abundant. There was a smooth elegance to the way they walked. It made me question my gait as I straightened my shoulders and stuck my chest out.

Mum gave me a look. "What are you doing?"

Drooping my shoulders back to normal, I answered her question with silence.

Laura was ahead of us, her delicate white dress fluttered in the occasional breeze, showing off her perfect legs as she swayed gracefully through the flow of fashionistas. Her curly hair bounced playfully with each step. To see her comfortable in her hometown made me wonder how on earth she ever ended up in the Port Angeles.

And what she was doing with me.

I reached out and grabbed her hand. She glanced back with mild surprise before she flashed a smile that settled my spirits. I mustn't have screwed up that badly last night if she was willing to hold my hand in front of Mum.

"How do you know about this place?" I asked her as I glanced over to Mum who was ignoring us.

"I bumped into it years ago. It's been in Rome for a long time."

"Would you bring anyone else here?"

What are you doing? Didn't you learn anything from last night?

I couldn't help myself imagining her shopping with Giancarlo, holding hands and flirting while they tried on new shoes. I could see him taking off her pumps before replacing them with a sexy pair of heels. I bet she shivered every time he touched her. I could imagine him slipping his hand up her leg before she lost control and threw her lips onto his in the middle of the store.

What the hell are you doing?

She looked at me askance. "Who else would I come here with?"

"Oh, I don't know. Friends maybe?" Maybe all those boyfriends you didn't want to talk about. Maybe "shopping" was code for "making-out in public." Maybe I should just give up now and admit that Mum was right.

"I usually shop alone," she replied.

"I bet Giancarlo shops here. He had really nice shoes." Trust Mum to bring him up.

I shot her an annoyed look before realizing that, hey, I may want to hear this.

"Giancarlo? No, this place isn't expensive enough for him. He prefers Gucci or Prada."

"What do those shoes cost?" I asked, hoping to get another glimpse into what I was up against.

"Five hundred euros and up."

"Five hundred! I could buy twenty pairs of shoes at Walmart for that price!"

Laura only laughed. "So I can tell."

She'd meant it as a joke, but it only made me feel less worthy of her hand. My sulkiness returned in full force as we stopped in front of a shoe store prominently displaying all manner of leather footwear lounging around with supple vanity. Even shoes were lazily sexy in Italy.

"Here we are," she said.

"These are shoes? Why do they all look like they're missing something? They look like fancy slippers," I observed out loud. I was used to cushioned soles with plenty of padding for the pavement. These shoes looked anemic. Sickly almost.

"Style is not always comfortable. Looking good can mean a little sacrifice," Laura said proudly. "You need to toughen up for fashion."

I grew up as a Scout, where "tough" was living in the woods with just a knife. Bears wouldn't have cared if I was wearing Italian shoes or not. In fact, the scent of Italian leather may have made me a more appealing meal.

"You mean Italians are in pain when they dress well?" I asked.

"I wouldn't say pain. Discomfort, but not pain. Why do you think women get pedicures? Imagine walking an entire day in leather shoes on these cobblestone streets. Romans are tougher than you think."

"I'd say. I'm cringing just thinking about it."

Being attacked by a bear sounded better.

As Mum and Laura entered with me in tow, I caught a glimpse of my reflection in the store window. For the first time since I had arrived in Italy, I saw the tragedy of my appearance. The ugly duckling gazing into the pond.

Someone brushed past me, jostling me against the window. When I turned, I saw a Giancarlo look-a-like. In fact, most of the men around me were at least a four out of five. Even if they didn't have the most handsome faces, they made up for it in swagger and style.

"*Mi scusi*," the gentleman apologized as he entered the store, following Laura and Mum. In that instant, I wondered how I was going to do this. Every single man here was a better match for Laura. How was I going to win her heart? How was I going to bridge the gap between what I was, and what I would need to be? It seemed like a chasm so wide that only fate could possibly allow our union to happen.

You can't live in her world. You belong in the woods with nature. You're not a city guy.

Could she ever accept a young, foolish Camerican kid who didn't even own a suit? I tried to think of Anne and Pierluigi as encouragement, but at least Pierluigi was Italian. He had style. And Anne was gorgeous. What did I have to offer Laura except romantic dreams of falling in love? How on earth could I ever conquer love if I couldn't even conquer myself?

My reflection stared back at me, a specter in baggy beige shorts and a blue T-shirt—

Is that a stain?

Leaning in closer to the window, a blotch stared back at me without shame.

Ketchup!

I was really starting to hate that stuff.

Quickly, I scraped at it with a fingernail turning it from red to pink, only making it worse.

You need water. Stat!

Looking around, I caught sight of a *nasone* across the street, like the one in Piazza Cavour. Running through the crowd, I frantically knelt down to wash the blotch away with water. Instead, it landed right on my crotch.

Great!

Now it looked like I had a bladder problem.

To hell with it.

I whipped off my shirt, and doused the stain under the nasone. I held my shirt up to give it a closer glance.

Good. All gone.

This reminded me of that time when I fell in a river while hiking through the Olympic Mountains. In order to dry my clothes more quickly, I wrung them out and laid them on the hot stones by the riverbed.

Testing the top of the sun-drenched *nasone*, its steel casing was sizzling hot. Perfect. If I draped my shirt here, it would be dry in no time. Laying it over the top, vapour steamed like a hot clothes iron as I put my plan into action.

Now for my wet crotch. Would anyone notice?

Yep. Definitely.

I needed to get this thing dry before I went into the shoe store. Maybe if I fanned it, it would dry faster. Sticking both hands in my pockets, I started fanning my shorts as fast as I could. I could feel fresh wind breeze up my legs.

This could work.

I flapped harder and harder, occasionally testing the dryness with one hand. I gave it a good squeeze to make sure that it was working.

It's getting there. I need a little more speed.

I looked for a corner where no one could see me, and with the force of frantic frustration, I flapped my shorts as fast as I could. Warm wind blew up my shorts, slowly evaporating the moisture-spot.

Getting there. It's coming. Faster. In. Out. In. Out. Faster. C'mon. In. Out. In. Out. Faster. Faster damn it! You can do this.

As I was staring down at my moist nether area, I felt a tap on my shoulder just as I heard Laura call my name. When I turned, a *carabinieri* was looking at me with a raised eyebrow. He looked down at my shorts that were still wet, and then over an my shirt that was still hanging on the *nasone* before locking my gaze.

"*Che cazzo stai facendo?*" He asked me. I didn't know many Italian swear-words, but I knew that one. I looked past the carabinieri to see if Laura had noticed me.

Good. Not yet. I could still survive this moment of temporary insanity if I remained hidden behind the eclipsing officer. Quietly, I tried to explain why I was rapidly thrusting my hands in my pockets while my shorts were wet.

The look he gave me was one that asked "Are you on drugs?" Thankfully, Laura ducked back into the store giving me an opportunity to put my shirt back on without her seeing me.

"Mi scusi," I told the officer as I dressed myself, and ran into the shoe store, looking for shadows to hide the water marks on my clothes. The officer kept a close eye on me through the store window as I rejoined Laura.

"Where were you?" she asked. I tried to hide the stain on my shirt by pretending to scratch an itch. Knowing that scratching my loins at the same time would have looked strange, I pulled my T-shirt down as low as it could go.

"I was just getting a drink of water at the *nasone.*" I turned my back to cover her from the peering officer.

"Okay—" she said before handing me a pair of shoes. "Here. Try these."

The officer, seeing that I was behaving normally, turned to continue his beat. I shook my head with anger at myself. I would have to do a lot better than that if I was going to win Laura's heart.

Chapter 29
The Carousel

Laura

"How do they feel?" I asked.

It was hard to take him seriously as he flailed his arms to keep his balance.

"They're slippery."

"You've obviously never worn leather soles before"," I laughed out.

The stains on his clothes were nearly as ridiculous as his flapping arms. How on earth had he managed to get himself soaked with water? Turning this goofy prince farming into a prince charming was going to be tougher than I thought.

And you want to choose this guy over Giancarlo?

"Whoa!" He nearly lost his balance. "No. Definitely not. If they're like this, then I'm glad I haven't. Where are my comfy runners when I need them?"

"Off your feet, where they belong," I chided.

It was cute to see him trying so hard, even though he looked like a giant bird flapping its wings. Given the length of his arms, he managed to clear most of the sidewalk around him as people dodged his flailing limbs. I should have been embarrassed, but instead, I found his determination endearing.

If sophistication wasn't learned it was earned. When I was young, Papà used to scold me when I wasn't walking like a proper princess, or eating like a lady. It was embarrassing back then to be chided for my inelegance. It must have been the height of humility for Alex to be learning at his age. He was definitely earning sophistication points today.

"But I'll get it. I'll learn," he said as though he could hear my thoughts.

"Just give it time. Once the soles scuff up a bit, they'll be a lot easier to walk in," I encouraged. "How about you, Mrs. Baker?" I asked, turning to where Alex's mother was proving far more adept at walking in leather shoes on the cobbles. "You've done this before. Where did you say you grew up?"

"I grew up in London, lovey. Italians aren't the only ones with nice shoes, you know." She had a sharp edge about her, and it was getting more honed with every passing moment.

"How come you don't wear them at home, Mum?" Alex asked.

"When you grow up with four men in the house, you forget how to be a lady. Besides, I stand on my feet all day. These shoes wouldn't work," she responded. "We'll see what your father says, Alex."

"I think Dad would like them. He always wanted you to dress up for him," Alex said.

"Your father? I don't know. We're not young anymore."

"I think they look great. And trust me, your husband is going to love them," I smiled. If Alex and I did somehow pair up, it would be nice to be friends with her. I didn't have a lot of lady friends. When I was younger, my girlfriends would often try to steal my boyfriends. It got to the point where I drove as far away from Rome as possible, where none of my friends could get their competitive claws into them.

One old flame, Marcello, was a mountaineer from the Dolomites. He was tall, charming and muscular. The sexiest thing about him was his northern accent, which yodeled and lilted with a masculine melody that made the nine-hour drive more than worthwhile. Unfortunately, even he fell prey to the allures of other women when he ended up cheating on me with one of the concierge girls I had befriended.

A blonde Slovenian named Natasha.

Too cliché?

Not as cliché as catching them in my bedroom while he yodeled her name at climax.

That's why I didn't trust women.

Or like the name Natasha.

With Angela, I wouldn't have to worry about her trying to steal my boyfriend. What I had to worry about was a mother's jealousy. So far, I had never found a mother who wasn't protective of her son. Italian mothers were all I had ever known, so an English mother was an unknown quantity. My hopes were slim that she would be any different. So far, she had been as cool and subtle as a scalpel.

"Why are people staring at us?" Alex asked as he held his arms out to keep his balance.

"Maybe because you look like you're walking a tightrope," I quipped. He automatically pulled his arms down, and just as soon nearly fell flat on his determined face.

"Are we done shopping?" he asked hopefully.

"You mean you're not enjoying yourself?" I asked.

"I'd rather hike up Hurricane Ridge barefoot than try on more shoes," he said.

"Don't worry. It's my turn now. I need a new dress. We're nearly there," I said over my shoulder.

The evening-wear store I had in mind wasn't a place where I would normally shop (it was about a decade too young for my taste) but it should have what I needed.

"I'll wait outside," Mrs. Baker said as she plunked her flat bottom down on a black bench outside. The pained expression on her face told me that Italy was too much for her London sophistication.

Peering through the store's clear window, I spotted exactly what I was looking for. Dancing around sensually, dozens of beautiful, dark Italian girls were trying on the skimpiest of dresses, buzzing like a hive of queen bees. Full of sexy, giggling, youthful energy, this was the perfect place to test my little prince.

"Are you sure? There are some nice dresses here," I told Angela.

"I'm sure. You two have fun. I'll sit and watch the world go by," she smiled, hiding her discomfort.

"Okay. We won't be long," Alex said.

Better this way. We didn't need any distractions.

As soon as we stepped into the store, all the girls fell silent as they scanned Alex carefully. I knew my people. Alex had an American charm that made him exotic to Italians. This was the perfect time for my little test. Predictably, they cast their stares to bait Alex. The question was: would Alex resist the sight of such ravishing, tanned beauties?

I grabbed the nearest dress.

"Do you like this, Alex?" I asked, spinning around flirtatiously while holding the skimpy cherry-red dress over my body. I looked to see if his eyes were still on me.

So far, they were.

"I don't know. I'll have to see it on," he said very wisely.

"Do you want me to try it?" I asked seductively.

"If you think you'll like it, sure."

I spun my back on him and the vulture-chicks, and headed to the fitting area. I could feel their eyes watching me as I disappeared into the changing room. As soon as I drew the curtain, I heard them whispering to each other.

"Hey. Check out the American," one of them said.

"What's he doing with that *signora*?"

"Maybe she's his aunt or something."

Bums and boobs perked up like helium balloons as the carousel of preening mares circled sweet Alex. They flicked their hair and fluttered their lashes hoping to attract him onto their flirty-go-round. Dropping a garment close to him, one plopped her voluptuous cleavage down in the hopes that he would peek a peep.

When had Italian women lost their subtlety? The entire sight made me ashamed to be a woman.

Pathetic.

With a clenched jaw, I watched for Alex's reaction. Would he look? Would he snoop? Would he be what I had expected him to be? Tucked behind the curtain, I hoped for a surprise.

He'll look. Every man does.

As he looked down at his shoes, the girl jiggled her cleavage in front of him again. Smoothly, he averted his gaze to avoid her charms.

Wait...what?

Then, with kingly grace, he turned his back on her, and the other chicks, and thoughtfully combed through the store's dangling inventory.

I don't believe my eyes.

Alex hadn't slipped up once. Passing my little test proved that he was truly the gentleman I thought he was.

Don't get your hopes up.

I knew this wasn't the last test I would throw his way, but in that moment, I saw a man I could have confidence in; a man who wasn't like every other man I had been with. I had learned a lot of things in the past, and one of them was obvious. A man with a wandering eye was a man with a wandering heart.

When I came out from the fitting room, I gave Alex a sensual touch on his arm. He looked up from his perusal in surprise—as did the group of girls who suddenly looked like flustered hens trying to look busy. I gave them each a warning glare.

Back-off, bitches. He's mine.

My silent femme-speech worked as each girl pretended not to care about Alex anymore.

"What do you think?" I asked, doing a twirl on my bare tippy-toes. He may have been able to avoid looking at the girls, but he wouldn't be able to avoid looking at me in this dress. The stunned look on his face said it all. "Well?"

Is he going to pass out?

"Yeah. It's nice. I mean really nice," he stammered.

"Better than last night's dress?"

"It's different. Last night's was more casual. This one is much more . . . revealing. But is it appropriate for a fundraiser?"

Not a bad assessment from someone who didn't know much about fashion.

"It is a little much, but let's see what your Mum thinks." I wanted to send an obvious message to Mrs. Baker and to all the women staring at us: I may be older, but I wasn't old. But when I went to find her, she had vanished. "Hey, where is she?"

"I thought she was sitting outside." He scanned the busy street nervously. "I don't see her. Where the heck is she?"

Running back into the fitting room, I threw my clothes back on, and joined Alex outside, leaving the dress behind. His agitation was palpable as he scoured the bustling street. Headlights and screaming scooters heralded the coming of dusk. Heavily bagged daytime shoppers weaved in and out as evening called everyone to the security of their homes or hotels.

Mrs. Baker was nowhere to be seen.

"Where the heck is she?" he asked again.

"Maybe she's in another store," I suggested.

We both scrambled down the street, looking into each store as we went. After we had covered the entire block without finding a single trace of her, Alex's panic took a turn to frenzy.

"Where is she? Where the heck is she?!"

"I hope she hasn't wandered off too far. Rome is a maze if you don't know where you're going. Even I get lost here," I said.

"I can't believe she would just take off like this," Alex said.

"Has she done this before?" I asked.

"She's done some weird stuff, but nothing like this. What do we do? Should we wait here?"

"I think we have to. If we try to find her, she might come back and not find us."

"What if I go looking for her, and you stay here?" He asked.

Scouring the streets for a missing English woman was making my blood boil. It was official: Mrs. Baker was pissing me off.

"I think it would be best if I go," I said. "The last thing we need is both of you lost in Rome. You wait here in case she comes back."

He nodded in agreement, the wrinkle between his eyebrows sank into a dark crevice of concern. "All right. Sorry about this. I don't know what's gotten into her."

"We'll find her," I reassured him.

As I left, I thought about where she would go. I doubt she would have wandered off the main strip, but the street was getting busy now. It was seven thirty and many Romans liked to shop when the heat of the day had cooled. Women walked arm in arm, as did men. It was nice to see Italians still showed affection for each other. I nearly forgot this in the States.

A nice-looking couple of men wearing refined suits walked ahead of me. One had his arm over the others shoulder. They were waving their hands as they talked. There was no awkwardness in their embrace. No loss of masculinity. In fact, their comfort made them more masculine.

As I looked more closely at the man on the right, I couldn't help but feel that he looked familiar. White hair capped his lean, athletic frame, and the sun had sensually kissed his taut skin with a golden tan. As I approached, his nose unmistakably leaned downward just like his brother's.

"Luca?"

He took his arm from around his friend's shoulder and turned. It took him a split second to realize who I was.

"Laura?" His face was nearly as perfect as his brother's, though it was a little more wrinkled and a little less pensive. He leaned over to give me a kiss on each cheek. "Laura, nice to see you again. It's been a while. This is a very good friend of mine, Diego. This is Laura. She and my brother were very good friends."

"Who, Giancarlo?" Diego asked.

"Well, that was a long time ago," I explained quickly as I shook Diego's hand.

"What are you doing back in Rome? I thought you were in America?" Luca asked.

"I was, but I've had enough. I'm thinking of moving back."

"Why? What happened?"

"I just miss Italy. I miss my people."

They both scoffed.

"Really? You miss the corruption and the traffic?" Luca asked.

"That's all Italians ever see. Corruption and traffic. After being abroad for so long, I'm willing to put up with that if I can laugh and see beautiful towns and eat good food. I miss all of this, even the chaos."

"Well, the chaos is still alive and well," Luca noted just as his phone started to ring. "Excuse me one second. It's a client." He answered his phone and promptly placed the caller on hold. "Listen, Laura, I have to take this call."

"That's okay. I have to find someone anyway," I said.

"By the way, did you hear that Giancarlo is having a fundraiser tomorrow night? You're invited if you want to come."

"Trust me. I know. Your brother has already invited me."

"He did? Good then. Hopefully I'll see you there." He leaned over and gave me two parting kisses. I stared at their backs until they disappeared into the Roman crowd.

I was torn between two worlds. One was the world I had grown up with. It offered wealth. Power. Fashion. Refinement. Glamour. The other had a lost English woman and a sweet young man with a ketchup stain on his shirt. My life was at a crossroads. I knew that the next decision I was going to make would shape my life forever. I also knew that making the wrong decision could cost me dearly.

Where the hell is Mrs. Baker?

Chapter 30
Mum's Super-Power

Alex

Why was Mum doing this? Why would she just wonder off? Was she mad at me? Maybe she wanted me to worry about her so I wouldn't pay so much attention to Laura. Either way, I was getting tired of her games. She never acted this badly with my dates. I was used to misleading lies, but not this.

I heard Laura's irritated voice call my name from behind. When I turned, frustration etched her features. Maybe Mum was doing this to sabotage my chances with Laura? If Michela ever acted like this, it would certainly get under my skin. It wouldn't hinder my desire to be with Laura, but it would chip an otherwise smooth vase. I hoped Laura wasn't too chipped off.

"Did you find her?" I asked.

"No. Not yet."

"I don't know where she is. What do we do?" I asked.

Just then, I heard a voice call us from across the street. Mum was waving at us like nothing had happened. I could barely see her through the beaming headlights that flowed between us like a river of yellow streaks. As we watched, she sauntered across the street with all the casualness of someone out for a Sunday stroll.

"Where were you? We've been looking for you for an hour!"

"I just went for a walk," she replied. She smiled almost too kindly. I knew that smile. It asked a simple, silent question: what are you going to do about it?

That was enough to pop my top.

"What the . . . Are you kidding me!? We were worried to death! I've been standing outside for an hour and Laura has been walking all over Rome trying to find you. Why didn't you tell us? I can't believe you did that!"

She shrugged. "I thought you two were having fun. I didn't think you would miss me."

"Is that a guilt trip? Are you trying to guilt me into something?" I was far too pissed off to feel any kind of onus. "What are you, ten years old? You don't just go wandering off in a foreign country, especially when you don't know your way around or the language! What the hell were you thinking?"

I knew my mother could be aloof, but I had no idea she could be bereft of feeling all together. I couldn't imagine anyone showing such a lack of consideration for her loved ones. Laura was shrinking away from us as we "discussed."

"What if I had done that? How would you have felt?" I asked her.

"I would have had faith that you could take care of yourself."

"What!? Really!? Holy shit! Thanks, Mum. Nice to know you care! What about Laura? Didn't you think that maybe she has other things she would rather be doing than looking all over Rome for you?"

She glanced at Laura. "I didn't think you would miss me, that was all."

"You're my mother! Of course I would have missed you. Who do you think I am? You!?"

Mum flinched. A chill so frigid froze even the late Roman air. I regretted it as soon as the words left my lips. I had never seen her show weakness before. Regret filled every cell of my body as a sickening shockwave of remorse blasted through my entire being, even if there had been truth to the words.

"I'm sorry. I didn't mean that."

"No. It's all right." Her face was pinched. "You're right. I should have told you."

She stood, arms crossed, like a berated child looking down with heavy shame, pulling on the strings of my guilt.

Don't fall for it! She's turning on her super-power.

Too late. The combination of guilt, duty and family-first was an emotional cocktail I couldn't resist. With a single expression, she managed to make me feel badly for her wrongdoing. How did she do that? I hated it when she did this to me, especially when it wasn't my fault.

Laura interrupted the silence. "Why don't we head on home? It's getting late. Mamma will be wondering where we are, and I don't want her roaming the streets looking for us."

Even though the light quip deserved a laugh, I couldn't summon the mirth to give it a chuckle. "C'mon. Let's get going," I said, turning in the direction of the nunnery.

Everything was happening so quickly, starting with Laura accepting my courtship, then learning that I was a virgin, and now Mum was acting like an impetuous child forcing me to lash out in anger. I hoped Laura wouldn't see me any differently. The last thing I wanted was to be seen as a man quick to flip out. The past twenty-four hours were starting to feel like an emotional coal mine, with the pickaxes of change chiseling away at my resolve.

I glanced over my shoulder to access the temperature of Mum and Laura's feelings. Laura hastened her step to catch up with me, and for a second I thought she was going to reach out and take my hand. I wanted to feel the warmth of her silky fingers interlaced with my own. I wanted to know that I wasn't alone and that everything was going to be all right.

Instead, she walked ahead of us as the distance between us grew. She never looked back, and even though the night was warm, it was a cold walk home.

Chapter 31
Motherly Advice

Laura

Electricity cost a fortune in Italy, so only one feeble light flickered from Mamma's gloomy kitchen. I could hear her talking with herself as I entered the apartment, locking the deadbolts that sealed the door with eight different iron rods. Safety had a different perspective in Italy, and a door was more of a portcullis than a means of going in and out. In Port Angeles, everyone left their front doors unlocked, and usually open.

The sound must have alerted, because she emerged from the kitchen, her fearlessness a testament to a woman who had lived on her own for the past two decades. I admired her for that. She'd had many suitors, but she never compromised out of fear of being alone.

"So? How did it go?" she asked, wearing a faded rose house coat and matching peachy slippers. Throwing my bag onto the nearest table, I walked to join her in the kitchen.

"You won't believe it." I sat down at my usual wooden stool. Even though it was the most uncomfortable seat in the entire apartment, the kitchen always seemed to be where we congregated. In fact, the kitchen didn't have any of the easy-to-use Amercian appliances, which was why Mamma was cleaning dishes by hand.

"What happened?"

"Alex's mother. That's what happened. She's driving me crazy! I can't believe she just left us like that!" I hadn't been able to vent on the walk home, so now, my emotions were like Vesuvius ready to explode. "She just left us. Right in the middle of Rome. She took off, wandering around the streets without even telling us. Alex and I were worried to death about her. I mean, who does that?"

Mamma was confused. I was too angry to be coherent, so I started from the beginning.

"Alex and I were shopping—oh, you should have seen him, Ma. He was so sweet. There was a group of girls there that were trying to get his attention, you know how they are here."

Recounting the story to Mamma poked old wounds as it made her think of Papà who would have easily succumbed to the allures of other women. Hearing that Alex showed greater resolve made her nod with admiration.

"Yeah, but his mother is a real doozy. She's worse than Enzo's mamma. Remember?" I asked, mentioning my first boyfriend whose mother came with us on our first date and sat between us the whole night!

"How could I forget? She clung to her son like no other."

"Well, I think we may have another one on our hands, only sneakier. The only consolation was that Alex was pissed. I never saw that from Enzo and his mother."

"Good. It sounds like he has some guts."

"I know, but the age difference is a tough one for me, Ma. I can't get over it. I feel like I'm with a child. The girls in the store thought I was his aunt."

"They're just jealous. I lived through that with Patrizio. Remember? Even you gave me a hard time for dating a younger man."

"Oh my god. I just realized something. You were my age when that thing with Patrizio happened."

Mamma's mouth twitched. "I was thirty-four."

"And here I am now, dealing with exactly the same situation."

"Karma," Mamma said. Coupled with her Catholic background, her time in India had given her a very different perspective on things. Everything had a spiritual significance. "This is why I'm encouraging you to pursue it. I wish I had someone telling me that when I was your age. I missed my soulmate and I regret it ever since."

"What ever happened to Patrizio?"

"He's married now, with two kids. I heard that he's not very happy. It just goes to show that we only have one soulmate. I've never found anyone like him since. You know that. Now I would rather just be alone than with someone that doesn't complement me."

"You mean fulfill you?"

"No, I mean complement. Nothing will fulfill you except your own heart. A soulmate helps you discover that fulfillment, but he can never be your fulfillment. That's an illusion."

Mamma had moments like this, when she spoke wisdom that seemed divine. I could tell she was inspired because her mouth stopped twitching. It was as though another voice had taken over hers and was speaking the truth.

Sort of like what happened to you at Fregene when you said "yes" to Alex.

"Remember that God loves you, and your reason for being is to realize that love. He sends us challenges to strengthen us. A soulmate can help you identify the blocks in your life that prevent you from experiencing God's love. He can help you overcome these obstacles by challenging you to grow. And you must do the same with him. If Alex is your soulmate, then you will need to be strong for him, and he will need to be strong for you. . . Heck, if you could spend the last two years with your last useless boyfriend, Luke, then you could give this kid a chance!"

Mamma may have been right. I sat silently for a while to let the lesson soak in. I wish I fully believed her. It was hard to overcome this age difference, especially if Alex's mum was going to be a pain. I wasn't in the mood for that.

Why can't it just be easy? Simple?

"Oh! And then guess what?" I asked.

"What?"

"I met Luca while I was looking for Alex's Mum."

"Luca? You mean Giancarlo's brother?"

"Yeah. What are the odds?"

"Hmm. That sounds a lot like temptation to me."

"Or is it a sign? Maybe I am supposed to go and meet Giancarlo. Maybe I'm supposed to see where that path goes."

"Or maybe it's a distraction from your soulmate? You know what Giancarlo is, but do you know what Alex is?"

"I don't know, Ma. I'm so confused. One side of me wants to go back to things that are familiar and comfortable. And the other side of me wants to try with Alex."

"Love is found in the strangest places and don't forget, Giancarlo is still married."

"Yeah, I know, but he said he'd leave Lucinda for me. This is what I've been hoping for. Maybe it can finally come true?"

"Do you really think he'll follow through? Don't forget, he had plenty of opportunities to leave his wife before."

"He mentioned the "L" word Ma. That's a lot different than four years ago."

"Is it? Do you forget that he stood you up after misleading you? We often forget the bad things. With your father, I forget the beatings and the prostitutes and only remember the good things."

"He seemed so sincere this time though. It felt real. Besides, he's got everything I want. I won't have to start from scratch like I would with Alex. I could just settle in and start enjoying life."

"Don't kid yourself. You'll be eternally partnered with Lucinda if Giancarlo leaves her. Don't look at me. When I left your father, I was done with him. I cut all ties to him and never talked to him again. You should expect Lucinda to put up more of a fight. Remember: she's more connected than he is. She'd make both of your lives a living hell. Is that really what you want?"

I knew Mamma was right, but I still wasn't convinced. If there was a real chance that Giancarlo and I could be together, I had to pursue it. The problem was, what was I going to do with Alex?

Chapter 32
Suit Yourself

Alex

Mum had ducked into her room last night without saying goodnight. I had every reason to be angry with her, but I couldn't understand why she was annoyed with me. Knocking on her door the following morning left little doubt that she wanted to be left alone.

"Mum? Are you all right?" I asked as a tall nun swooshed by on her way to her duties.

"I'm fine, Alexander. Go ahead without me," she murmured.

Hearing my full name meant only one thing: I was in trouble, and to be honest, I didn't care. I was tired of her games, so without a single response, I stormed out of the nunnery and onto the insomnious Roman streets.

The smell of stagnant dog droppings and exhaust mingled with the fragrance of baked bread and coffee. Tiny parked cars sparkled with damp dew drops as gray pigeons pecked the cobbles clean. Wooden window shutters flapped open as yawning Romans blinked at the morning light. Seeing their red rimmed eyes reminded me that I wasn't the only one who hadn't slept.

"What are you doing up so early?" Laura's voice startled me. She must have snuck up on me.

Turning to face her, I could tell last night's events weighed on her as well, but her aura was still open, which meant that not all was at a loss.

"I could ask you the same question," I replied, wishing I hadn't sounded so defensive. Mum's cantankerous mood was having a contagious effect.

"I'm always up early. Life's too short to sleep all morning. I'm getting a coffee. You wanna come?" she asked, warmth glowing from her chocolate-colored eyes.

"Are you sure? After last night's outburst, I thought that maybe you wouldn't want to see me anymore?"

"Outburst? You obviously haven't been around Italians long enough. It'll take more than that to put me in a bad mood."

"So you're not upset about last night?"

She shook her head without answering my question. "Where's your mum?"

"She wants to sulk right now. We can get her later."

"She's not going to retaliate if we don't include her?"

"Probably, but she needs to smarten up. She's acting funny these days." I reached for Laura's hand. "Let's not worry about it now."

"Are you sure? I don't want to stand in between you two," she asked while wringing both hands around her white purse strap.

"I'm sure. She just needs to cool off," I replied as I let my hand fall, untouched. Something had noticeably shifted after last night. "Where are you going for coffee?" I asked.

Laura pulled a worried gaze from Mum's closed bedroom window, and looked at me uneasily. A spiff of wind caught a curl on the edge of her temple. She pushed it aside with a manicured finger before answering my hanging question.

"I was going to Antonini's, but let's head downtown and finish your shopping. You still need pants and a jacket, right?" she asked.

"But what about a coffee?"

Again, anxiety pinched her forehead. "Um. That's okay. I can get something on the way. We have a lot to do today before the fundraiser tonight." She paused in thought again. "We better get going."

She barely waited for me as she took the lead into the heart of Rome.

I never knew walking beside someone could feel so lonely. Just two nights ago, we were flirting and holding hands. Today, it felt like a giant, invisible wedge had been jammed between us. A Mummy-sized wedge that needed to be banged out with a hammer.

Preferably a big one.

I scoured my mind, frantically searching for an answer and a way back into Laura's good graces. This wasn't the first time Mum had held me back from expressing my true nature. Every time I tried to date someone, she stood in the way.

"Are you okay?" Laura asked. My silent seething must have been louder than I thought.

"I'm fine." I lied.

"Right," she said sarcastically. "You've been glum ever since I saw you this morning. What's up?"

"I'm just a little tired. What about you? You seem a little distant today?"

"I'm fine," she replied before falling into a pensive silence. I could tell she was also lying.

So there we were. Two fine people, finely walking the fine thread of a lie. If only Pierluigi and Anne could have seen us; what a pair we would have seemed. Anne must have been shaking her head at me from heaven, and I was positive that Pierluigi would have kicked me in the rear end. I needed to think of something to regain her trust.

Something bold.

That was when the glitter of gold caught my eye.

"Isn't that Archangel Michael?" I asked pointing to the top of a stone fortress. Round stone walls circled the glimmering archangel, impervious to the assault of age.

"Yes," she replied. "That's my favorite castle in Rome. *Castel Sant'Angelo.* I always wanted to get married along this bridge. It's such a powerful spot. How do you know about him?"

"He keeps popping into my life these days."

First at Anne's place. Then Pierluigi's bar. Now this.

Are you following me?

"Well, he's the slayer of Satan, and the head of all the archangels. Do you see the spear in his hand? The scales in the other? See the serpent under his feet?"

Wide-eyed tourists were gawking at the marble statues along Ponte Sant'Angelo as I squinted at Michael hovering in the cerulean sky.

"That's supposed to be the devil?"

"Yep. And Michael is about to slay him with his spear."

Staring at the statue pulled me into another realm as I fell under its mesmeric gaze. Struggle. Conflict. Pain. The sins of belief beckoned from the crevices of the past, pleading with me to hold tightly to tradition. But what if I didn't want to anymore? What if I wanted to spit in the eye of convention and be someone different?

"Are you okay?" Laura asked again.

I shook my head. "Yeah. It's nothing."

Laura sloughed off my indifference with apathy of her own as she shrugged her shoulders. Seeing her emotionally removed drove a cold dagger through my heart. If I kept this up, I would be booted from potential boyfriend status back into the friend zone. From there, it wouldn't be long until she referred to me as "some-guy-I-knew-once."

You need a plan – now. And don't mention Giancarlo this time!

"Well, we're almost there," she said after more walking and no talking.

Back in the old days, it seemed so much easier to win the heart of a lady. All I would have had to have done was slay a Minotaur, or climb a bean stalk to kill a giant. Everything included a sword and poking something with it.

Preferably to death.

Nowadays, I had to be sensitive and emotional and understanding of a woman's feelings. Having only grown up with brothers and suffering the female castration of my mother had left me particularly ill-equipped for sentimental subtlety.

Why couldn't I just kill a bear to prove that I cared for her? That would be so much easier. Or hell, give me a cyclops. That would do the trick. If Archangel Michael could kill Satan, I could kill a cyclops.

As we kept walking, we stepped into the most vacuous piazza I had ever seen. It was as cavernous as my empty head, incapable of coming up with a good idea. There were plenty of bad ones, but I was done with those.

"Where are we?" I asked.

"*Piazza del Popolo.*"

"Square of the people?" I asked.

"Yes. Good translation. You always were my best student."

"It has a strange feeling about it. Most piazzas I've seen feel full, but this one feels hollow." Like the empty space between my ears.

Why can't I come up with an idea?

"This is the beginning of Via Del Corso, where you'll find some of the most amazing shopping in the world. Are you ready?"

"Ready for what?"

"Ready to shop 'til you drop!"

If there were violins playing, they would have come to a screeching halt. "Really? You're going to use that cliché on me?"

At least she's being playful.

"Oh, c'mon. You need to lighten up a little. Look at yourself. When was the last time you went clothes shopping?"

"A few weeks ago," I lied. It had been several months.

"Yeah. Where? Value Village?" Laura's eyes widened when I didn't correct her. "I knew it! I knew you shopped there! I can't believe it! That place is a rip-off."

"Hey! I found these pants for five bucks."

"And they look like five-dollar pants."

I looked down at my corduroys, which had definitely seen better days. "No they don't."

"You're right. They look more like two-dollar pants." Laura said.

"Well. I guess they do look a little tired," I conceded.

"Tired? They look fast asleep. C'mon. I'll show you how to shop. It's time I started making you look like an Italian."

"You mean like…" I shut my mouth.

"Like who?"

"Um, like everyone else," I said.

"No. I'm going to make you look like the best version of you."

And then like a soldier heading for battle, she spun and marched into the fray of tourists.

•   •   •   •   •

Wearing Italian clothes was like wearing shrink wrap. As I sat in Franchi's bar, I longed for my old, loose clothing, now stuffed into one of the bloated shopping bags on the ground. I may have looked more Italian, but I certainly didn't feel like one.

Franchi's Bar was full of life as I waited for Laura. Hungry Romans stuffed the bar, all looking for an afternoon snack or an escape from the heat outside. Laura was getting us a bite on the other side of the bar as I staked out a corner where we could eat. Italians tall and small pushed up against my back, many asking if the seat next to me was taken. Luckily, my broken Italian was brutal enough to scare most inquirers away.

Talking with Laura so far had been horrible. It was as though we didn't even know each other anymore. Thinking of Archangel Michael made me contemplate a sword, and how a pen was often mightier.

Inspired by the Archangel I found a romantic card while Laura wasn't looking. If I could find the right words, perhaps a poem could win her over.

This might me your best idea yet.

Furiously, I wrote down the words before they were forgotten and folded the card into its envelope. The clutch she had bought for tonight seemed like the perfect hiding spot. With any luck, she would find it before we left. The poem wasn't an expensive gift, but I was hoping that she would see the wealth in my words.

Once it was carefully hidden, I had a chance to scan the audience of people around me. Being a head taller than most Italians in the bar, I could see above the tapestry of hats and hairdos. Soon, Laura emerged from the throng at the bar holding two finely shaped balls in white napkins.

"Here, try this." She handed one of the balls to me.

"What is it?"

"*Suppli.* Deep-fried rice balls stuffed with mozzarella."

I took the suppli, and with the impatience of a hungry child, bit down hard. Scalding pain burnt the roof of my mouth as steam and spittle collided in a cauldron of exclamation.

"Ow! This is hot!" I spat half the suppli back onto the napkin.

"Careful." Concern painted her face like a Modigliani abstract; I wasn't used to feminine sympathy, so it made the pain somehow desirable. "Of course they're hot. They just made them," she continued.

"Let me know next time, would ya? I just about burnt my mouth off."

"Aw. Do you want a kiss to make it feel better?"

I looked up with hopeful surprise as Laura moved in a little closer, her chest pressing against my arm. The pain in the roof of my mouth dissolved at the thought of my first kiss with her. Her lips were only a hand's length away from mine where she stopped and looked deeply into my eyes.

"Because if you do, that lady over there is checking you out." She pointed to a generously girthed lady in her eighties wearing a large floral dress.

"The one wearing the moo-moo? Nah. Too young. I prefer more mature women," I said. "But I did spot someone for you." I pointed to a chocolate stained kid licking a gelato.

"No way. Too old," she replied. Thank God we were both laughing again.

"Are you sure? You kind of act like a five-year-old," I said.

In response, she did what any refined woman of thirty-five would do. She stuck her tongue out at me. "Are you sure you're not eighty-three? You sure act like it," she retorted.

We both chuckled as she bit into her *suppli*. A long string of mozzarella cheese stretched from her mouth as she pulled the last half away. When it broke and slapped against her cheek, I instinctively took my napkin and blotted it away.

She laughed, before a sudden clap of silence broke the wall between us. Up until now, we hadn't laid a single finger onto each other; the frigid Mummy wedge had been standing firmly all morning. However, with that single touch, the ice between us shattered. All that remained was the longing of realization, yearning for the serenade of love.

How could a second feel like an eternity?

How could a thousand words be told in an instant?

When our eyes locked, I knew precisely how.

In that moment, there were no thoughts, nor judgments. There was only the purest of understanding. All my doubts and fears dissolved in the warmth of divine recognition. The connection was so deep that there was little doubt she felt the same way.

I had found my soulmate.

Chapter 33
Decisions, decisions

Laura

My entire body shivered when Alex touched my cheek. It was like a can of *Chinotto* had opened up inside, filling me with fizzy realization. Not even my first kiss felt like this. Trying to compare the bizarre moment to anything from my past left me without words, which was saying a lot.

So now what? Was he going to kiss me? Should I kiss him? I've never made the first move before, but it felt like this should be the time. Was this what it was like to meet your soulmate?

How the hell should I know? I've never met him before.

Maybe now I had. Strange. I never thought it would have ended up being him, especially since he was everything I didn't want in a man. But after *this*, how could I question my feelings any longer? This was beyond anything I ever felt before. It was deeper. Spiritual almost.

You need to tell him about Giancarlo.

After this? No thanks. I'd rather walk around Rome with Lulu-lemons, red flannel and wool socks than tell him what was going to happen when I showed up to the fundraiser.

He needs to know the significance if you attend tonight.

No problem.

Hey Alex. Guess what? If I show up to the fundraiser tonight, Giancarlo is going to leave his wife and carry me off into the sunset. Did I know this before you asked me out? Yeah, but that's okay. My inner voice told me to date you so that I could break your heart into a thousand little pieces. You understand? Right – soulmate?

Looking into Alex's eyes, I felt the fragility of romance, and how a lie could ruin it all. I couldn't tell him. Not now.

Then cancel tonight.

But he needs my help, and after this starry-eyed gaze, I wasn't sure of anything anymore.

"Are you going to get that?" Alex asked, pointing at my purse on the bar table.

Like a hypnotist snapping her fingers, my ringing phone broke the depth of our trance. Shaking my head, I tore my eyes away from Alex, wishing the moment could have lasted forever, but in a way, thankful it hadn't. This was the one time I was grateful for my phone interrupting me in the middle of something.

Something? That wasn't just something. That was something *else.*

Yes, and that something else has a shrew for a mother.

And he doesn't have a job.

And he puts ketchup on carbonara.

And his hands sweat.

And people think you're his aunt.

Oh, and in case you forgot, he's a virgin.

My heart was muddled. I really didn't know what to do, and the last thing I expected was Alex's soft touch to muddy my decision even further.

So instead, I answered my phone.

"*Pronto?*"

"Laura? *Ciao.* It's Fabio. Il Grande."

From sweetness to over-sweet. Mr. Kissy-kiss was not who I wanted to talk to right now. I shifted in my stool.

"How are you? What are you up to?" he asked.

"I'm just at Franchi's with Alex."

"You should have told Fabio. He could have joined you," he replied. "He can be there in five minutes."

The last thing I needed was a Fabio to add more confusion to my distress. Two men was already one too many. Adding a third wouldn't be a charm.

"We were just heading out, Fabio. Alex and I have to get ready for tonight." Any excuse would do to keep him away.

"Oh. Okay. Well, don't forget to let me know if you need a lift. I can pick you up," he replied, ever hopeful.

"I won't forget. I'll call you later. Ciao for now."

"What did he want?" Alex asked when I hung up. He seemed annoyed.

"He wanted to know if I needed a ride tonight."

"But we have my car. You don't need a ride," he said.

It was time to tell him the truth. He had to know about Giancarlo.

"Listen, Alex. About tonight . . ."

My phone rang again.

"That thing sure has bad timing, doesn't it?" Alex said.

I bit my lip from the revelation I was about to share.

Saved by the phone. Maybe fate was stepping in again. I looked down at the caller ID. It was Mamma. Fate's messenger.

"Just a sec. Ciao, Mamma," I answered.

"Laura. Is Alex there?"

"Yeah — why?"

"His mother wants to talk to him. It's important." I looked at Alex, puzzled. "Here. It's your mother."

He took the phone, bewildered.

"Um. Hello? Mum? What's up?" Lines etched his features as his gentle face became a grey pencil drawing. "You spoke to him? When? Just now? What did he say? You can't tell me over the phone? Okay. I'll be right there. No. It won't take us long. Okay. Bye."

He hung up, looking downwards.

"Mum just met with Giancarlo."

"When? Where?" I asked. "I thought she said he didn't have any time until tonight!"

"Apparently, time became available."

"Really?"

Yes!

"I have to get back." He stood to get his bags off the ground.

"Well, I'm coming too." I jumped from the stool and grabbed my bags.

I couldn't believe my luck. Just when I thought I would have to tell Alex about Giancarlo, fate gave me the perfect excuse not to. If Mrs. Baker had already spoken to Giancarlo about the will, then we wouldn't have to go to the fundraiser tonight. This solved all my problems. I could stay home which would send a clear message to Giancarlo without hurting Alex with the truth.

Good old fate. Good old Mamma. I should listen to her more often; she always encouraged me to have more faith.

Stepping onto *Via Cola di Rienzo*, I breathed in the thick Roman air, feeling as light as *schiumetta* on top of a *macchiato*. As we walked, side by side, I reached for Alex's hand. For the first time since our date — for the first time in my life — I felt like I had finally found the romance I had been looking for. And all it took was to have faith in fate.

It was about time. It only took thirty-five years.

When are you going to tell him that you're staying in Italy?

Shoot! I forgot. Nothing was easy, was it. Should I tell him now? If I did, I could ruin this one moment of peace.

You'll have to tell him eventually. He's leaving tomorrow.

Deciding to wait and see what Mrs. Baker had to say, I kept my little secret to myself. Fate had taken care of me so far, perhaps it would give me a good opportunity to tell him later.

Right now, I just wanted to enjoy walking with my soulmate. I had earned it.

Chapter 34
Family first?

Alex

Anxiety was corrosive, and right now, Mum's phone call was dripping emotional acid on my euphoria. I couldn't enjoy holding Laura's hand as we walked back to the nunnery. I couldn't savor the sights and smells of Rome, nor could I saunter with a lover's amnesia as I forgot the cares of the world. Instead, the obligation of familial duty once again obstructed my heart's desire.

Family first.

What had Mum learned from Giancarlo and why couldn't she tell me over the phone? Did this mean that everything was finalized and we wouldn't be attending tonight? Judging by her tone, I doubted it was that easy.

I couldn't let Laura walk into that fundraiser all by herself, especially with the likes of Giancarlo waiting for her there. She had been telling Alberto and Fabio that she was going, and I knew she would keep her promise.

She isn't a liar.

And what about Pierluigi? There was a slim chance he was involved with Anne's will, but what if Mum found out that I had spoken with him? Should I have told her the truth about Anne? Would she have even believed me? Or would it have made her more defensive?

If there was one thing I abhorred, it was challenging Mum. Family was always first, and as the head of the family, Mum could never be challenged. But after learning a different side of Anne from Pierluigi, I was starting to doubt even my own mother.

Mum is the liar.

I hoped not.

Hopefully, the news she had was straightforward. Hopefully, Anne had left a clear heir to her legacy, allowing me to focus on Laura. After the transcendent stare we just shared, nothing could change my mind now. The way she was holding my hand proved she cared for me as well.

Laura broke the silence.

"Do you think it's good news about your aunt's will?" she asked.

"I really don't know. Mum said there was too much to tell over the phone."

"How did she sound?"

"What do you mean?"

"Well, did she seem worried, or happy?"

"It was hard to tell. You know Mum. She's tough to understand."

"I'm sure it'll be fine. If she spoke to Giancarlo, then everything should be under control," she replied with more bubbliness than the situation called for.

"I hope you're right," I said.

"It'll be fine. Have faith."

She snuggled her head into my shoulder again. Finally. An affirmation to what I was feeling. This could mean only one thing: I was good enough for her. Even with all the gorgeous Italian men to choose from, she was choosing me. Not Giancarlo, nor Fabio. She obviously didn't care about my lower mating score. Yep. Three-out-of-five was good enough for her.

I must have earned some bonus points without knowing it. Was it the new clothes? I thumbed my blazer which felt like a straightjacket. Instead of loosening with wear like good old flannel, it seemed to have vacuum-sealed itself to my body over the course of the day.

Is this why she likes me now? My clothes?

I hoped that wasn't the reason, because deep down, I would always be a Camerican who loved flannel. Shaking my head, I convinced myself she was deeper than that. She had to be. She was my soulmate.

When we arrived at the nunnery, I squeezed her hand gently. "Let me talk with Mum. I'll see you in about thirty minutes."

"Okay."

Staring into her eyes again, I nearly forgot my anxiety.

Go on. Kiss her. She wants one.

Not now. I had to deal with Mum first. After a quick ciao, I bounced through the nunnery entrance ready for anything.

"Slow down, young man," Sister Greta said with her usual reverse smile as I saluted. It was impossible to be happy around her. She could scare the joy out of Santa Claus.

"*Salve Madre,*" I replied cheerfully. She harrumphed.

After bounding up the stairs to Mum's room, I found her bedroom door ajar. My ray of cheer quickly turned to a cloud of worry as I pushed it open with a foot and found Mum sitting on her bed.

"Come in, lovey, and close the door," she said when she saw me.

Lovey? What happened to "Alexander?" Had I suddenly been scratched out of her bad books? Or was there something else at work here?

"Okay," I said cautiously, closing the door. "How did it go with Giancarlo?"

"Well, you're not going to like it."

"Like what? Is it about Anne's will?"

"No, lovey. It's not. It's about that girl of yours." She crossed her arms as she stood into lecture-mode. The shadow of Mum's pulpit was the last thing I wanted to be standing under.

"Look, Mum. I don't need a spiel on who you think I should be dating."

"You might change your mind after you hear what I learned from Giancarlo about your little Italian tutor."

She still couldn't say her name. It was infuriating.

"Her name's Laura. L-A-U-R-A. Laura. And what about the will? After all this, you seriously didn't talk about it?"

"What I learned was more important—and I don't care what her name is. Hopefully after this, you'll never want to hear her name again. Did you know that Giancarlo proposed to her two days ago?"

A slap across my cheek would have been less surprising. "What do you mean 'proposed'? He's already married. How can he propose?"

"I knew it!" she crowed. "I knew she was a liar! You see. You can only trust your family. Two days ago, Giancarlo asked L-A-U-R-A to run away with him. He said he wants to leave his wife for her and he was going to announce that tonight at the fundraiser."

What was she up to? Was this another one of her manipulative lies? None of this made any sense. If Mr. Perfect had proposed to Laura, why had we shared such a beautiful moment together. She would've told me.

Wait a second. She did try to tell me something at Franchi's.

Nah. This was too big of a deal to keep quiet. If Giancarlo had proposed, I would have found out tonight anyway. Laura wouldn't do that. Mum was lying.

"Why are you doing this? Are you jealous? Angry? Why won't you just let me choose who I want to be with?"

"Keep your voice down, young man. I'm telling you the truth!"

"The truth? Why do you always have to control everything? I see why Anne left you and Grandma. She probably got sick of all the manipulation."

She stiffened. "What has Anne got to do with any of this?"

"Anne has everything to do with this! She's the reason we came to Italy. She's the reason we're in Rome. And if it wasn't for her, I wouldn't be falling in love with my Italian tutor!"

Tears nearly ran away with me, but my anger was strong enough to bridle them.

Spit in the eye of convention. Conquer love!

"I won't let you control me anymore!"

"Control you? What's wrong with you? I think this girl is making you crazy. I can't believe my own son is silly enough to fall for a hussy."

"A hussy? You mean like Anne?"

"How dare you talk about my aunt that way!"

"Your aunt?" I thought about that for a split second. "You're right. She is your aunt, especially since you never mentioned her to me until she died! You keep talking about family first, but you never talked about anyone in the family, and when you did, it was always negative. But guess what? I know the truth about Anne. I know why she left you and grandma."

She wasn't expecting a challenge as her arms tightened around her waist, defensively. For a split second, I saw a frightened, little girl standing in front of me, before the mother I knew returned. "What are you talking about?"

"I found Pierluigi. I found Anne's soulmate, and he told me everything." I pulled the photo from my pocket, flapping it in front of her. "Anne's "boy-toy." Remember what you called him? He lives in Rome. And guess what? His description of Anne was the complete opposite of yours. She loved you guys, but grandma's mental problems drove her away."

"And you believe a W.O.P. over family?" she sneered.

I had never raised my hand to anyone before, and I certainly wasn't going to start now, but it took all my will not to lash out.

"Yes. I do. You seem to believe Giancarlo easily enough. He's Italian!"

"I don't need to believe Giancarlo because I have this..."

Silence fell on the room slowing the passage of time as she walked over to her dresser, and lifted a thick file folder.

"That's all for Anne?"

"Not all of it. When I was looking through the forms I need to fill out, I found this." Like plucking a single white feather from a black goose, she pulled a sheet of paper from the folder. A smile tried to conceal itself, but her lips twitched, betraying a hidden satisfaction. A silent doom filled the room as Mum dangled the sheet in front of me. "Here. Read it."

Slowly, I reached out and grabbed the lone sheet. Eyes darting from Mum to the paper, I read the importunate letter.

Cara Laura,

Ever since you left for America, I realized just how important you are to me. Life had no meaning until I saw you the other night at Tesone's. When I saw your beautiful face and your smile, my heart leapt back to life.

I now know what I had lost, and I won't let you go again. Four years ago, I wasn't ready to do make the right sacrifices to keep your hand, but now I'm ready. I'm ready to give you the commitment you need and leave Lucinda forever.

If you'll be my guest at the fundraiser, I'll let everything go for you. My wife. My children. My political aspirations. Everything. All you have to do is show up, and I will be yours forever. I hope that I can earn your love again. I know this is just a letter, but every journey begins with a step of faith. I hope you will take that step with me.

With the deepest affection,
Giancarlo.

"Where did you get this?" I shook the letter.

"Giancarlo must have accidentally stuffed it with Anne's things."

I crumpled it into a ball. "Yeah, right. Accidentally. Just because Giancarlo wrote this doesn't mean that she knows or that she's even agreed to this."

I wished I could have believed my own words.

"If that doesn't convince you that she's playing games, then did you know that she's staying in Italy?"

"C'mon, Mum. Stop. I get it. You don't like Laura, but you're not going to stop me from dating her."

"Go ask her. I talked to Michela. She told me. L-A-U-R-A is staying in I-T-A-L-Y."

Nothing made sense anymore. I wasn't angry now. I was confused. Squishing the letter in my hand, I threw it to the floor as I tried to make sense of everything. Was the letter real? If it was, how did it get into Anne's things? Could Giancarlo have planted it to drive confusion and dissuade me?

And what about Laura staying in Italy? She never told me this. How could we possibly be together if we were thousands of miles apart?

"This girl is playing games with you. She's not serious. You're just a fling before she resumes her love life with him. It's obvious to me."

Disbelieving my mother with cold hard facts was usually a mistake, especially ones that could be confirmed. If Laura was staying in Italy, this changed everything.

"This doesn't make any sense. Why wouldn't she tell me?"

It didn't explain what we shared at Franchi's, or how she held my hand and looked into my eyes. Unless she really was just toying with me.

Told you. She's a flirt.

"No. No way. This is different," I said, suddenly less certain.

"You don't believe your own mother? You don't trust your own family. Then you're not the son I thought you were. Fine," she said, smoothing out the paper and then placing it back in my hand. "Don't take my word for it. Ask her yourself, and hopefully you'll never doubt how important trusting your family is again. We are the only ones who care for you. No one else."

I couldn't listen anymore. Family first. Pierluigi's words. Laura's loving gaze. I needed to find out the truth. With a storm of emotions, I spun on Mum and marched out to find Laura.

Chapter 35
Answers

Laura

"Mamma?" I called out, slamming the door behind me. Hearing my own words over the blaring TV was next to impossible. "Mamma!"

"*Laura? Che c'è?*" Her voice was drowned out by *Rai Uno Telegiornale.*

"I've made up my mind."

The sound of news rambled from the living room to the right of the entrance. Mamma sat up from her favorite faux-leather recliner reaching for the remote. The walls that had been carpeted back in the seventies only added to the suffocating heat. "What?" she screamed over the falling volume as she muted the TV.

"I said: I've made up my mind!" I shouted.

"About what?"

"About Giancarlo and Alex. I've decided to give it a try with Alex. You're right. He's so sweet, and we shared a moment today that I've never shared with anyone. It was as though he could read my thoughts. Or maybe our thoughts were the same. It was hard to tell, but I know he felt it too."

"That's . . . good," she said, less enthusiastically than I liked.

"That's good?" I crossed my arms. "That's all you have to say? I thought you'd be more excited than that. You're the one who told me to be unconventional. To have faith in fate."

Avoiding my eyes, she looked around the living room.

"What is it, Ma? What's going on?"

"There's just one tiny little problem."

Problem? Mamma. Missus Positivity herself. The one who pushed me to have faith in fate was suddenly being negative. "So?" was all I asked, shaking my head inquisitively while tapping my left foot on the granite floor.

"I may have accidentally told Mrs. Baker that you were staying in Italy."

"What?" Mamma was wrong. This wasn't a tiny problem, this was a huge problem. If Alex learned from his mother that I may be staying in Italy, then he might blame me for not being honest. Mrs. Baker would use this to drive him away from me. "Ma! I was going to tell him tonight. Why did you tell her now?"

"I don't know. You know how things get. It just slipped out. Anyway, it shouldn't be too big of a deal. All you have to do is explain it to him. You'll work something out. Besides, I shouldn't have to lie for you. Why didn't you tell him at the beginning?"

"It's not lying if you don't say anything!" I should have told him. Now I looked like I was hiding something.

You were hiding something.

"Well, you better get down there and smooth this out. Who knows what she's telling her son?"

Oh my god. She was right. Poison dripped from a mother's hand could be the most venomous kind. Especially this mother.

Before another drip could be dropped, I flew out the door and down the stairs to the building's ground level. Desperately, I flung the main entrance door out onto the street, just in time to hit Alex squarely in the face.

"Ow!" He fell backward onto the warm concrete, clutching his nose.

"Oh my god! Alex! Are you all right?" I crouched down to look closer, but all I could see was his hand covering his face "Where did you come from?"

A group of pigeons clucked clear of us.

"You just hit me in the face, and you're scolding me? What about you? Why are you throwing doors open?" He sounded more frustrated than the moment called for.

The afternoon heat radiated from the sidewalk as I knelt down beside him. He pushed my hand away when I reached to help him. The gentleman I had shared an eternal glance with had suddenly turned into an un-gentleman. The love from Franchi's bar had turned to confusion.

"You still like Giancarlo, don't you? Admit it. You want to get back together with him. Why wouldn't you? He's good-looking. Rich. Powerful. Hell, I even have a crush on him. If you've slept with that guy, why the heck would you ever want to be with a virgin," he said, jumping to his feet with enough force that it made me take a step back. The pigeons flew away as he threw his arms in the air. "You'll do just what every other girl does when they realize they're with a virgin. You'll break my heart. You'll pull it right out of my chest, and squish it with your Pradas. I'm just a joke to you, aren't I?"

"What are you talking about? Keep your voice down. You're making a scene." After being with Luke, I knew how to identify panic, and Alex was completely consumed by it. Pedestrians steered around us as though we *both* shopped at Value Village.

"I'm too young! I don't have job. I still live at home. I'm surprised you even want to be around me. This is all just a game to you, isn't it? What am I? Just some quick flirt to pass the time? I'm no Giancarlo. I'm just a two out of five. Why would you give up on Mr. Five Out of Five for Mr. Goofy!"

I tried to calm him down as people stopped veering and started leering. "What are you talking about? 'Mr. Five Out of Five?' 'Mr. Goofy?' You're not making any sense. Calm down!"

"You're used to lawyers, and actors. I'm used to bears and bugs. I'm just some hillbilly from Washington State. What the heck would we have in common? Nothing! You're from Rome, with your fancy clothes, and anorexic shoes, and tight pants that strangle my crotch, and cars that beep all the time! Why do Italians beep so much? What is it with you guys and noise? You know it doesn't make anything go faster, right? You know that it only adds to the frustration? I've heard more beeps here in two days than I've heard in a lifetime back home. There's no way. This can't work. Go back to Giancarlo. Go back to your fancy-schmancy life where everyone looks down at me. I'll run back to Port Angeles where there are more bird droppings than people. At least they won't beep at me!"

"Have you lost your mind? Fancy-schmancy life? Bird droppings? I knew this was too good to be true. I told Mamma. What the hell am I doing with a skinny country bumpkin who has to ask his mummy for money to buy me a rose?" I shook my head at myself. "Who do you think you are? I came to Rome to be with my friends and my family, and instead I dedicated my precious time to be your 'little' tour guide. I wasted the last two days showing you and your stupid mother around, and for what? To be subjected to this? An unfair judgment based on nothing—or worse—based on your mother's hateful theories? I can't believe I was actually thinking of dropping Giancarlo for you! What's wrong with me? I must be losing my mind. America is definitely bad for me. I knew there were no decent men in this world. Not even sweet young ones like you. What changed anyway? How did we go from having a great day to us shouting at each other in the street? What's gotten into you?"

"What's gotten into me? This."

He shoved a crumpled piece of paper in my face, which I scanned quickly before shaking my head. I couldn't believe it.

"Where did you find this?"

"Mum found it with Anne's papers. Giancarlo wrote you a love letter."

I gave a dark chuckle. "Oh. Your mother. How convenient. I should have known. She's been looking for a reason to keep us apart since we first met. She's a manipulator, and you can't even see it. You're just like every other mamma's boy. Besides, how dare you read into something that you don't know anything about? For crying out loud, you've known me for three months and you think you can judge my life?" I smushed the paper into a ball and threw it at him. "I can do and date whoever I want. I thought about Giancarlo, and yes, I was thinking of getting back together with him. But when you asked me out, I saw something special in you. I thought you were different from all the Giancarlos of this world, even with your sweaty hands, and scruffy clothes. Instead, you're a pathetic, gullible manipulated kid who's just trying to be a man. What a disappointment! I can't believe I just told Mamma I found someone different and that I was going to cancel tonight. What a mistake. Better now that later, I guess. Have a great life with your mummy back in country bumpkin land!"

Turning my back on Alex should have been harder, but after he revealed his true character, I knew fate had stepped in. Once again, it was pushing me back to the place I had been running from since I left for America. I was a Roman, and would always be a Roman, which meant there was only one place where I could be understood.

In the arms of a Roman.

Chapter 36
A Revelation

Alex

After Laura left, I had nowhere to go except back into the lonely confines of the nunnery. It felt like a part of me had just been ripped from my soul, and I was alone again with the dreariness of my own existence. How could someone do that? How could someone tear down all my walls and leave me feeling so vulnerable?

This was what happened when I trusted someone. I needed to be more careful. Trusting was dangerous. The only people I could trust was my family. I hated admitting it to myself, but Mum was right. Family first.

As I dragged myself up the stairs, my head bobbing with each step, I came to the top and froze. The middle hallway stared at me. Calling me. Tempting me. Faintly, nearly imperceptibly, orange light flickered from its recesses. The cold, eerie familiarity that I had experienced when I first arrived at the nunnery now beckoned with a strange warmth. A voice called to me from the silent gloom before I looked down the hall to the left where Mum's room was.

Should I talk to her?

The last thing I wanted to deal with right now was a gloating mother, so instead, I swallowed deeply and took a step towards the soft light. The only comfort I had were the hollow echoes my new leather shoes made on the marble floor .

As I moved deeper into the obscure darkness, not a sound could be heard, nor a movement seen. The voice I had heard before must have been an imaginary one, but everything seemed familiar to me. A distant comfort willed me further as the pain of losing Laura was lost in curiosity and forgetfulness.

When the hall turned sharply to the right, the source of the light was revealed. A bright candle waved rapidly at my presence as currents of air wafted its warm flame. Freezing to a standstill, it wasn't the candle that paralyzed me with fear and wonder.

It was it's subject.

With wings as wide as the end of hallway, a giant angel spread it's glory with dazzling feathers. A golden crown sparkled around its flowing hair as eyes of universal vastness pierced deeply through the spectral stillness. A muscular hand held tightly to an iron sword that pointed menacingly downwards. Its chest heaved beneath a leather breastplate as spaulders protected its round shoulders. Powerful legs stood effortlessly, snaring a hideous dragon under its feet.

Even though I was fully clothed, I had never felt as naked or alone as I felt in that moment. A paralysis locked my gaze with his as I reveled in awe at the standing form of Archangel Michael.

I was suddenly transported to Anne's apartment where I had first met him painted gloriously on her wall. Then to Bar Arcangelo Michele, where the angel had guided me to Pierluigi and the courage I needed to ask Laura on a date. Then to the golden statue standing on top of Castel Sant'Angelo; Laura's desired location for matrimony.

Throughout this entire journey, Michele had been there. Silently. Patiently. Showing me the path that I needed to take. Guiding me with subtle love and eternal compassion. I had never believed in angels.

Until now.

Spit in the eye of convention.

Pierluigi's words echoed loudly as the Archangel loomed before me, daring me to listen.

How could I spit in the eye of convention? I had tried and here I was, alone and miserable. How could I trust anyone other than my family who had just discovered Laura's betrayal?

To trust your beliefs is noble. To surrender them is love.

Shadows flickered, the darkness taunting me.

Why? What good would it do to pursue her? Even if she would listen to me, I wouldn't fit in the sophisticated world she lives in. I was too different. Too Camerican.

Surrender.

Pierluigi encouraged.

"Surrender to what?" I whispered in the darkness. "I don't have anything to surrender. I'm just a young, stupid kid who believes in love, but can never seem to find it."

Surrender what you believe.

"What I believe?"

Family first.

"No. Never. I could never turn my back on my family. I won't do it!"

Pierluigi's voice faded away and was replaced with my father's.

"Son. Find 'em. Fuck 'em and forget 'em."

Then my mother's.

"You're no Giancarlo, son. They're just wops."

An anger began to boil.

What had family gotten me?

Family had just forced me to send Laura into the hands of her ex-lover. Family was probably ready to pat me on the back for not choosing the "wrong" girl. Family was threatening my potential happiness all for what? For an idea? For the family?

You're not thinking straight, Alex. Just stop thinking. You're angry. Anger never solves anything. Turn your brain off.

But I couldn't. A revolution had started. A mutiny. My mind and thoughts were fighting the forces of my heart and intuition. Everything I had ever believed was being challenged under the gaze of Archangel Michael. I didn't know what to do. I didn't know who to talk to. With the statue of an angel as my sole companion, questions bombarded my ideas of reality.

Until a single inspiration broke through the ravages of my mind.

How had Mum talked to Giancarlo today?

Being always against technology, she didn't own a cellphone. And even if she did, she told us she lost his card with his number. So how was she able to get an appointment with him today after he had made it clear that he was unavailable all week?

Something wasn't adding up.

Suddenly, a noise came from the direction of the staircase. Turning my back on the Archangel, I peaked around the corner to see if Sister Greta had discovered my snooping. Curiosity quickly turned to surprise as Mum's hunched form paused as the top of the empty staircase before looking over her shoulder and slinking downstairs.

Looking back to Michele for final encouragement, the candle flame flickered a wink from his marble eye. Then, sleuth-like, I pursued Mum as she left the nunnery.

Moving quickly, she turned down a street I had not been before. I thought she would have been nervous walking alone in the darkness of Rome, but instead, she moved with the confidence of someone who had walked a path before.

Finally, at the end of the block, she ducked into a phone booth. With haste, I ran to catch up to her and slid to a stop behind a tiny parked car barely big enough to give me cover. Peeking from behind its tail lights, I watched Mum dial from a payphone. With Rome settled into a strange stillness, I held my breath to overhear what I could.

"Hello, Giancarlo? Yes. Laura should be coming tonight. Alex won't be a problem. The letter worked like a charm. You really think you can get around this Pierluigi character? . . . Good. I knew I could count on you. Okay. Enjoy your reunion with Laura."

I couldn't believe my ears. Giancarlo? She knows about Pierluigi? Before I could analyze what I had just heard, she hung up and dialed another number.

"Hello, lovey. It's me. Yes. Don't worry. It worked. Alex won't be seeing that Italian tutor anymore. You can tell him when we get home. He needs fatherly direction right now. He's forgetting that only family cares for him."

Is she talking to Dad?

As I listened, she huffed at something said from the other end.

"Anne was a stupid fool. She left everything to someone by the name of Pierluigi, one of her silly fancies. The lawyer here has given me a name of someone back in the States who can help us out. We won't have to come back to Italy ever again. . . All right. We'll see you in a few days."

As she hung up and turned to leave, I ducked as low as I could to hide my presence, reeling from what I just heard.

Mum is in on this whole thing?

I couldn't believe it. How had she done this? It looked like Laura was right. My mother was sabotaging us. But why? Why wouldn't she want me to be happy? What happened to family first?

Not to mention Anne left everything to Pierluigi? I had to tell him. But first, I needed to confront Mum. As Pierluigi warned, it was time to conquer love. It was time to spit in the eye of convention with the biggest loogy I could come up with.

Chapter 37
Ara Pacis

Laura

The slam of Mamma's door made even the old Mussolini building tremble with fright.

"That's it! I'm going!"

Mamma's slippers slapped the granite floor as she came running from the kitchen. "Going where? What happened? I heard a bunch of screaming through the window. Was that you?"

"Yeah. Me and Alex. He thinks I want to be with Giancarlo, so guess what. I will! His wish is my command. Get ready, fundraiser, here I come!"

Mamma put a hand to her heart. "But what happened? I thought you were getting along so well?"

"I'll tell you what happened: his mother. That's what happened. She's another conniving cow who wants to keep his son under her thumb. And I thought Alex would have had the guts to stand up to her. Well, I guess I was wrong!" I told Mamma everything, from Giancarlo's letter to Mrs. Baker's insidious role.

"The problem wasn't the letter, the problem was how Alex reacted. He was a lunatic, completely crazed by jealousy. I don't want to deal with that. I refuse to deal with that!"

I stormed into my room, tearing my clothes off. I needed to get ready for tonight, but first I needed to call Alberto. Snatching the phone from my bedroom dresser, I dialed furiously. "Ciao, Albi! Can you still pick me up tonight? . . . Good. I'm coming. . . My student? Forget about him. It's over. You were right. He is a *carciofo*. I'll see you soon."

Throwing my phone onto the bed, I headed for the bathroom to shower. Twisting the tap on, cold water streamed out like liquid ice. "Ma! Is the water heater on?"

"Are you sure you're doing the right thing? Don't you want to let things cool off a bit before you jump to conclusions?"

"Forget it! Nonna was right. *Mogli e buoi dei paesi tuoi.* It's time to stick to my own people. Is there any hot water left?" Darn Italian water heaters. They were never ready when you needed them. "Never mind. I'll take a cold shower. I need to cool off anyway."

Sliding the shower door shut, I jumped under the cascading water, shutting out Mamma's protests. I forgot how cold the water could get here as I scrubbed as quickly as I could before my limbs froze. It was the fastest shower in Italy, and soon I was drying off and dressing for the big night.

"At least I got something good out of the day," I said to myself as I looked at the beautiful sequined navy dress I had bought. It was too bad it reminded me of Alex.

Forget him. Giancarlo's your man. Fate has spoken.

Before long, my phone was ringing and I was giving myself one last look in the mirror.

"I'm outside," Alberto said over the phone.

With a final rush, I grabbed my new clutch and flung a few things inside along with my phone. As I dashed downstairs and into the evening's humidity, I gave one last glance over to the nunnery. Despite everything, a faint glimmer of my longing for Alex remained. I wished things had worked out differently, that he'd turned out to be the gentleman I thought he was, but it seemed I had put my faith in folly instead.

No more.

It was time to think of Laura now. No more dreams of romance or delusions of faith. The angelic voice that had spoken to me at Fregene was nowhere to be heard, and good riddance. I didn't need faith or fate. Reason was my guide now and Giancarlo was the most reasonable choice.

"Are you getting in?" Alberto called through the passenger window of his black Maserati.

I gave one last hopeful glance in search of Alex, and then climbed into the car, closing the door on him forever.

"What happened to the *carciofo*?" Alberto asked once I was settled in.

"You were right. He doesn't belong in our world."

"Good, because tonight, your life is going to change forever. I want you to meet some people…"

I didn't hear most of what he said, the words drowned out by the restlessness of regret. The problem with romance was that it involved two people who cared for each other, and after today, I only cared about me.

•   •   •   •   •

The Ara Pacis museum was packed with the world I had grown to resent. Glittering diamonds and shimmering sequins disguised the slick pretense necessary to survive a world that prized status over genuineness. Fake smiles and flabby bodies overly tightened with extra-small Spanx reminded me the reasons I left Italy four years ago.

Walking amongst the refinery I had grown up with felt oddly surreal. The peace of Port Angeles vanished as the memory of the lapping ocean was drowned out by the rush of gossip. Fragrant pine trees were pushed to the back of my mind as the miasma of over-sprayed perfume poisoned the air.

Feeling like a stranger in a known land, I scanned the shimmering crowd for the one thing that could save me from loneliness. When I caught sight of Giancarlo, my body surged with pride. This was it. He was mine now. He hadn't chosen me. I had chosen him.

I wouldn't be the other woman. I would be the only woman.

As the distance between us shrank, thoughts of prestige grew. He looked beyond amazing, even better than before. His black hair was pushed back with a light shine. His tuxedo would have made James

Bond ask for fashion advice. Golden light shimmered from his tanned skin.

Goodbye romance.

Hello Laura.

That was when I saw Lucinda off to one side. She seemed happy to see me as I headed towards her husband; a sly smile slid across her face. She'd always been forgetfully pretty. How she had ever won Giancarlo's heart was beyond me. Judging by the look Giancarlo gave me, it was obvious that his heart was never Lucinda's. She may have gained his hand in marriage, but I was the one who had the key to his heart.

And I was about to use it.

Chapter 38
Surrender

Alex

Never before had I felt so violently angry. Like a blistering volcano buried beneath deep layers of guilt and duty, fury groaned for freedom.

Family first.

Find 'em. Fuck 'em. And forget 'em.

These were the tenets of my upbringing. They had molded the man I was today.

And they had just been obliterated.

How could Mum have done this? How could she have plotted against me? Why had she pushed Laura out of my life when she'd seen how happy I was? More importantly, why would she not respect my choice?

This wasn't about family first.

It wasn't about honor. Or duty.

It was never about me. I understood now that family didn't include me.

It was about Mum and what she wanted, and for some reason, she wanted me to be alone.

I could feel the wings of Archangel Michael as they flapped behind me with the conviction of righteous anger. The sword of truth burned in my right hand, and the weigh scales in my left. The devil had taken the form of an unexpected figure, and I was about to excommunicate her from my presence.

Laura had once called me an angel and tonight, I was the angel of redemption.

Like a fiery sprite, I flew up the nunnery stairs. I was beyond the reproach of subtlety. I was perfect, harmonious wrath.

Without knocking, I pushed open Mum's door to find her standing by the window. She peered down towards the street through the curtains unaware I stood behind her.

"Why did you lie to me?"

She jumped from surprise. "Oh. Alex. You scared the living daylights out of me."

"Why did you lie to me?" I asked again. My heart was beating like the drum of a warship. Strong and sure.

"Lied? What on earth are you talking about?" She tried to meet my eyes, but she must have felt the danger there as she whisked her glance away quickly.

"Why were you speaking to Giancarlo on the phone?"

"What? I didn't..."

"I was there! I heard you on the phone!"

My voice boomed. The horn of war.

"Ah. Oh yes. I was just following up on our conversation today..."

"No more lies!"

Her breathing stopped. Even the wind outside seemed to halt its growing lament as the ensuing silence tingled with tension. Blood surged through my veins as the dams of damnation opened their gates.

"What..." She bit her tongue.

When the realization dawned that I knew everything, she crossed her arms, preparing for one of her condescending sermons once again. "Well, what did you expect? She's too old for you. Did you honestly think we would let that happen? She's an Italian cougar for crying out loud! Did you really think that she'd fit in with the family?"

"I don't care! If this is what family is, I don't want it anymore! Don't you want me to be happy?"

She tried to answer before I bulldozed her with words. "You have been against Laura and I from the very beginning. In fact, you've been against all my girlfriends. You never wanted me to date. You pushed them all away. And the silly thing was, I let you do it. I trusted you. I believed in you. I had faith that you knew what was best for me. But now I understand. You don't care about me. You care about you!"

It was as though Medusa stood behind me, turning Mum to stone. She didn't move. Not even a wink. She stood paralyzed, her mouth agape and her eyes wide as she stared at what I had become.

The hallway lights turned on as voices came from upstairs. Angry, disturbed Sister-Greta-voices. I didn't care though. Nothing could frighten me now. Not even Sister Greta.

"I am tired of being lonely! I am tired of being the 'good' son! I am tired of family!"

"You don't mean that, Alex. Family is all you have."

"Exactly! It is all I have! And I'm tired of it! I don't want to be alone anymore!"

Tears welled up. They were not of fear, but of loss. I knew what was happening. I was saying goodbye to my past. I now understood the true meaning of love.

Love wasn't weak or feeble. Nor was it passive or gullible.

Love is strength in the face of deception.

Love is conviction in the truth.

Love is righteous justice.

Placing family first had distracted my line of sight. It had trapped my feelings in a cage poisoned with false trust and honor.

To surrender your beliefs is love.

Pierluigi's words sang to me like cherubim.

Love was surrender.

Surrender everything.

My life.

My thoughts.

My words.

My deeds.

Even my family.

I could hear Sister Greta from down the hallway. Her feet thundered on the marble floor as she stormed towards Mum's room.

I need to find Laura.

Pushing past the startled nun, I ran downstairs and into the warm Roman night hoping to catch Laura. Finding only vacancy, I thought of how I could reach her before she met with Giancarlo. I could have driven there, but I didn't even know where the fundraiser was.

It was then that the most unlikely of angels appeared out of nowhere. I didn't think it was him at first. Like an overly plump Fonzie, he swaggered around the corner, his heels clacking like snapping fingers. An obsidian motorcycle jacket creaked tightly as he raised his arms to place a helmet over his stylish hairdo. He seemed annoyed as he huffed a puff.

"Fabio!" I called out.

His head snapped toward me as he squinted through the darkness. "Alex? Is that you? What are you doing out here?" He stopped short. "You look terrible. What happened?"

"It's been one helluva night. Are you looking for Laura?" I asked.

"Yes. She never phoned me back if she wanted a ride tonight. So I stopped by to see. Fabio never forgets his friends." He puffed his chest with pride. "Is she here?"

"No."

"Oh. Why are you still here then? Aren't you going?"

I paused for a second.

Was I still going?

It was Pierluigi's voice that answered.

Get going, dummy! Listen to your heart!

"Yes," I replied with full confidence. "I'm going. I can come with you?"

My question came out more like an order. He must have noticed the fury in my eyes because he jumped with compliance. "Sure, sure. Have you been on a scooter before?"

"No, but who cares? Let's go."

The helmet he threw my way landed with a hollow thud against my stomach.

"Let's get going then."

•   •   •   •   •

Careening down the busy streets of Rome on the back of Fabio's scooter, all I could think of was Laura. I didn't try to guess how she would react to seeing me. I didn't think about what Giancarlo would do, nor what Alberto would say. I didn't even think of how strange it was to have my arms wrapped around Fabio's chubby waist.

I was consumed by passion. I felt alive. I felt free. Headlights danced around me like sparkling fairies cheering me on. For the first time, the thoughts of my beliefs were silent. I knew what I needed to listen to now, and it was beating strongly in my chest.

Overcome by a new found freedom, I let go of Fabio's waist, stretching my arms wide like the wings of an angel. Wind caressed my face like feathers as the lightness of joy carried me to my soulmate. I felt like Jack Dawson on the bow of the Titanic, sailing into the sunset. All I needed was my Rose.

I was free.

I was in love.

I was...

"What the hell are you doing, you idiot!?" Fabio screamed at me. "Put your arms back around me! You're gonna to get us killed!"

Snapped out of my revelry, cars beeped at us as Fabio nearly lost control of the scooter. Like a frightened koala, I threw my arms back around his waist as he recovered the wobbling scooter, saving us from becoming a Roman pancake.

Then finally, after several minutes, Fabio brought us to a stop.

"Here we are," he said.

"Thank God." I swung off the scooter and pulled the helmet from my head.

We were standing in front of the most modern fountain I had seen in Rome. Water bubbled with yellow-lit luxury. Like a giant cube, the building behind it was starkly modern and made entirely of marble and glass.

"Where are we?" I asked Fabio when he'd dismounted and come to stand beside me.

"This is the *Ara Pacis*," he replied.

"Look at all those people inside."

"This is a big night. Giancarlo has a lot of influence. How else do you think he was able to do a fundraiser in a public museum? The Ara Pacis is a relic from ancient Rome. Politics and corruption go hand in hand."

"Are those security guards?"

"There are a lot of important people here."

The line up to the museum looked like a sparkling river of sequined dresses and black tuxedos as security guards checked a list.

"I must be on the list. Giancarlo would have put me there. Right?"

Fabio shrugged. "Let's go and find out."

Swallowing a nervous knot, I followed Fabio to join the line. This was real now. I was doing this. My heart beat rapidly. My hands were clammy. But the fire of my passion had not been extinguished.

Yet.

•   •   •   •   •

The guards were taller than most Italians and had obviously been chosen from the most intimidating stock of Roman men. One had a thin beard across his chin like a streak of war paint, and the other was as bald as Mr. Clean. When they saw me, they both moved to block the entrance.

"*Nome, prego*," the bald one said.

"Um. I'm a friend of Mr. Giancarlo Deluca. I should be on the list. My name is Alex Baker."

They shared a moment of doubt and without looking at the list, turned their gazes back to me like unconvinced tigers about to pounce. I had to be more persuasive.

"Could you please check? My name should be on there."

The bearded guard gave me a long, suspicious look. Checking the list, he shook his head. "You're not on here, and you're holding up the line. Please step aside."

That wasn't possible. Either Giancarlo forgot, or he intentionally didn't put me on the list. I had to find out. "Is my friend on the list? Laura Di Stefano?"

Biceps bulged from underneath his coat as the bald guard crossed his arms with impatience. The bearded one checked the list for Laura's name.

"Yes. She has already arrived."

Why would Laura's name be on the list and not my own? That could only mean one thing. Giancarlo had intentionally omitted my name. It was all starting to make sense. I tried to look past the guards to see if I could spot Laura.

"Please. I only have to talk to one person, then I'll leave. I won't be long."

Their backs straightened as the guards moved to grab me. It was Fabio who came to my rescue.

"Guys, guys. There must be a mistake. The kid is with me. Give him a break."

"And who are you?" asked the bearded one.

"My name is Fabio Il Grande," he puffed up in an attempt to seem bigger that the guards, and even though he was a lot shorter, Fabio Il Grande was living up to his name.

The guard drew his stare from Fabio to the list while Mr. Clean kept me pinned under his eye. "Yes, Mr. Il Grande. You're here, but your friend is not."

"Well, I know for a fact that Giancarlo invited this young man. Is there a way that we can check?"

The line behind grew restless, like a dark, luxurious caterpillar bristling its coat. Words like "andiamo" and "dai, su" encouraged the guards to be better men. "He's just a kid!" one voice shouted out. "Let him in" said another. Before I knew it, almost everyone was cheering for me to pass.

The last thing I expected was Roman sophisticates coming to my rescue. Italian snobbery would not be outdone by their hospitality. With mounting pressure from behind, the guards were forced to make a hard decision.

"All right, but you have five minutes," the bearded guard said while Mr. Clean snapped his fingers to a young waiter inside the museum. "He will be your escort. He will follow you in until you speak to your friend, and then he will bring you back here in exactly five minutes. Understood?"

I looked at the waiter, who seemed proud to be given a security detail. It was probably going to be the most exciting part of his night.

"Okay. *Grazie. Grazie,*" I said.

They stepped aside, allowing me to pass. As I entered, the volume jumped several decibels as a string quartet played above the social chatter. In scanning the crowd for Laura, I couldn't help but notice the Ara Pacis sitting in the center of the room.

It was a masterpiece of ancient art, figures of Roman antiquity etched into marble with enough grace to have been done by Neptune himself. Despite the noise echoing all around, a patient presence emanated from its meticulously etched engravings. At the heart of Roman chaos and noise, it stood with an air of peace.

That was when I saw Laura. Across the room. Her blue dress glittered like a starry night as she laughed in a group that had their backs to me. With naive exuberance, I called out her name. Called and waved.

"Laura!"

My voice rose above the tumultuous chatter, quelling the room like a thrown blanket over a fire.

"Laura!"

Slowly, conversations silenced and heads turned as violins whined to a halt. Everyone stopped to gawk at the strange kid who dared disturb the joviality of the night.

Then Giancarlo appeared behind Laura, who froze at the sight of me. Pleased to see me in my desperate state, a cold smirk of satisfaction grinned across his flawless face. Like a serpent, he wrapped an arm around Laura's waist as he gave a smug, devilish grin. With his tuxedo, Mr. Perfect easily scored another bonus point, leaving my Mating score buried under the dust of his magnificence.

Searching the hall for anything of familiarity, a pool of silence closed in around me, drowning me like a simple minnow in an ocean of polished, powdered piranhas; black sequins as scales, glittering diamonds as teeth. A whirlpool of death for my simple ways. I knew how to survive the animals of the wild, but not the intangible beasts of human pretence.

Their stares pressed in, suffocating me, pulling me down a dark abyss of insecurity and shame, pressing for etiquette, demanding composure. My tight jacket and pants, Laura's thoughtful attempt to help, squeezed in with their glares, suffocating me. Strangling me. Pressing me like a cube into a peg's hole.

Laura did nothing. Too stunned to react, she barely blinked. Her differences glared back at me, measuring carefully. Soulmates? A foolish notion. Naive. Stupid. I didn't belong in this world. She deserved a man who understood her and could give her the things she needed. I was no Giancarlo.

I'm too young.

Too inexperienced.

Too country.

Feeling the weight of my presence, I took a step backwards. Then another. Then two more. Before I realized what I was doing, I pushed back in retreat, between the ogling crowd and a confused Fabio, into the night, and away from my foolish passion.

Chapter 39
Folly? Or Fate?

Laura

I heard my name, but hoped the voice wasn't calling for me. There was only one person silly enough to make a fool of themselves by screaming at a fundraiser, and I had left him with his annoying mother an hour ago.

"Is that your student?" Alberto asked, taking a sip of his bubbly prosecco.

I started to blush, praying to God that it wasn't true. Hadn't he embarrassed me enough outside the nunnery? Why was he doing this?

"I think it is him. Look," Alberto insisted.

Praying that my cousin was wrong, I slowly turned to see Alex standing in the middle of the museum. All eyes, painted and plain, were on the Camerican kid who was ludicrous enough to embarrass me in front of Rome's most influential. A security guard was moving towards him as a waiter tugged at his arm, imploring him to be quiet.

"What on earth?" I whispered to myself.

His eyes were pleading with me, not with pity, but with conviction. The jealous kid I had argued with had vanished, and the idealistic romantic had returned. There seemed to be a new confidence about him. As we locked eyes, I knew there was only one thing remaining between us and our fragile romance.

Me.

I motioned towards him, but something held me back. Alex's gaze shifted to my left. It only took a second to notice that Giancarlo had wrapped his arm around my waist.

When I looked back to find Alex, he was gone.

The shimmering spectacle around me slowed to a dreamlike smear and before I realized what had happened, my phone vibrated in my clutch. Scrambling to see if it was Alex, I tore Giancarlo's arm away before my hand clasped a thin, surprise rectangle. Pulling it free, an envelope with my name inked with careful writing begged to be torn open.

Rip.

As the social murmur returned to the museum and my phone kept ringing, I opened the card inside. The words read:

Soulmates

Two souls lost in the ocean of life.
Fighting the waves of loss and strife.

They plead with cries to the endless sky,
To find the one that will help them fly.

Above the turmoil of screaming confusion.
The noise of life is the greatest illusion.

Blind from the deception of our harried thoughts,
Searching the forgotten depths of our longing hearts.

The lighthouse stands shining its beacon of light,
Seeking our mate in the darkness of the night.

Close your eyes and you will soon see,
That faith in your heart will set you free.

I stared at the words for a long time. No one had ever written me a poem before. I wanted to dive into those words and feel the freedom that he spoke of. I repeated the last line.

Faith in your heart will set you free.

"Laura?"

Giancarlo called me back to reality.

"Are you all right?" he asked.

I shook my head. "What are we doing?" I asked as I pulled myself out of his arms.

His puzzlement was only trumped by Alberto's. The circle of sycophants glittering around us tightened with objection as they all shifted their gaze from the silly shouting boy to the now sillier girl. After all, who would ever object to having Giancarlo pick her as his *bella*? For the first time since I had known him, I saw nervousness. "Being together. I thought that was why you came?"

Looking past Giancarlo, my reflection stared back at me from the glass museum wall. Seeing myself, adorned with jewels and sequins, surrounded by wealth and power, made me realize why I ran away to America.

"Do you know why I went to America?" I asked.

Giancarlo shook his head, confused. "No. Why?"

"At first, I thought I was running away from you."

"And now?" He asked.

"Now I realize I was running away from myself."

"I don't understand."

"Of course you don't. You never could, and you never will because you see everything with the eyes of power. I did as well. Power is very alluring. You are very alluring." I gently caressed his clean-shaven cheek. He smelt of musky-spice cologne. "But I realize now that I was wrong about me. I deserve more than just power. I deserve more than just wealth or prestige. I deserve love."

Giancarlo continued his stern simmering all the while never offering the words I was waiting to hear. They were simple words, yet so hard for some to say. After what he had said at Antonini's, I had hoped he had the courage to speak them now. Instead he depended on a more reliable approach: flattery.

"*Amore.* You're so beautiful. You deserve the best, and I'll make it my life's mission to make sure you get it."

"I'm not sure that you can. Where is Lucinda?"

He stepped back from my question, surprised that I would ask about his wife.

"Lucinda? She's somewhere, I'm sure. Why?"

"And your children?"

"The kids? They're probably playing with their friends by the Ara Pacis."

"And us? Where are we?"

"Well, we are supposed to be having a good time."

"No. That's not what you promised. You promised you would call this all off and give up everything for me."

"And I'll keep my promise. Once I get elected, I'll end it with Lucinda."

"What do you mean 'once you get elected'? You said you would announce it tonight."

Giancarlo shifted uneasily, looking around to see if any of his donors were eavesdropping. "You're right. I did say that. But, to be honest, I thought you would understand. If I get elected, this could be good for both us."

"You mean for you."

"No, I mean us."

"Then do it now. Tell Lucinda that it's over."

His unease was growing more obvious by the moment as he looked to see if anyone was overhearing.

"Don't you have faith?" I asked.

"Faith?"

"In us. Don't you believe that we can do it together, without Lucinda's influence?"

"C'mon, *amore*, be serious. You're a retail clerk. You couldn't possibly have the connections Lucinda has. Besides, once I'm in, I won't need Lucinda. I'll just need you."

I scoffed loudly to make sure everyone around us heard. Then reaching over, I ripped Alberto's glass out of his hand, and drenched Giancarlo's five-thousand euro tuxedo with five-hundred euro prosecco. Normally, I would have cried for ruining such fine wool, but like I said earlier. . .tonight was about me. With a final nod, I turned my back on Giancarlo and his world—forever.

•   •   •   •   •

Lightning sliced the sky above the Ara Pacis as I tried to decide which way Alex had turned on the Lungotevere. Rome's street lights were turning the clouds a deep orange.

"Laura?"

The voice startled me. I turned to see the least expected person.

"Fabio? What are you doing here? Oh my god! I forgot to call you!"

"Never mind that. Are you all right?"

"I . . . I don't know."

"You need to go after him. He's young, but he has a kind heart. He needs someone who appreciates that, otherwise this world will eat him alive."

It was the most perfect advice I could have received in that moment. I couldn't believe it came from Fabio the Great.

"You're a very sweet guy, Fabio." I leaned up and gave him a kissy-kiss on his cheek. "You deserve a woman that will give you all the kissy-kisses you could ever want."

He blushed, his macho exterior faltering just a little. He looked like a giant teddy bear. And was I imagining things, or was that a small tear at the corner of his eye?

"You better get going." He composed himself before his reputation could be tarnished. "I saw him heading towards the Vatican."

With one last smile, I turned and ran to find Alex. Trying to run in heels would have been suicidal along the bumpy cobbles, so I tore the Pradas from my feet and threw them to the curb. Now barefoot, I ran as fast and as hard as I could—tearing through the blurry streets of Rome, pushing past exclaiming tourists, dodging all manner of cars and traffic, I ran. I ran until my legs gave out. I ran until my dress had turned into an "undress." I ran until I was blind with exhaustion and any hope of finding Alex seemed impossible.

I couldn't give up though, nor would I let fear and doubt cloud my judgement ever again. To hell with Mrs. Baker. To hell with our age difference. To hell with his inexperience. To hell with everything that stood in our way.

Fate had brought him to me, and faith would take me the rest of the way.

As the night became darker, plump drops of rain spattered on my face, washing away my makeup. Within seconds, a cleansing downpour inundated Rome, freeing me from the varnish of my past.

Finally, pain gripping my bare feet and lungs, I skidded to a fatigued halt. Tilting my face toward the sky, I closed my eyes to feel heaven's shower finish its fall. The woman I had been was no longer the woman I was, and as a final blessing from above, a flash of lightning blasted across the sky, shuddering my eyes open. Thunder rumbled as God cleared his throat.

Flying high in the night, a shining angel floated above me. Flapping its wings in the inky sky, its body shimmered with golden light. In one hand, a lance was set to plunge, in the other, a scale measured the balance of life. It was set to strike the dragon that squirmed beneath its feet. I couldn't move, frozen in awe.

Another flash of lightning lit the sky pointing to a singular soul hunched down on Ponte Sant'Angelo. The figure had slumped to his knees as his head quivered. I looked back up to the top of Castel Sant'Angelo, staring into the eyes of Archangel Michael. I tried to hear its voice, silently pleading for advice.

Faith.

God had given me the choice and now I had to have the courage to follow it.

"Alex!" I called out through the dark night as thunder rolled above, drowning my voice. Moving closer to the hunched form, Alex's features were lost in shadow.

"Alex!" I screamed again.

His head moved. Like a flower growing through stone, he opened his stance to a stand. His face was covered with rain and as I approached the lightning revealed the blue of his eyes.

Drenched from the top down, he captured my gaze, holding it tightly with gracious humility. Fear and faith bruised his face as he struggled to be the man I knew he was.

Strong.

Fragile.

Timeless.

The words of his poem sang to me through his stare. There we were, two souls lost in the night of life who had found each other. I couldn't contain my tears. I wouldn't contain them. I was a strong woman, but I wasn't afraid to show Alex my weakness.

I wasn't afraid to show him my fragility.

Water dripped from his nose and hair. He stood confidently as his chest heaved beneath his jacket. Lured by his confidence, I took a step closer. Lightning thrashed the sky, turning night to day. Thunder roared and bellowed like wailing demons.

Time stood still. Eternity passed between us. Power. Knowing. Understanding. Recognition. The words of his poem echoed in my mind.

Two souls lost in the ocean of life.

Fighting the waves of loss and strife.

"What are we going to do?" I shouted over the rainfall.

He shook his head. "I don't know. I think the question is, *how* are we going to do it?"

I knew the answer now. "Faith."

His eyes sparkled as rain dripped from his long lashes. I didn't know how it happened, but the distance between us disappeared. When our lips met, and his arms wrapped around me, it was not just a kiss. It was *the* kiss. It was the kiss I had dreamt of all my life. It was the completion of all my searching.

Close your eyes and you will soon see,

The faith in your heart will set you free.

So I did. I closed them. Lost in the eternity of his embrace, all pain and worry dissolved in the perfection of his tender lips. His arms were strong. His chest pressed against mine. He no longer felt like my younger student. In that moment of sweet recognition, I understood that faith was the choice to surrender to fate, and fate had brought me the man I would spend the rest of my life with.

The End

About the Author

Born on the dusty Canadian prairies, Steven Bale spent most of his life in the Pacific Northwest. After earning a Bachelor of Science from the University of Victoria, he opened a small business which he has run successfully for twenty years. Inspired by his Roman wife who shares her passion with fearless abandon, he spends his time between Canada and their villa in Tuscany, where the contrasts of life spur his creativity with clashing enchantment.

Note from the Author

Word-of-mouth is crucial for any author to succeed. If you enjoyed *Ketchup & Carbonara*, please leave a review online — anywhere you are able. Even if it's just a sentence or two. It would make all the difference and would be very much appreciated.

Thanks!
Steven Bale

CPSIA information can be obtained
at www.ICGtesting.com
Printed in the USA
BVHW072319110221
599954BV00001B/4